DARK WIDOW'S CURSE

THE CHILDREN OF THE GODS BOOK 24

I. T. LUCAS

THE CHILDREN OF THE GODS ORIGINS

1: Goddess's Choice

2: Goddess's Hope

THE CHILDREN OF THE GODS

Dark Stranger

1: Dark Stranger The Dream

2: Dark Stranger Revealed

3: Dark Stranger Immortal

Dark Enemy

4: Dark Enemy Taken

5: Dark Enemy Captive

6: Dark Enemy Redeemed

Kri & Michael's Story

6.5: My Dark Amazon Novella

Dark Warrior

7: Dark Warrior Mine

8: Dark Warrior's Promise

9: Dark Warrior's Destiny

10: Dark Warrior's Legacy

Dark Guardian

11: Dark Guardian Found

12: Dark Guardian Craved

13: Dark Guardian's Mate

Dark Angel

14: Dark Angel's Obsession

15: Dark Angel's Seduction

16: Dark Angel's Surrender

DARK OPERATIVE

17: Dark Operative: A Shadow of Death

18: Dark Operative: A Glimmer of Hope

19: Dark Operative: The Dawn of Love

DARK SURVIVOR

20: Dark Survivor Awakened

21: Dark Survivor Echoes of Love

22: Dark Survivor Reunited

DARK WIDOW

23: Dark Widow's Secret

24: Dark Widow's Curse

25: Dark Widow's Blessing

TRY THE SERIES ON

AUDIBLE

2 FREE audiobooks with your new Audible subscription!

STOKE-ON-TRENT LIBRARIES	
3 8080 01805 2249	
Amazon	18/06/2019
	£10-17

Copyright © 2019 by I. T. Lucas
All rights reserved.

No part of this book may be reproduced in any form or by any electronic or mechanical means, including information storage and retrieval systems, without written permission from the author, except for the use of brief quotations in a book review.

Dark Widow's Curse is a work of fiction!
Names, characters, places, and incidents are products of the author's imagination or are used fictitiously and are not to be construed as real. Any similarity to actual persons, organizations and/or events is purely coincidental.

1

VIVIAN

A shiver of unease rolled through Vivian's body as Magnus turned into a fast-food drive-through. Perhaps it wasn't wise to stop for coffee before dropping their belongings at the donation center.

She shouldn't have asked.

As long as the tracker Romeo had planted was still with them in the car, Gorchenco's goons could be right behind them and closing in.

"I'm sorry that I made you stop." She put her hand on Magnus's arm. "When the goons realize that the tracker is no longer in the cabin, they will change direction to follow the signal. If they didn't already. They might be right behind us."

Magnus's smile was tight as he cast her a sidelong glance. "It will only take a few minutes. And if they show up, I can handle them."

"You're sure about that?"

"I'm sure. I'm hungry. And I don't like to fight on an empty stomach. It makes me mean." He winked at her before pulling up to the window and placing their order.

Talk about an overinflated ego.

The guy had impressive athletic skills, she had to give him that, but he wasn't Superman. The goons were most likely armed, and as far as Vivian knew, all that Magnus carried on him was one knife, which was strapped to his calf. If he was hiding a gun under his suit jacket, he was doing a great job of concealing it. She hadn't caught a glimpse of it during all the time they'd spent together.

"Your drinks." The girl at the window handed Magnus a cardboard carrier.

Taking the two coffees out of the container, he put them in the cup holders and then handed the hot cocoa to Parker. "Here you go, buddy."

After stirring in the cream, Vivian took a sip and closed her eyes in bliss, even though it was a shitty fast-food brew she would've never ordered under normal circumstances. But beggars couldn't be choosers, and there was nothing normal about what was happening to her and her family.

As of ten days ago, her ordinary life had been turned into a nightmare that was bizarre enough to make an action movie or two.

One could be about Ella—a girl lured into a trap by a pretend boyfriend and bought by a Russian mafia boss, then coerced into cooperation by threats to her family.

The other movie could be made about the girl's mother and brother running away from the mafioso's minions, and the handsome bodyguard aiding them.

Surreal.

How was she supposed to deal with that?

There was a saying that bad things came in threes, but in Vivian's case it seemed like there was no limit to bad luck. The tragedies of her husband's death and then her two boyfriends weren't enough.

Now the curse had gone ahead and also claimed her daughter.

Like the biblical Job, Vivian's calamities kept piling on. Except, she doubted God had anything to do with that. There were other forces at play.

What were they?

Why were they targeting her?

Vivian couldn't imagine. She was a good person, and she'd never harmed anyone on purpose or even gossiped maliciously. She didn't deserve all the disasters fate was heaping upon her.

There was nothing she could do about it, though, except take one day at a time and try to survive as best she could.

"Here you go." The sandwich Magnus handed her was so greasy that the wrapper was soaked through.

After handing the second one to Parker, Magnus put the third one on the center divider and pulled out of the drive-through.

"Aren't you going to eat?" Vivian asked.

"In a moment. You were worried about the goons catching up to us. I want to get on the freeway first."

"Yeah, you're right. Thank you."

Her knight in shining armor, or rather in a pair of custom-tailored slacks and a dress shirt.

It was astounding how much she'd come to depend on him in such a short time. It had been ten days since Ella had gone with Romeo to New York, but only seven days since Vivian had started suspecting that something was wrong, and only four days since Magnus had picked her up at a mall parking lot and taken her and Parker to the cabin. Not even a full four days, and he already felt like an integral part of her family.

Falling for the bodyguard was so cliché.

Magnus was so much more than just a protector. She shouldn't typecast him in that role because it was too limiting. However, Vivian could easily cast him in the role of a life partner and a father figure to her children. But that was taking it to the other extreme.

The truth was probably somewhere in the middle.

Magnus was a great guy that any woman would've fallen for. Circumstances had thrown them in together, making the connection so much more intense and immediate. Add to that the looming danger, and it was the perfect recipe for a fast, pressure-cooker romance.

The problem was that she couldn't allow herself to think of him as husband material, and not only because of her curse. Once this was over, and Ella was rescued, they would part ways, and Vivian would go back to her old life and her old job.

Her job. Damn.

Vivian slapped a hand over her forehead. "It's Monday. I need to call in and cancel my appointments for today. What am I going to tell the office? When am I going to be back?"

Magnus put his sandwich down. "I don't know. My guess is that it will take a while. In case Gorchenco's people are monitoring the dental office, you need to come up with an excuse that will require taking a long vacation. Maybe something about winning a free ticket?"

"To a cabin? I don't think so."

"Do you have a better idea?"

"It has to be something about Parker or me getting

sick. A contagious disease that requires me to stay away from people."

"And leave your car at the mall?"

"Right. I need to incorporate it into the story."

"Good luck."

It was too early in the morning for anyone at the dental office to pick up the phone, but she could leave a message.

It was even better that way.

Dolores would have started asking questions, and then Vivian would have had to come up with more lies on the spot.

Pulling the phone out of the ziplock bag, she hesitated. Up until now, she'd used the phone Turner had given her only to check things online, not for calling anyone. "Are you sure using this phone is safe?"

"It is."

She dialed.

The recorded greeting came on. "Thank you for calling Bright Smiles dental office."

Vivian tapped her foot and waited for it to finish playing.

"We are closed right now. If this is a dental emergency, please press one, and you'll be redirected to a call center. Otherwise, leave us a message, and we will get back to you as soon as we can."

"Hi, Dolores. It's Vivian. I'm sorry to spring it on you like this, but you'll have to reschedule all of my appointments for the coming week. Parker came down with a bad case of chicken pox. He's been so miserable that when a friend of mine offered to take us on a road trip in her motorhome, I gladly accepted. It helps take his mind off the itching. I'll call you as soon as I can come back to work."

"Wow, Mom, I didn't know you were such an awesome liar."

She put the phone back in the bag. "It's not something to be proud of. Besides, this is probably going to get me fired."

The way things were going, she wouldn't be surprised. Jobless and on welfare were the next blows her curse would deliver.

"Why would they fire you?" Magnus asked. "Do they expect you to leave a sick kid alone at home?"

"No, but they expect me to leave a phone number they can call me at."

"Why didn't you? This phone is safe."

"I almost did, and then I thought better of it. If Gorchenco's people were listening in, they could've gotten the number. Then, he could have called me and threatened to hurt Ella if I didn't show up with Parker. I would have been forced to do what he told me. But if he has no way to contact me, he can't do that. Right?"

Magnus nodded. "I'm impressed, and I'm also ashamed of not thinking it through myself. You're a smart woman, Vivian."

"Thank you."

In the back seat, Parker cleared his throat. "So your calls are not getting forwarded to your new phone. How did Ella manage to call you?"

Her son was too sharp for his own good.

"I promise to explain later."

2

MAGNUS

When Magnus pulled out of the donation center's parking lot, Vivian let out a breath. "It's such a relief to know it's gone. Knowing that the tracker was right here with us in the car felt like sitting on a ticking bomb."

He put his hand on her knee. "Now that this is taken care of, we can go shopping and get you some clothes and shoes."

"Let me check what's near here." She pulled out her phone and started scrolling. "There is a Walmart Supercenter ten minutes' drive away from here. You can get us something there. All I need is a pair of black leggings, a T-shirt, and a pair of simple flip-flops. Parker can do with the same, except for the leggings, of course. Just get him some sports shorts. We will get the rest at the mall."

Magnus chuckled. "My partner likes shopping in Walmart."

"Your partner?" Vivian narrowed her eyes at him.

Was she jealous? It sure sounded like it. Should he

tease her? He could say that his partner was a tall, gorgeous redhead with a great sense of humor.

Nah, the woman was under enough stress as it was.

"We usually work with partners, but not always, and right now we are spread thin."

"What's he like? I assume he is a guy?"

"Yes, he is." Magnus cast her an amused glance. "His name is Anandur. You'd like him. He lives for making people laugh. Well, he did. Now he also lives for making his mate happy."

"Mate?"

"Girlfriend. Future wife. I guess fiancée is the most appropriate term."

"It's nice that he wants to make her happy."

"Doesn't everyone in a committed relationship want their mate to be happy?"

She shrugged. "No, not everyone. Some people are more concerned about making themselves happy than their partners. I think most people are like that. It's the 'me, myself, and I' generation."

He wondered which kind her late husband had belonged to. Vivian had said that they'd been in love, and since she'd brought his framed picture along for the weekend, that hadn't been a lie. That picture was also one of the few things she'd had him check for the tracker because she wasn't willing to leave it behind.

Still, Magnus was curious. Not that he was going to ask her while Parker was sitting in the back seat and listening to their conversation, but maybe later when they were alone.

"I texted you our sizes," Vivian said as he parked in the Supercenter's huge parking lot.

"Thanks. Lock the car while I'm gone."

"I will."

Thankfully, the entire shopping expedition took less than fifteen minutes, and that included standing in line for about five. Magnus could see the appeal of fast shopping in a place that had almost everything a human needed for survival, provided said human was not very discriminating about quality. It was quite low.

When he was done, he found a quiet corner next to the optometry center. Since the place wasn't open yet, chances were that no one was going to bother him while he talked to Kian.

Before leaving the cabin, Magnus had sent the boss a quick text about the tracker and the urgent evacuation, but he still needed to discuss with him a new safe house for Vivian and Parker. Hopefully, the boss had figured it out and had already made arrangements.

Or rather Bridget had. Perhaps he should call her instead?

Except, it still felt weird to have the doctor in charge of rescue operations. Bridget was very capable, but she had zero military background.

He dialed Kian.

"Where are you?" the boss asked.

"In a Walmart about an hour and a half drive from the cabin. We dropped all of Vivian and Parker's belongings at a donation center, so I had to get them some clothes. They need to replace everything and more. It seems like this is going to take much longer than any of us had anticipated."

"Tell me about it. As if I need another headache. Engaging the Russian mafia was not part of the plan."

Magnus shifted the phone to his other ear. "Do you want to pull the plug?"

"I can't even if I wanted to. If I do, Julian will hate me for the rest of our immortal lives. But even if that wasn't a consideration, once I commit to something, it goes against my nature to withdraw."

That was a relief. "Thank you."

"What is it to you?"

Glancing around, Magnus checked that no one was listening in. "Vivian might be a Dormant. She and Ella share a telepathic communication. That's how we knew about the tracker. Ella was blocking her mother because they were threatening her just as we expected. Early this morning, she finally opened the channel to warn Vivian that Gorchenco knew where she and Parker were hiding."

"You mean to tell me that they can actually converse telepathically?"

"That's what Vivian told me."

"I thought you'd just found the tracker. How long have you known that Vivian and Ella can do that?"

"Since this morning, when she woke me up and told me that we had to run because Gorchenco's goons were on the way. She had to fess up so I'd believe her."

"Interesting. Anything else?"

"Yes. Ella also told Vivian that she is on a plane to London."

"You should have mentioned it in the text."

"I was in a rush. Besides, there is still plenty of time to abort the mission."

"True. But in the meantime, Turner and the guys are wasting time on planning an operation that isn't happening."

"Yeah, you're right. My bad. All I was thinking of was getting them to safety. Should I call Arwel now?"

"I'm texting Turner as we speak."

"I need a new safe place for them. Since Vivian and Ella are potential Dormants and naturally Parker is too, is there a chance you'll allow them into the village?"

The long silence on the other side of the line didn't bode well for an affirmative answer.

"Under the circumstances, I'm not willing to compromise the village's location. Vivian and Ella might be innocent victims in this, but they might also be plants. With their knowledge or without. We know that the Doomers have connections with the Russian mafia as well as others. They can also compel people to do things they otherwise wouldn't. It could be a ploy to flush us out."

Talk about paranoid.

Magnus had no doubt that Viv and Ella were innocent. No one was that good of an actor. Still, Kian was right that there was a remote possibility that someone was using them as a Trojan horse.

"Where can I take them? We need a new safe house."

"You can take them to the keep. I don't have any apartments vacant at the moment, so you'll have to use the underground ones. I'll send Okidu to prepare them for you. Park in one of the adjacent buildings' parking lots and use the underground tunnel to get them to the keep's underbelly. As you get near, blindfold them. When you're there, you can load them into a mobile cart. I don't want them to see the passage and how to get to it."

It seemed like Kian had caught the paranoid bug from Turner. The parking was nothing new. Clan members who suspected that they were being followed, or those who didn't wish to use other evasive maneuvers, parked in one of the adjacent buildings and used the underground tunnels to get there.

Magnus could see the logic in that. But the blindfolds were overkill.

"I can be there in about two hours. Or later if Vivian wants to go to the mall. It's still closed right now."

"That's plenty of time for Okidu to get the rooms ready."

"I hope you're not talking about the dungeon. I'm not putting Vivian and the kid in a prison cell."

Kian chuckled. "The apartments are on the same level, but they are nicely appointed just like any other space Ingrid decorates."

That would do. "Good deal."

"Call me if you need anything."

"I will. Thank you, Kian." Magnus clicked off the call and headed out.

Seeing him approaching, Vivian unlocked the car. "Did you find everything?" she asked as he got in.

"I did. I hope that this is what you wanted." He handed her the store bag.

"Thank you." She pulled out the pair of leggings and her flip-flops.

After handing the bag to Parker, Vivian shimmied into them, pulling them on without showing a thing.

Which was a shame.

"Aren't you going to put on the T-shirt?"

"Nope. Changing shirts in the car is a bit problematic. The leggings work fine with your dress shirt."

He had to agree. It was long enough to serve as a dress for Vivian's petite frame, and even though it was much too big, she looked sexy in it. Hell, the woman looked sexy in everything.

"Not a problem for me," Parker said. "I'm ready for the mall and all the games that you guys promised me."

"Absolutely. But we still have a couple of hours until the mall opens. We can go and have a decent breakfast somewhere, and then we can watch a movie in the car."

"Sounds good to me," Vivian said.

Magnus turned on the engine.

After their second breakfast, he drove into the mall's parking lot and put a movie on. Even before the coming attractions were over, Parker dozed off with Scarlet curled up in his lap, and a few minutes later, Vivian fell asleep too.

Content to just watch over his little pretend family, Magnus turned the movie off and waited for the mall to open. When it did, he nudged Vivian. "Time to shop."

She opened her eyes. "When did I fall asleep?"

"As soon as the movie started."

Stretching her arms over her head, Vivian yawned. "I didn't realize how tired I was."

"You didn't get much sleep last night."

"That's true."

He pulled out his wallet and handed her several hundred in cash. "Don't use your credit cards."

"Why? I'm supposed to be on a road trip. It will make more sense if it shows that I bought a few things. We are just passing through. It's not like they could zero in on our location by checking my credit card charges. By the time they post, we will be long gone."

She had a valid point, but Magnus wanted to pay for her and Parker's new things. It was his fault that they'd had to toss everything out. He should've checked their stuff for bugs before taking them to the cabin.

"A few things are fine. But it would be suspicious if you buy an entire new wardrobe." Not really, but he wanted her to take the money. "You need more stuff than what you brought with you. This might take a while."

"Fine. But I'm going to pay you back."

"Nope. Not happening."

She narrowed her eyes at him. "We'll talk about it later. So what's the game plan? I don't suppose you guys want to go clothes shopping with me?"

"No way," Parker said. "I want to go to the gaming shop and get my equipment back. I don't care about clothes. You buy them for me anyway."

"I'll take you," Magnus volunteered. "Let's meet back here in an hour? Is that enough time for you, Vivian?"

"It should do. If not, I'll call you."

"Good deal. I can't leave Scarlet in the car for too long. Parker and I will do our shopping quickly and come back to wait for you here."

They parted ways at Macy's. Vivian headed inside, while Magnus and Parker continued to the gaming store.

"I'll wait outside," Magnus said. "Pick whatever you want and then come to get me when it's time to pay."

Parker grinned from ear to ear. "Whatever I want? No budget limit?"

"Go crazy, kid, just do it fast."

"Oh, I will."

3

ELLA

Ella lay awake in bed, too shaken up to fall asleep, but also too terrified to make a sound.

Dimitri Gorchenco, the scariest man she'd ever met, had told her to go to sleep, and Ella didn't dare to disobey, or rather disobey in any way he could discern. Even though she was in his bedroom, on his jumbo jet, she was sure there was a surveillance camera hidden somewhere.

He was probably watching her every move.

Huddled under the blanket, she forced her breathing to sound as even as if she were asleep and tried to talk herself into calming down. Telling her mother to run had been a major act of defiance. Even though Dimitri could never suspect her mode of communication, Ella was still scared that he would blame her for their escape.

Hell, he might punish her regardless of her supposed innocence. This wasn't a guy who played fair. He might take out his anger on her.

But even if he did, it was worth it.

It had felt so good to finally communicate with her mom. For the first time since her ordeal had begun, Ella felt like she had some control over what was happening to her and her family.

Hopefully, they had made it out in time. She was almost afraid to find out. In any case, Ella wasn't ready to open the channel again until she got her nerves under control.

Vivian would sense her panic and freak out.

There were so many questions Ella wanted to ask her mom. Who were the people helping Viv and Parker? Why were they helping them? And how were they planning on rescuing her?

She couldn't imagine who could be powerful enough to get her away from Dimitri Gorchenco. The people helping her mom probably thought she was still being held by Romeo or Stefano.

Those two were small fry, petty criminals who tricked silly girls like her into following a handsome guy like Romeo, and then sold them to the highest bidder, while ensuring their cooperation by threatening their families.

Getting her away from them would've been easy.

Unfortunately, the people helping her mother were too late. Now that Ella had been sold, her fate had been sealed.

Gorchenco was too powerful.

If she tried to run, he would find her. Perhaps if she played her part well and convinced him that she was happy with him, he would forget about searching for her family. If he wanted to, Ella had no doubt Dimitri would find them no matter how well they were hiding. It wouldn't even take him long.

Especially since the people helping her mom were obviously amateurs. Otherwise, they would've checked her things for bugs and trackers.

It seemed that the best way to salvage the situation was to accept her fate, play nice with Dimitri, and convince him that she was actually happy about him buying her. If she succeeded, he might not feel the need to hold her family hostage.

The question was whether she could pull it off.

Perhaps if he weren't so scary, she could warm up to him. Gorchenco wasn't a bad looking guy. From the little she'd noticed while being scared out of her mind, it seemed that Dimitri was in good shape. Obviously, he exercised regularly and took good care of himself. Except, he only looked good for someone his age, which was more than double hers. Much more.

Could she stand a man that old touching her?

Did she have a choice?

Since she didn't, she'd better convince herself that she could. As Rose had said, many generations of girls had been married off to men they hadn't chosen. If they'd survived it, so could she.

At least now that she could communicate with her mother, Ella wouldn't be as completely isolated.

After another hour of lying awake, Ella opened the channel.

Mom? Did you guys get out? Are you safe?

Yes. What about you? Are you okay?

I'm in bed, in a bedroom on a private jumbo jet. Can you imagine that? It even has a second floor with a bar, a dining room, and staff sleeping bunks.

Hopefully, she sounded excited and not scared.

Is he there with you?

He is in the living room portion of the plane. He told me to go to sleep.

You know who he is, right? Vivian asked.

His name is Dimitri Gorchenco. I think he is a Russian mafia boss.

He is. The people helping me found out who bought you. Oh my God. Saying that sounds so awful. How are you holding up?

I'm fine. At first, I was scared, but I'm getting used to it. Dimitri is treating me really well. He got me a whole new wardrobe of classy designer clothes, and even a coach to teach me which forks go with what. That means that he wants me to accompany him to business meetings and show me off. He's not going to keep me locked in his bedroom. And I'm flying around the world in a private jumbo jet. It could've been worse.

Ella heard her mother's internal sigh. *You're so brave, my Ella. I'm so sorry you got sucked into the family curse. And don't tell me you still don't believe in it.*

No, I do. You are right. We are cursed. I don't know why, but we are. Did you piss off a witch?

Not that I'm aware of.

Did Dad have a girlfriend before you? Someone you stole him from?

He dated a few girls, but none of them was serious. I was his first steady girlfriend.

Still, it could be that one of them was a witch, and she cursed you for taking him away from her.

That sounds silly. Life is not a television show.

Oh, really? And believing that we are cursed is not silly?

You're right. But it's not like I can do anything about it.

Maybe you can get another witch to remove the curse.

Her mother chuckled. *I'll do some research once I get to the safe house.*

Where are you now?

I'm shopping for clothes. We dropped all of our things at a donation center, even the clothes we were wearing. Magnus, the guy who is helping us, gave us his clothes to wear until we buy new ones.

Why didn't you just leave everything behind?

Because we didn't want it to look as if we were warned. We packed, cleaned up, and we even made the beds. The idea was to make it seem as if we were just continuing with our vacation and donating a few things. That way no one can suspect you or blame you.

Wow, that was smart. Ella felt a huge weight lift off her chest. If Dimitri believed her family was just taking a vacation, chances were he wouldn't punish her.

You need to be very careful, Mom. I don't know anything about the people helping you, but they must be amateurs for not checking your stuff for bugs. If Dimitri decides he wants to find you, he will. He is incredibly rich and powerful.

They know that. It was a mistake to underestimate Romeo. No one expected the weasel to be so thorough.

By the way, how did you explain knowing about the tracker?

I had to fess up about our telepathic connection.

Isn't it dangerous? You've always told me how important it was to keep it a secret.

Vivian sighed. How else was I going to explain it? Female intuition? But that's okay. I trust these people. And besides, there was no other choice. Right now, the overriding consideration is getting you out. I hate thinking of what you're going through.

As long as I know you and Parker are safe, I'm okay. I can handle everything else.

Oh, sweetie. Just hang in there. Help is on the way. Things are more complicated now, but we will figure it out. You are not doomed to life as this mafioso's possession.

There are worse fates than that, Mom. I don't want anyone

getting killed over this, and I don't want you or Parker getting hurt.

As they kept the back and forth going for a little longer, the familiar banter with her mother managed to achieve what all the self-talk Ella had done before opening the channel had not. Her anxiety was mostly gone.

She yawned. *I'm tired, Mom. I should get some sleep.*

When are we going to talk again?

Maybe when I get to London.

4

TURNER

"It was a half-assed plan anyway." Yamanu clapped Julian on his back. "Now we can come up with something better, right, Turner?"

"Yeah." Turner glanced at Julian.

Ever since hearing the news about Ella, the kid looked like he'd aged twenty years. Sitting with his elbows propped on his knees and his head leaning on his knuckles, he was the picture of despondency.

Not that Turner was faring better. He'd failed the kid, and he'd failed Ella, and Victor Turner didn't do failure well.

It had killed his appetite the same as it had Julian's. That's why he was in the executive lounge with Yamanu, Arwel, and Julian, while the rest of the Guardians and the rescued girls were having breakfast down in one of the reception halls of the hotel.

Turner was supposed to be the pro, the best in his field, and Ella's situation was exactly what he'd been hired to do countless times in the past.

Usually, the people he rescued were hostages held for

ransom or for prisoner exchanges, not sex slaves, but other than that it was the same. What he needed to do was to switch mental gears and treat this the same as any other extraction operation he'd ever masterminded.

"Do you have a new plan?" Julian asked. "Are we going to follow her to London?"

"I wish it was that simple. Things like that take weeks to plan, and this one is more complicated than most because Gorchenco never stays in one place for long. I don't have enough information about him to come up with a plan yet."

Julian groaned. "That's what I was afraid of. I can't stop thinking about how much Ella is suffering, and how terrified she must be. It's eating me alive."

Arwel lifted the half empty bottle of whiskey he'd gotten from the hotel's bar, took a long swig, and pushed to his feet. "I have to get out of here. I can't handle the emotional overload of Julian's misery, and Turner's anger and guilt."

"Where are you going to go?" Yamanu asked.

"I'll ask Ragnar where his accounting department is. I love accountants. They have the quietest and least emotional minds."

"I'm not emotional." Turner waved a hand. "An operative can't allow emotions to cloud his or her cognitive pathways."

Yamanu cast him an amused glance. "Perhaps you need some of Arwel's medicine?"

"My mind needs to stay sharp. Besides, I don't drink so early in the day."

Swaying on his feet, Arwel lifted the bottle and waved it in front of Turner's face. "Try to live in my head for a few minutes. You'll be fighting me for the booze."

"What about florists?" Yamanu asked. "Aren't they even calmer than accountants?"

"I've never hung around florists, so I wouldn't know," Arwel said. "But I'm sure that no one is more stoic than bean counters. You see, they need to focus on the numbers, and they can't let their minds wander like someone arranging flowers can. The beauty of this is that numbers don't evoke emotions. Their minds are quiet and serene."

"Right." Yamanu chuckled. "Tell it to the Enron people."

Arwel waved a dismissive hand. "I'm talking under normal circumstances." He opened the door. "Call me if you need me. I'll be schmoozing with Ragnar's accountants."

"I don't know how you can make jokes at a time like this," Julian said as the door closed behind Arwel.

Yamanu walked over to the windows lining the wall of the executive lounge. "It's no joke to Arwel. Try to imagine feeling everyone's emotions as if they were your own. You wouldn't know if you were feeling depressed because of something relevant to you, or because the guy sitting next to you was depressed. It would drive me crazy. I admire Arwel for his sacrifice."

"What do you mean? It's not like he has a choice."

"Yes, he does. He doesn't have to be a Guardian. Imagine how much happier he would've been working in the accounting department. But he is a Guardian because his telepathic ability is an important tool. He chooses to protect the clan instead of opting for the easier way out."

Julian nodded. "I get it. Even though I'm only mildly telepathic, I couldn't stand the human hospital because I could feel everyone's misery and anxiety. Emotions get very powerful in a place like that. It was one of the main reasons why I quit my residency and came home. Unlike Arwel, I'm affected only by strong human emotions. Immortal minds are closed off to me."

Since Yamanu's speech about Arwel had nothing to do with Ella, Turner wondered whether Julian looked and sounded calmer because the hypnotic quality of Yamanu's voice had worked its magic on him.

Apparently, in addition to being a master thraller and shrouder, the guy could also inspire calm.

An interesting fellow, no doubt.

Would he have the same effect on the girls? Or would his size and his weird eyes intimidate them?

It was worth giving it a shot.

"So what now?" Yamanu asked. "Are we going home?"

"Yes, we are. We need to take our prisoners to the keep and deliver the girls to Vanessa. Then I need to go to my office and start organizing Gorchenco's file."

Julian pushed to his feet and walked over to the coffee carafe. "Can't you do it from here?" He poured himself a cup. "What if Gorchenco comes back in a day or two? You said he never stays in one place for long."

"You are right, and I plan on having a team stationed here. Including you, Yamanu."

The Guardian lifted a brow. "I don't think Onegus or Kian will approve."

What Yamanu had probably meant to say was that he didn't like being away from the village. Turner was well aware of that. But he might have no other choice.

"Right now, all of us are going home. If we have a large team stationed here, I don't want their time to be wasted waiting for Gorchenco to come back. We are going to reshuffle things and plan other rescue operations in this area. The logistics of that are not simple, although having Ragnar and his hotel helps. We can stash the weapons here instead of schlepping them back and forth."

"Bridget is going to pull her hair out," Yamanu said. "That's a lot of reshuffling you're talking about."

"I know. And that means that you, Julian, need to get your shit together and manage the clinic, so your mother can focus on that instead of trying to do both jobs."

"I will. And if I can help her to reorganize the schedule, I'll do that too."

"Good." Turner clapped him on his back.

Having something to do would make it easier for the kid. Especially when he found out about Ella's telepathic ability. Turner hadn't told anyone how he knew Gorchenco had taken Ella out of the country. People had just assumed that he'd learned it from one of his sources, and he hadn't bothered to correct the misconception.

The setback was difficult enough for Julian to swallow while he thought of Ella as just a girl he didn't know but cared about for some inexplicable reason.

It would be much worse when he learned that she was a potential Dormant.

5

VIVIAN

*A*fter talking with Ella, Vivian had a hard time concentrating on shopping. Her eyes were misted with tears and she couldn't see where she was going.

What a brave girl Ella was, and so selfless. Reminded of all their arguments, big and small, the little annoyances, the frustrations, Vivian realized how trivial they were, and how much she'd depended on her daughter throughout the years.

Even as a little girl, Ella had always been there to help out with Parker, holding him when he was fussy, feeding him, and changing poopy diapers—which had been the only thing she'd complained about but had done anyway.

Later, when she was older, Ella had babysat her little brother countless times, having an issue with it only when it was on the weekend and she wanted to hang out with her friends.

Vivian had taken all of that for granted, but she shouldn't have. Next time they talked, she was going to tell Ella how much she appreciated her.

Brushing a hand over her eyes, Vivian pulled out her

phone and glanced at the list of items still missing from her shopping bag. Since she hadn't bothered trying anything on, she'd limited her wardrobe purchases to three pairs of leggings, six T-shirts, and one sweatshirt. She still needed to get shoes, socks, underwear, a couple of pushup bras, toiletries, lotions, a brush or two, an eye pencil, and mascara. There were so many things a woman needed for proper grooming.

Right, she needed to get tweezers or her brows would turn into one.

An hour was not enough to get all that and also buy things for Parker. She'd need to move faster.

Taking a deep breath, Vivian started speed walking through the various departments.

Somehow, she managed to be done almost on time, rushing out the doors five minutes past the hour. Hefting several bags in each hand, she scanned the parking lot for Magnus's car.

When she'd gone into the store, there had been hardly any cars parked out in the lot; now there was an ocean of them, and she couldn't make out which one was his.

As he drove up to her, she sighed in relief.

"Let me help you with these," he said as he got out.

"Thank you. I bought as little as possible and still ended up with six full bags."

"Did you find all that you needed?"

She shrugged. "I bought basic stuff to hold us over for a week. It's not like we need fancy clothes."

"We can order things online." He opened the trunk of the SUV, which was already full of shopping bags.

"What did you guys buy? The entire gaming store?"

Parker turned around with a big grin. "Magnus told me to go crazy. So I did."

"You're spoiling him."

"I figured he needed the entertainment." Magnus opened the passenger door for her. "I don't know how long we are going to be cooped up in hiding." He waited for her to put the seatbelt on before closing the door.

"Where are we going to stay?"

Magnus grimaced. "You're not going to like it."

"As long as it's safe and has a bed and a bathroom, I don't care about anything else."

"I'm glad to hear that because the safe place is underground." He pulled out of the parking. "Some people get claustrophobic when there are no windows. I hope you're okay with that."

"Cool," Parker said. "Is it in your secret lair?"

Magnus chuckled. "Good guess, kid. It is. And that is why I will need to blindfold both of you before we get there."

Was he joking?

Except, Magnus wasn't smiling. In fact, he looked uncomfortable.

"You can't be serious."

He cast her an apologetic glance. "I trust you, but my boss is paranoid."

Oh, wow. He was serious.

Vivian shook her head. "I feel like Parker and I stumbled into a James Bond movie."

She glanced at Magnus's slacks and dress shirt. The top buttons were open, and he'd rolled up the sleeves, displaying muscular forearms with a light smattering of hair. His suit jacket was hanging from a hook in the back.

"You fit the part perfectly, but I don't." She looked down at her nonexistent cleavage. The James Bond hotties were usually well endowed.

"Of course you do. You're the gorgeous undercover spy who is trying to infiltrate my headquarters."

"Is that what your boss thinks?"

Another grimace confirmed it. "He's just being overly cautious. The way he explained it is that someone might be using you without your knowledge. Personally I think it's ridiculous, but he's the boss, so what he says goes."

She put a hand on his arm. "That's okay. I don't mind. It's just a bit odd. I don't want you to feel bad about a minor detail like that. Your organization is helping me so much without asking for anything in return. It would be ungrateful of me to complain about anything at all."

"Yeah, well. I'm not happy about it. We have a kid and a dog and they need sunlight and fresh air. Besides, living underground is depressing."

"We will manage for a few days."

Grimace number three. "That's the thing, Vivian, it might take much longer than that. Turner is good, but he needs time to plan."

"I'm hungry," Parker said. "Can we eat first?"

"Sure. And we should stop by a supermarket as well. The underground apartments don't have kitchens, but there is a bar with a fridge in each. It's kind of like a hotel suite."

Vivian wondered what kind of guests were entertained in the organization's underground quarters. If they came equipped with bars and fridges, they were obviously not meant for prisoners or people held for interrogation.

Were those like panic rooms? Except, instead of rooms they had entire apartments? How well funded were they to afford that? And who were their backers?

She had so many questions, but knowing Magnus, he'd give her evasive answers that wouldn't tell her anything. She didn't even know what these people called themselves. It couldn't be just the organization, or Turner's organization. Except, Turner was not even the big boss. Julian's mother headed it, and she answered to some other nameless boss.

"What's the name of your organization, Magnus? Can you at least tell me that?"

After a long moment of contemplation, when Vivian thought she wasn't going to get an answer even to that simple question, Magnus sighed. "We call ourselves the clan."

"Like a Scottish clan?"

"Yeah. That's where most of us came from."

"Just the clan. Not clan McSomething?"

"Just the clan."

Obviously, it was a nickname, but it was better than nothing or just calling it the organization.

A clan implied family.

Magnus had mentioned uncles and cousins who served in the same organization, so maybe the clan was indeed a family, and not just a group of people working together.

6

ELLA

A knock on the door woke Ella.

"One hour to landing," Misha opened the door a crack but didn't poke his head inside. "Get dressed and come out to eat lunch with boss."

Mentioning Dimitri was like dropping a bucket of dread on her head. An effective way to have her fully awake in under a second.

But lunch? She hadn't had breakfast yet.

Ella sat up and rubbed her eyes. "What time is it?"

"New York time or London's?"

"Both."

"It's twelve-thirty in the afternoon in New York, and five-thirty in London."

Ella didn't want to sound ignorant, but she had no idea what the time difference was. "Is that a.m. or p.m.?"

"It's p.m. Afternoon in London. You eat lunch, we land, and you go to boss's house."

"Oh, okay."

She'd been under the impression that Dimitri Gorchenco lived on his jets. But evidently not exclusively.

Was his house in England a sprawling estate like the one in New York?

The thing was, it didn't make sense for him to live in anything smaller. He would want a large estate that didn't have any close neighbors to spy on his illegal activities. And with the number of security people he employed, he needed a place big enough to house them.

Was it too much to hope that he had business meetings scheduled for the evening and wouldn't be back until the small hours of the night?

She needed more time to get used to the idea of him putting his hands on her.

And more.

Shivering, Ella hugged herself. She was such a damn scaredy cat.

What she needed to do was take one step at a time. First, she needed to get out of bed and into the bathroom. Then she needed to get dressed and remind herself of the proper eating etiquette Pavel had taught her.

Perhaps the lunch with Dimitri was a test to see how well she retained her lessons. Pavel had told her that if she always did her best, she would be fine. Did it mean that if she failed at something, Gorchenco was going to punish her?

Another shiver rocked her body as she imagined him slapping her across the face. No, he wouldn't do that. Dimitri Gorchenco seemed too cultured for that. He would tell Misha to do it.

Misha would apologize, but he'd do exactly what he was told.

I'm being silly.

No one was going to slap her around for choosing the wrong fork.

Just in case, though, she chose one of the Chanel skirt combos to wear, adding a conservative silk blouse under it. If she looked like a lady, maybe there was less chance of her getting slapped.

The combo was cream and pink-hued, so she put on a pair of red-soled cream-colored high-heeled pumps. Pinning her shoulder-length hair up in a chignon, she considered putting some mascara on but decided against it. Instead, she put on lip-gloss and sprayed herself with one of the perfumes Pavel had gotten for her.

Before leaving the room she opened a channel to her mother. *Everything still okay?*

Yes. What about you?

We are landing in London in about an hour. I can't talk because Dimitri is waiting to eat lunch with me. I just wanted to check on you guys.

We are safe.

Good. I'll talk to you later.

Misha waited for her by the stairs. "Very nice." He gave her the thumbs up. "Boss is going to like."

For a girl who was used to pants and sneakers, climbing the narrow staircase in a tight skirt and high heels was a perilous endeavor. Misha was right behind her, so if she fell, they were both going to tumble down.

On second thought, though, Misha would probably catch her and not even sway on his feet.

The guy was built like a brick house.

When she got to the upper deck, Dimitri surprised her by getting up and pulling out a chair for her. "Good afternoon, Ella. Did you sleep well?"

Even when he was being polite, the man was scary.

"Yes, thank you. And good afternoon to you too." She sat down.

He pushed her chair back in and walked around to the other side of the table.

Since he hadn't joined her in bed and was still wearing the same suit he'd had on the day before, Ella assumed he hadn't slept at all. Then again, he could've slept on the plane that had brought him to New York. It had been early in the morning when they'd taken off.

But maybe he'd done it out of consideration for her?

Not likely. He probably had lots of paperwork to go through, and stocks to check, or whatever else rich people did to manage their money.

"Would you care for coffee?" Dimitri asked.

"Yes, thank you."

A waiter, or was it a flight attendant, jumped to pour it for her. "What would madam like to eat for lunch?"

"I haven't had breakfast yet."

Dimitri waved a dismissive hand. "Just tell him what you want, and he'll have it prepared for you."

Ella wasn't hungry, but she had a feeling Dimitri would be upset if she refused food. "Two scrambled eggs with toast, please."

As those deep-set pale blue eyes bore into her, Ella was sure Gorchenco was going to say something about her family's escape.

Averting her eyes and holding her trembling hands in her lap so he wouldn't notice, she pretended to look at the large selection of liqueurs in the bar cabinet behind Dimitri.

"You look very nice," he said. "Pink is a good color on you."

"Thank you."

"Look at me when I'm talking to you."

"I'm sorry." She forced herself to do as he commanded.

"Am I so displeasing to you that you can't bear looking at me?"

Her eyes widened in fear. "No, not at all. You are very handsome." *For an old guy with thinning hair.* "You're just very scary."

Dimitri laughed, a deep-bellied laugh that shook the table. "I have this effect on people. Or at least on those with good survival instincts." He reached across the table, motioning for her to take his hand.

With an effort, she unclasped her hands and put one in his. It trembled only slightly.

He lifted her hand, looked for a moment at her short nails, grimaced, and then brought it to his lips for a kiss. "You have lovely hands, Ella. But you need proper nails." He held on to her hand for a moment longer before letting go.

"Your breakfast, madam." The waiter put a tray in front of her.

"Thank you."

There was a plate with scrambled eggs, a stand with a selection of different toasted bread slices, two jams and a small container of butter. Thankfully, there was only one fork and two knives, one of which was clearly for spreading butter and jam on her toast. Not that she wanted either. As nauseous as she felt, dry toast would be best.

Should she cut the toast, though? There had been no toast with the meal she'd shared with Pavel.

It was safer to start with the eggs.

"Regrettably, I have a meeting scheduled for this evening, so I'm unable to accompany you to the estate. Misha will take you and show you around. I'll probably get home late. You'll have to eat dinner without me."

"Yes, sir."

"I suggest that you rest. Maybe even take a nap. I want to enjoy your company when I come home."

Ella nearly choked on the little bit of scrambled egg she had in her mouth. Without spelling it out for her, Gorchenco had made his meaning crystal clear. Tonight, he intended to have sex with her.

Reaching across the table again, he took her hand and looked into her eyes. "You are a very beautiful girl, Ella, and you are smart. So far, you are meeting and even exceeding my expectations. If you continue to do so, I'm going to treat you like the rare treasure you are. You have nothing to fear from me."

7

MAGNUS

Magnus parked the car a few streets away from the keep. "Okay, guys. I'm sorry about that. But it's time for the blindfolds to come on."

"I already know that we are in downtown Los Angeles," Parker said.

"It's a big place." Magnus opened the trunk and pulled out two neckties from his duffle bag. "Vivian, I need you to move to the back seat. The windows in the back are darkened." He walked around and opened the door for her.

They were less than five minutes' drive away, but it was broad daylight and someone might notice a woman wearing a necktie around her eyes.

As Vivian took his offered hand, the small touch felt like an electrical shock. She must've felt it too because she chuckled nervously and pulled her hand away as soon as she was out of the car. "If the police stop us, we can say that we are on a scavenger hunt."

"I'd rather not have to provide explanations."

Opening the back door, he offered her his hand again, but Vivian pretended not to see it.

"Yeah, that would've sounded silly. Who does a scavenger hunt blindfolded, right?"

He handed her the ties. "I trust you guys to do it yourself."

"I can do it for both of us," Parker said.

"Thanks, buddy." Magnus closed the door and got behind the wheel.

"Is that good?" Parker asked.

Magnus looked at him in the rearview mirror. "Perfect. But how are you going to blindfold your mother when you can't see?"

"Oh, right. Can you do it, Magnus?"

Ah, to be young and innocent.

If Parker only knew what his suggestion had done to Magnus. The image of Vivian with nothing but a blindfold on, one that he'd tied on her himself, was damn erotic.

Vivian put a hand on her son's shoulder. "That's okay. I can do it myself."

Had she sounded a little breathy, or had he imagined it?

"Is that okay?" she asked after a moment, and this time, he wasn't imagining the husky tone.

"It's good." His own voice got a lot deeper.

Damn. Magnus hadn't played these kinds of games before. He had never had the desire or the inclination, but he was definitely inclined to play them with Vivian.

If she would have him.

The attraction was there just as strong if not stronger than in the beginning, but she seemed adamant about ignoring it for some reason.

Well, he could imagine a couple of them.

One was her daughter's perilous situation, and the other one was her so-called curse.

There was little he could do about either. Ella's rescue was up to Turner, and Magnus knew nothing about lifting curses, real or imagined.

As per Kian's instructions, he drove into the underground parking of one of the other clan-owned high rises. In each of them, the lowest level was reserved for maintenance and administration staff and closed off by a rolling gate. In reality, it was a restricted area only clan members had access to.

The newest additions to the system were the golf carts.

The tunnels connecting the buildings were long, but not so long as to necessitate motorized transportation. Except, ever since Turner had implemented the new evasion tactics, Guardians and any other clan members visiting or staying at the keep and later going to the village were required to park in the adjacent buildings and take the tunnels.

Currently, though, only a few civilians were using the keep's offices. Mostly, it served the Guardians. The village's training facilities were insufficient for the large number of Guardians, so they had to rotate between the two centers.

"We are here," he said as the gate closed behind them. "Don't move. I'll get a cart."

After loading their purchases in the back, he opened Parker's door. "Hold on to Scarlet. I'm going to carry you both to the cart."

Even the blindfold couldn't hide the kid's indignation. "I can walk."

"I don't want you to stumble and fall. This is going to be faster."

Without waiting for any more grumbling, he swung Parker into his arms, took two steps, and deposited him inside the cart.

Scarlet whimpered.

"Don't let her get away."

"I got her."

Vivian got out of the car and tried to follow the sound of their voices to the cart.

"Oh no, you don't." He swept her off her feet.

With a squawk, she wrapped her arms around him. "You should have given me a warning."

Her lips were so close, he felt himself being pulled to them as if by an invisible string. And then she went ahead and parted them.

"Who is heavier, Mom or me?" Parker broke the spell just in time.

Magnus released a breath he hadn't been aware of holding and put Vivian down next to her son. "You both weigh nothing. I'm going to spend the coming week fattening you up."

Getting behind the steering wheel, he pulled out his phone and opened the hidden door to the tunnel with the app William had designed. "Hold on to the side bars," he said before putting his foot on the pedal.

"Are we in a tunnel?" Parker asked as the hidden door closed automatically behind them. "My voice sounds weird in here."

"Yes, we are."

"How long is it?"

"I'm not going to tell you."

"Pfft. I can figure it out."

"You can try."

Just for the fun of it, Magnus drove around the

connecting tunnels, making the trip three times longer than it should've been.

"Wow, that's a long tunnel," Parker said.

"It's a labyrinth. If you don't know the way, you can get lost in here for days."

"Really?" Vivian asked.

"Yes. Never go into the tunnels without me."

The tunnels had motion-detecting sensor lights, and anyone with minimal orientation skills would know how to navigate them, but he didn't want Parker getting any ideas and trying to find his way out.

When he was sure Parker was thoroughly confused, Magnus turned into the keep's tunnel and entered the clan's reserved parking level.

"You can take off the blindfolds now."

Parker yanked his off and looked around. "This is just another parking garage."

Vivian took hers off and smoothed her hand over her hair. "What did you expect?"

The boy shrugged. "I thought Magnus would drive into a big elevator that would take us like twenty floors down into an underground complex full of scientists working on secret stuff."

"You watch too many action movies," Vivian said.

Offering her a hand to help her out of the cart, Magnus chuckled. "Actually, he is not too far off. There is an elevator that will take us down. But we have to walk to it. And right now I'm not sure there is anyone there. Except for the boss's butler. He was supposed to come and tidy up."

Parker's eyes widened. "Your boss is really like Batman, a rich dude who helps people, and he even has a butler. Is his name Alfred?"

Magnus picked up all the bags from the back of the cart and headed for the elevator bank. "If you're asking about the butler, his name is Okidu. Can you pick up Scarlet? She looks scared."

The dog was sniffing in a frenzy, trying to figure out where she was.

"Sure." Parker scooped her up. "What kind of a name is Okidu? It sounds like one of the munchkins from *The Wizard of Oz*."

"Appropriate," Vivian muttered under her breath. "I feel like we've been sucked into the land of Oz."

8

VIVIAN

"This is really deep," Parker said as the elevator kept going down.

Instinctively, Vivian looked up even though all she could see was the elevator's ceiling.

"Are you bothered by the depth?" Magnus asked.

"Is there ground above us, or is it just the building?"

"It's all built up. The underground has several floors. On top of those are the parking levels. And on top of the parking there is a high rise."

"Then it's fine. Having tons of earth on top would've bothered me. But I don't care how many floors are above me. It doesn't have the same oppressive feeling."

As the lift finally came to a stop and the doors opened, Vivian was startled by the smiling face of a butler. He was so stereotypical that there was no mistaking him for anything but. Okidu was short and stocky, in his mid-forties, and wore a suit and tie.

"Madam, Master Magnus, young master, and of course Scarlet." He bowed. "Welcome to the keep. May I show you to your apartments?"

He also spoke with a lovely British accent.

Magnus hefted a pile of shopping bags. "Lead the way."

"Oh, no." Okidu rushed to him. "Let me carry the bags, master." He wrestled them out of Magnus's hands without too much resistance.

Scarlet sniffed at the butler's feet and then retreated into the safety of the elevator.

"Thank you." Magnus lifted the dog into his arms. "It's only Okidu. You know him."

"Please, follow me." The butler smiled his big fake smile and rushed forward as if the bags were filled with inflated balloons and not lots of heavy stuff.

"He is very strong," Vivian whispered.

Magnus chuckled. "He is. Also, don't let that charming smile fool you. He is more stubborn than a mule. That's why I let him carry the bags. Resistance is futile. Okidu sees it as an offense when someone refuses to let him do his job."

"And I guess he decides what's included in that definition."

"You got it."

After the luxuriously appointed elevator, stepping into the industrial-looking corridor was somewhat of a letdown.

Not only that, the doors they were passing by were strange. First of all, they were made of metal, not wood, and they were about a foot thick. She could tell because each came with two windows, one on top and one on the bottom. Were those prison cells? Or was Magnus taking her to an insane asylum?

She wasn't the only one discomforted, though. Baring her teeth, Scarlet growled at the doors.

Dark Widow's Curse

"Shush, girl." Magnus patted her head. "There is nothing to be afraid of."

"What is this place?" Vivian looked up at him.

He grimaced. "This is the dungeon level, and some of these rooms are cells. But don't worry. Yours is going to be a well-appointed apartment. The same interior decorator who worked on the cabin did the underground apartments."

"Here is yours, madam." Okidu stopped in front of a door that didn't have the dual windows, but was made from the same metallic-looking material as the others.

He punched a code into a keypad and the door swung open. Just like the other ones she'd seen on the way, it was about a foot thick.

"Please, madam, after you." The butler bowed.

Despite the prison door, the inside was indeed beautifully done. It wasn't the same style as the cabin, which was furnished with more rustic looking furniture and colors, but Vivian could recognize the decorator's attention to detail.

The colors were light earth tones, the overstuffed couch was piled with pillows, and vibrant art reproductions adorned the walls. Except for the one over the couch. That looked like an original. It was a portrait of a gorgeous short-haired brunette with full red lips that were lifted in a suggestive smile.

Except for the lack of windows, the place looked like a luxurious hotel suite. It didn't look like an underground panic apartment.

"Where should I put the shopping bags?" Okidu asked.

Magnus pointed at the floor next to the entry door. "Just leave everything here. We will take care of the rest."

After arranging the bags in a neat row against the wall, the butler bowed. "There are soft drinks and snacks in the refrigerator, and there is more dry food in the cabinet on top."

"Thank you, Okidu."

"Where am I going to sleep?" Parker called out from the bedroom. "There is only one bed and I'm not sharing it with you, Mom. I'm too old for that."

"The sofa opens into a bed," Okidu said.

Parker didn't look happy. "I guess I can sleep on the couch. But what about you, Magnus?"

The butler bowed again. "Master's bedroom is next door."

Now that he had spelled it out, Vivian remembered him saying apartments and not apartment. She didn't like the idea of Magnus not sleeping in the same place as her and Parker.

It was an irrational feeling. No one was going to find them in this place. Not even Gorchenco with all of his resources and his goons. But she didn't feel safe without Magnus near.

"Can I see?" Parker asked.

"Sure." Magnus picked up Scarlet and followed Okidu out.

If Parker was going, Vivian saw no reason to stay behind.

It was literally the next door over, which made her feel a little better. It was a single room, not a living room and bedroom combo, but it had a sitting area right when entering and the bed was in the back. There was also a wet bar with a fridge.

"Nice," Magnus said. "Scarlet can sleep on the couch."

Which reminded Viv that it had been a while since the

dog was walked. "Don't you need to take her out to do her business?"

"Oh, yes." Okidu smiled. "Doctor Bridget suggested that I purchase pee pads for Scarlet. I put a big box in the bathroom."

"Gross," Parker said. "You should put them somewhere else."

"Yeah, I should." Magnus walked out into the corridor. "Any suggestions, Okidu?"

"I am afraid I would not know, master. I have not been programmed with a dog care routine."

What an odd choice of words. The more time she spent around the butler, the weirder he seemed.

"I'll find a solution. In the meantime, would you mind bringing the rest of the things from the cart?"

The butler bowed. "Right away, sir."

"I also need the codes for the keypads."

"Both have the same code. It's Master Kian's birthday." The butler opened his mouth to continue, but Magnus lifted a hand to shush him. "I know what it is. I'll reprogram them to something that is easy for Vivian and Parker to remember."

Okidu bowed. "As you wish, master." The butler turned around and walked out into the corridor.

"He is such a strange dude," Parker said. "But I like him."

Vivian examined the room side of the door. There was no keypad. In fact, there was no handle either. "Can it be opened or locked from the inside?"

"Yes. I'll program your phone with the application that does it."

"You have an app for opening and locking doors?"

"Just these ones."

Now she was sure that even the fancy apartments were used to hold prisoners. "Who stays in here? Because without interior locking mechanisms for the doors, they would be useless as panic rooms, which I thought they were."

Magnus wrapped an arm around her shoulders. "Excellent observation. I'll tell you all about it over dinner."

9

ELLA

Dimitri left as soon as they had landed, leaving Ella with Misha.

As the bodyguard followed her into the bedroom, she rushed to collect the pile of garments strewn over the bed. "I'm usually not that messy. But you said to hurry up." She'd tried several outfits before deciding what to wear for lunch with the boss.

"I help you pack," Misha said.

"No." She put a hand out to stop him. "I can do it myself."

"Boss told me to help you. The limo is waiting outside."

"It won't take long. In the meantime, you can take the other suitcases down. I'll be done by the time you're back for the rest of it."

His thin lips pressed into a tight line, he didn't look happy. "Okay," he finally agreed. "I'll take the suitcases to the limo."

"Thanks."

Misha, as she was discovering, was an okay guy

despite his thuggish appearance. His misshapen nose and burly muscles didn't scare her. Dimitri, on the other hand, with his intelligent eyes and fancy suits, did.

Maybe the reason for it was that Ella believed she could manipulate and outsmart the bodyguard but not his boss.

After Gorchenco's comment about spending the evening with her, she'd planned on going into the bathroom and opening a channel to her mom, but there was no time for that. It would have to wait until they reached Dimitri's estate. Maybe by the time they got there, Ella would calm down enough to talk with her mom without freaking her out.

Hopefully, the drive was long because it would take a while.

How did she get ready for having sex with a stranger who thought he owned her?

Who was she kidding?

He did own her. Maybe not her soul, but everything else.

If only she could talk to Maddie. But, of course, she couldn't. In fact, she hoped Gorchenco didn't know about her friend. If he couldn't get his hands on her family, he might consider taking Maddie instead.

But since Romeo and Stefano had known about her, it was wishful thinking to assume that Dimitri didn't.

Except, Ella wouldn't give him a single reason to go to all that trouble. She was going to be the obedient little toy he wanted, and, hopefully, that would be enough to convince him that he didn't need to threaten anyone to ensure her cooperation.

As she finished putting her toiletries into the makeup bag, Misha returned and waited by the door with his arms crossed over his chest and a reproachful expression on his face.

"All done." She cast him a smile. "We can go."

He took the case from her, lifted the overstuffed suitcase with ease, and jogged down the stairs. Ella followed more carefully, holding on to the railing and watching her step.

Except, maybe she should fall on purpose?

If she broke a leg, Gorchenco couldn't have sex with her tonight. With only about six steps to go, though, she would probably just get banged up and not break anything.

There was enough pain in her future without adding that to the mix.

"You want to watch movie?" Misha asked as she buckled up.

"Sure. How long is the drive?"

"Two hours. Maybe more if there is traffic."

"That is long. Is Dimitri's British estate as big as the one in New York?"

Misha pursed his lips. "Maybe bigger. The one in Russia is the biggest. You drive for many miles from the guard gate to the house. He has a lake, with boats. Maybe he take you on a boat. He also has many horses. Maybe he take you riding."

"I don't know how. I've never been on a horse before. Besides, Pavel didn't get me any riding clothes."

Misha waved a dismissive hand. "Pavel is not the only guy buying clothes for boss."

"Does he have a Pavel in every estate?"

"Not the same name. But someone like him. Every house has a full staff."

Ella stifled a chuckle. Misha was so literal, and he

wasn't very smart. "It seems that Dimitri is providing employment for a lot of people. Does he pay you well?"

Misha shrugged. "It's okay. But I work for boss even if he don't pay well." He put a hand over his heart. "I have debt of honor."

"What does it mean?"

"It mean that boss helped me, and I owe him."

"Your life?"

"Yes." He smiled, showing his crooked teeth and a couple of gold crowns. "Now tell me what movie you want."

"You choose. I'm still tired. I wish I could take a nap until we get there."

Misha reached under the seat and pulled out a zipped up plastic bag. "Here is pillow and blanket." He unzipped the bag and arranged the things for her on the seat across from him. "You can sleep here."

"Thank you. That's wonderful." She kicked off her shoes, took off her jacket, and climbed under the blanket. "I wish I had pajamas. You don't happen to have some under that seat, do you?"

"No, sorry. But if you take skirt off under the blanket I don't watch."

"Don't mind if I do."

Turning her back to him, she thought about opening a channel to her mother. Misha wasn't the sharpest tool in the shed, and even if he noticed something off about her, he would assume she was dreaming.

What was the time over there?

They had landed at about six-thirty in the evening London time, and another hour or so had passed since then. Calculating the time difference, Ella figured it was eleven-thirty in the morning over in California.

The timing was good, but the subject Ella needed advice on wasn't something she felt comfortable talking to her mother about. Especially since she hadn't figured out a way to deal with it yet. Freaking her mom out wasn't going to help either of them, and it wasn't as if Ella was ignorant about sex and needed her mother to explain things to her.

Most of her friends had given up their virginity a while ago, and they'd supplied her with all the raunchy details. The rest had come from her mom's romance novels, which were quite explicit. What none of the books or her friends could've helped her with, though, and that included her mother, was how to handle a first time with someone she didn't desire.

Being a virgin didn't mean that Ella was naive. Love wasn't a prerequisite to sex, but attraction was. With Romeo, she'd had both, but it had all been an illusion he'd created to entrap her.

With Dimitri, Ella had neither.

The irony was that in order to cope, she'd have to create a mirage of desire and convince herself it was real.

10

MAGNUS

As the three of them walked back into the larger apartment, Parker started rummaging through the shopping bags.

"Where is my Switch? Here it is." The kid hugged the box to his chest. "Is there an internet connection here?"

"There should be. I'll have to call and check." Magnus knew that there was, but he didn't know whether it was okay to give the password to outsiders. "First things first, though, I need to take Scarlet out. In the meantime, start connecting your systems."

Parker eyed the big screen television hanging on the wall, then turned to look at the couch, and then back at the television. "Mom, is there a chance you'll let me use the bedroom and you take the sofa?"

"That's not very gentlemanly of you," Magnus said.

"I know. But the distance is all wrong. The couch is too close to the screen. And what if you and Mom want to talk? I will have to keep it quiet or use the Switch."

That was true. In addition, sneaking in and out at night would be much easier if Parker was in the bedroom with the door closed. Otherwise, Vivian would have to wait until he fell asleep and tiptoe around him.

Except, she might realize the same thing and use Parker as a chastity belt.

"We will talk about it later," Vivian said.

"But, Mom! I need to know where to connect my console. Do I hook it up to the screen in the living room or the one in the bedroom?"

Shaking her head, Vivian let out a breath. "How about a compromise? During the day you can play in the bedroom. But at bedtime you get the couch, and if you can't fall asleep, you can play with your Switch for a little while. I don't want you playing all night long."

His slim shoulders slumping, Parker muttered under his breath, "I'll hook it up in the living room."

"That doesn't mean I'll let you play until morning."

"I know."

By the smug look on Parker's face, the kid was going to wait until his mother fell asleep and then play to his heart's content.

"Master," Okidu called from the corridor. "I have the rest of the things. Where should I put them?"

"In my room. Those are all Scarlet's and mine."

"Very well."

Scarlet whimpered and nudged his leg.

"I'd better take her out. Are you okay here on your own? I can ask Okidu to hang around until I come back."

She waved a hand. "I don't need a babysitter, and this place seems more secure than the National Treasury. I'll get our stuff organized and check what's in the fridge and in the cabinets. You might have to get us some things from the supermarket."

"Good deal. Leave the door open. I won't be long."

"Okay."

"When I come back, I'll download onto your phone the application that controls the door's mechanism. Without it, if you close the door, you won't be able to open it from the inside."

"Yeah, you told me that. But you can open it if I call you, right? As long as there is reception." She winked.

Smart lady.

He put a finger to his lips and glanced at Parker. The kid was absorbed in hooking up his console to the screen and hadn't paid attention to their conversation.

Vivian gave him the thumbs up.

As Magnus walked Scarlet toward the elevator, he passed the two occupied cells. Vivian had glanced at them, but he doubted she knew anyone was inside. Her human senses couldn't have detected anything. Except, as a Dormant, she might have some extrasensory perception in addition to her telepathic ability.

In any case, though, he wasn't going to tell her unless she asked.

Since they hadn't captured any Doomers lately, the only ones who could be in there were Romeo and his uncle Stefano, which meant that the team was back from New York.

He texted Arwel from the elevator. *I'm in the dungeon level with Vivian and Parker. Are Romeo and the uncle our neighbors?*

A couple of minutes passed before his phone pinged with the answer. *Indeed. Don't worry. The cells are soundproof.*

When did you get here?

We dropped them off less than an hour ago. Good timing. It would've been awkward if we bumped into you.

Awkward was the wrong term. As gentle as Vivian appeared, Magnus had a feeling she would've attacked both scumbags and scratched their eyes out.

Hey, maybe he should let her. It could be therapeutic. The satisfaction from exacting revenge was underestimated.

Any new plans?
Not yet. Turner is in a meeting with Kian.
Keep me posted.
I will.

After going through the clan's parking garage's secret passageway and climbing the stairs to the next level up, he took the building's regular elevator to the lobby and stopped at the guard station.

"Hello, Jeff," he greeted the one human guard he knew by name. "I need to order dinner and have it delivered here."

"No problem. Nice dog." Jeff bent to scratch behind Scarlet's ears. "I didn't know we allowed pets in the building."

"We don't. Scarlet is the exception. She is training to be a guard dog."

Magnus had forgotten about the no pets rule. Obviously, it didn't apply to him, but the guards didn't know that. They also didn't know that he wasn't staying at one of the upper-floor apartments.

As far as they were concerned, Magnus and the other Guardians worked for a private security company that rented an entire floor in the building. According to Anandur, immortals used to work the guard station along with humans, but since the move to the village, only one immortal per shift supervised the entire building's security. The rest was handled by human guards.

While walking Scarlet down the street, Magnus texted William. *Can I give Vivian and Parker the access code to the underground's internet?*

The activity will be monitored. You should let the mother know.

I will. Thanks.

Next, Magnus placed a dinner order with a steakhouse he and the other Guardians favored.

The estimated wait time was an hour and a half.

Hopefully, Okidu had stocked the place with enough snacks to hold them over until the food arrived.

The question was what to do with them after that. Being locked up in the underground was going to feel oppressive. Although, if left to his own devices, Parker would play video games all day long and half the night.

Perhaps he could take the kid to the shooting range. There was also the pool. He could take Vivian and Parker swimming.

Come to think of it, he could teach Vivian how to handle a gun.

The woman was so small and skinny that he doubted self-defense moves were going to do her any good even against an untrained assailant. First, she would need months of weight training to build up some muscle.

Or, she could shortcut the whole thing by transitioning.

On the other hand, Tessa, Jackson's mate, who was built on a similar scale, was doing exceptionally well at the self-defense classes. The Krav Maga course she'd taken had been a big help.

A light bulb lit up in Magnus's head.

The traditional style they were teaching at the center was suitable for strong, immortal males. Guardians in particular. Krav Maga, on the other hand, could benefit the rest of the clan members who were basically a bunch of out-of-shape couch potatoes like his roommates.

Could Tessa teach it?

He fired up a text to Onegus. *I have an idea. Why don't we teach Krav Maga as self-defense instead of what we do now?*

Because we don't have a teacher.

What about Tessa?

She's a beginner.

Give it some thought. Perhaps we can send one of the Guardians to learn it and then teach it to the rest of us.

I'll think about it. How is the babysitting job? Ready to pull out your goatee?

I guess you didn't hear yet.

Hear what?

Vivian might be a Dormant. She has telepathic abilities.

You lucky bastard.

11

VIVIAN

As Vivian put away the last of their things in the closet, Parker finished setting up his gaming station and started shooting villains.

Being cooped up in a basement wasn't healthy for either of them. But at least Parker had plenty of new games to keep him busy, and with the amount of jumping around and yelling, he was even getting a bit of a workout.

"I'm going to get in the shower. When I'm done, it's your turn."

"Why?" he asked without pausing the game or looking at her. "It's not bedtime yet."

"I know. But we had a long day and you were holding Scarlet a lot. You're covered in dog hair."

"So I'll change clothes."

"Shower first. I don't want you putting on fresh clothes over a dirty body."

"Fine," he grumbled to shut her up.

What was it with boys and water avoidance?

Ella had never given Vivian trouble in that department. If anything, the fights had been over her taking too long because she loved soaking in the bathtub while reading a book.

God, I miss her.

With a sigh, Vivian turned the water on in the shower, folded her clothes on the counter and got under the spray. Hopefully, there was a washer and dryer combo somewhere in this sprawling underground. She'd bought enough clothes for a week, but if they had to stay longer, she would need to do laundry.

Perhaps Magnus could take stuff to a laundromat. Except, her underwear. She would wash her panties by hand and hang them to dry in the bathroom.

When she was done, Vivian wrapped herself in one of the big fluffy towels the butler must've brought, and padded to the closet.

She'd learned a few things while listening to Okidu. Like the name of Magnus's boss. Vivian had never met anyone named Kian, but it had a nice sound to it. She'd also learned that Doctor Bridget, who she knew was Julian's mother and the head of their rescue organization, had contact with the butler, which could mean that she and Kian lived near each other. Either that, or the big boss brought his butler to work, which was less likely.

Admittedly, it wasn't much. But Magnus wasn't forthcoming with information, and she had to glean as much as she could from other people in his organization, like Julian and Okidu.

"Dinner should get here in about an hour," she heard Magnus tell Parker. "In the meantime, I can show you guys around."

"Yeah, sure." Parker sounded as excited about Magnus dragging him away from his game as if he had been asked to do the dishes.

"I'll be right out," she called out.

"No hurry. Take your time," Magnus replied.

In the closet, Vivian took out a bright red T-shirt and pulled it over her black padded bra. She then added a pair of black leggings and slipped into the pair of flip-flops Magnus had gotten her at Walmart.

The red made her look less pale, and the tight leggings accentuated the few curves she had. Not bad, Vivian had to admit. But something with a little heel would've been nice, since Magnus was such a tall guy and she was so short. Except, the only other shoes she'd bought were a pair of sneakers.

Besides, she shouldn't be thinking about looking attractive for the guy. She was supposed to dissuade him from pursuing her, not encourage him.

Right.

And that was the reason she'd been so tempted to let Parker have the bedroom. Because it hadn't crossed her mind that sneaking out to go to Magnus's room would be easier if she slept on the couch in the living room.

Not at all.

She was such a damn hypocrite.

"You look nice." Magnus gave her an appreciative look-over. "Red is a good color on you."

"Thanks."

"Ready for the tour?"

"What is there to see?"

"Plenty."

"Can I stay here?" Parker asked.

"And miss the shooting range?"

That had gotten her son's attention. "There is a shooting range? Like with real guns?"

"And bows and arrows too."

"I'm coming."

She'd never seen him close a game faster.

In the elevator, she noticed that Magnus pressed his thumb on the display. He'd done the same when they'd arrived, but she hadn't thought it was significant. It had looked as if he was just pressing a number.

"Is the elevator coded with your thumbprint?"

"Yes."

"Cool," Parker said. "Are Mom and I going to get our thumbprints scanned so we can use it too?"

Magnus looked uncomfortable. "I'll have to check with the boss."

"You said we are not prisoners here."

"You're not."

The elevator stopped and they got out on another underground level.

"You are guests, but you don't get the keys to the house, so to speak." He led them down the corridor.

"But we can't leave without having access to the elevators."

"That's true. But I'm not leaving you alone here. So it's not like you don't have a way out." He pushed the doors open to a large gym. "This is our training center, and it's top secret. I can't give thumbprint access to nonmembers. And even if I wanted to, I don't know how to program it. Our tech guy takes care of things like that."

"It's empty," Parker stated the obvious. "Where is everyone?"

"Usually, people are training here this time of day, but right now everyone is assigned to a mission. Whoever had time off gave it up to go to New York. They've just gotten back."

Vivian swallowed. "Now I feel bad about complaining.

Here I am bitching about not having the freedom to come and go as I please, when you guys are going out of your way to help Ella and me."

Magnus patted her shoulder. "No one likes having their options taken away from them. I understand your frustration. But this is the best we can do."

"And I'm thankful for it."

"I know. Now let's go and check out the shooting range."

"Yay! Am I going to shoot a gun?" Parker glanced at Vivian.

"Isn't he too young? And don't tell me you were shooting guns when you were nine because I'm not going to believe you."

"Okay. I wasn't shooting at nine. I was eleven."

Vivian rolled her eyes. "Things must be really different in Scotland."

"Oh, I don't know about that. In the States, the minimum age for a shooting range practice is eight, as long as the child is accompanied by an adult."

"That can't be true."

"You can check if you don't believe me."

"I didn't bring my phone."

Magnus pulled his out, typed in the inquiry, and handed it to her.

"I'll be damned. It is eight."

Parker looked beyond smug, but he was wise enough not to say anything.

"If it makes you feel any better," Magnus said. "We can start with the bow and arrows practice. I just hope we have one that is small enough for Parker."

"Did the butler get mine from the car?"

"He did. But let's check first if we can find a small bow. Maybe Carol's would fit you."

"Who's Carol?"

Magnus wrapped his arms around her shoulder. "She is training to join our organization." The satisfied smirk on his face indicated that he hadn't missed the note of jealousy in her tone. "She is family."

"Oh."

12

EVA

Eva's living room was like a busy hive. Nathalie and Sharon were putting up decorations, while Tessa and Callie were organizing the buffet table.

Bhathian, Robert, and Jackson were rearranging furniture. To make room for the foldable tables and chairs, the couch and armchairs had been moved to the bedroom.

Oblivious to the noise, her little guy nursed at her breast, his tiny hand squeezing it in sync with his suckling.

So precious.

Pushing the glider back and forth, Eva sang softly to her baby while her adopted family and friends prepared a celebration in the little guy's honor.

"What shall we name you, my little one?" she whispered as he let go of her breast and let out a tiny contented sigh before falling asleep.

Everyone was making a big fuss about her not naming the baby yet, and maybe they were right. She should've done it the day he'd been born, but a week later he still remained nameless because she couldn't make up her mind.

He'd come into the world without much fuss. Less than two hours after her waters had broken, she'd held her bundle of joy in her arms.

Such a sweet baby he was, so peaceful, and in turn, Eva was at peace too.

With Nathalie, her life had been in turmoil. Pregnant and alone, Eva had left her job and married the first guy who she'd deemed a suitable father for her baby. Fernando had been a good choice in that regard, but he'd been a lousy husband. She hadn't been happy with him.

Except, not all of it had been his fault. She'd married a man she hadn't loved, had been forced to keep her immortality a secret from him and everyone else, and had lived in constant fear of discovery.

No wonder their relationship had been strained.

Still, despite all of it, Eva had been faithful to him, while Fernando had not been faithful to her. Nathalie had tried to persuade her to forgive him, but Eva couldn't. She just wasn't the forgiving type.

Heck, she was an avenger.

Or rather had been.

Her vigilante days were over. Bhathian hadn't been there for her when she'd raised his daughter, but fate had given them another chance at being a family, and she wasn't going to squander the gift. Until her precious one was old enough to start school, Eva was going nowhere.

As Bhathian had pointed out, she was an immortal, and as one she had all the time in the world to try new things. For the next several years, she was going to give domestic life a shot.

Hopefully, staying at home wouldn't drive her crazy,

and the craving for adventure and danger would stay dormant.

Right now, she was perfectly happy to sit in her rocking chair with her baby in her arms, immersed in a sea of love and tranquility.

"Where should we put the meat pies?" Ruth asked.

Behind her, Nick walked in carrying a warming bag that was so big, Eva couldn't see his face behind it.

Tessa pointed at the buffet table. "Everything except for the desserts goes there."

The party was a joint effort, with Sharon coordinating who brought what.

He put the thing down and came over to her rocking chair. "Hello, my little brother." Nick smoothed a finger over the baby's cheek.

Eva's heart swelled and her eyes misted with tears. Nick was like a son to her, but before transitioning, he hadn't known that she was old enough to be his grandmother and had teased her about her maternal attitude toward him and the other two crew members of her detective agency. Now that all three had become immortal, and all of them lived in the village, they were finally acting like a real family.

Damn. The hormonal changes were wreaking havoc on her brain. Since she'd gotten pregnant, Eva had been tearing up over nothing.

"Babies' skin is so soft," he murmured in wonder. "Did you come up with a name for him yet?"

"Nope."

"How about Rupert?" he teased.

"That's what you'll call your son."

"It's a good name. It's another form of Robert."

"We already have a Robert in the family."

"So what? Does it bother you that he's an ex Doomer?"

"No. Robert is a good guy. But I want an original name for my baby."

The thing was, a name was important, and Eva preferred to take her time and choose the perfect one for her perfect little guy.

"I still think you should name him Fernando," Nathalie muttered under her breath.

They'd been arguing over it for days. Fernando's health was deteriorating rapidly, which was affecting Nathalie. He didn't remember anyone and was refusing food. Bridget said it was the end.

Naturally, Nathalie wanted to honor his memory by naming her little brother after him. She loved her adoptive father, as well she should. He'd been wonderful to her. But it wasn't going to happen, and not only because Eva still resented her ex-husband for cheating on her.

It was bad luck to name a baby after someone who was nearing death.

The baby deserved a new beginning with no old baggage weighing down his destiny. Not to mention the fact that it would be beyond bizarre to name Bhathian's son after her ex-husband. What on earth could Nathalie have been thinking? Bhathian was an easy-going guy, but even he had his limits.

"Can I kiss his cheek?" Nick asked.

"Of course."

As his lips feathered over the baby's skin, Nick's eyes rolled back in his head. "I want one."

"Then you should talk to your mate."

"We are working on it."

That was news to her. "You are?"

"Well, since we are not using protection, it might

happen." His smile vanished. "We know not to expect anything soon."

Eva put a hand on his cheek. "The Fates will grant you a child when it's time."

"I guess." He pushed to his feet. "I'd better go help the guys with the chairs."

As she watched the open front door, more people came in. Eva smiled and waved at Amanda and Dalhu, and then at Anandur and Wonder.

Since Turner was probably busy with the rescue mission, Bridget came alone, although Eva had heard the operation had been aborted because the girl had been taken out of the country. A small rush of excitement ran through her as she imagined getting on board and helping out.

They could use a good undercover spy like her to infiltrate that Russian mobster's organization.

Not this time.

Leaning, she kissed her baby's forehead.

Sharon was too inexperienced to pull off a stunt like that, and Eva was not leaving her precious boy for any assignment.

"How are you doing?" Bridget asked.

"Are you asking as a doctor or as a friend?"

"Both."

"Breastfeeding is going well, and as far as my hormones, I'm emotional but in a good way. This little one is like a soothing balm on my soul. I feel at peace."

The doctor smiled. "I'm glad. Do you have a name for him yet?"

"No."

"Then I have a suggestion."

As did everyone else. "What is it?"

"Ethan. It means mighty or strong in Hebrew."

Eva looked down at her baby's sleeping face. He was still tiny, but she could sense the strength in him. One day he was going to be a mighty warrior, she had no doubt of that. With her as his mother and Bhathian as his father, he was not likely to become a poet.

"I like it."

Bridget grinned. "Are you going to put it to the vote?"

That had been the original idea behind the party. Sharon wanted to collect suggestions for names and have people vote for the one they liked.

"Yeah, I will. But I think I'll choose Ethan even if it doesn't win."

Bridget grinned. "You are the mother. It's your call."

13

VIVIAN

"That's a lot of food." Vivian eyed the two hefty bags Magnus walked in with.

"Whatever we can't eat we'll put in the fridge." He put the bags on the table. "We can heat up the leftovers for lunch tomorrow."

"I smell steak," Parker said.

Magnus pulled out a Styrofoam container and put it on top of the plate Vivian had set on the table. "You smell correct."

"Then there will be no leftovers." Parker rubbed his palms together. "I'll have a midnight snack."

"You're not staying up all night." Vivian opened the first container and transferred its contents onto the plate.

Magnus did the same with the other two. "I also got a salad for us to share and a dessert." He looked at her expectantly.

"Thank you for dinner."

"You're welcome." Given the disappointed look on his face, that wasn't what he'd been expecting.

It took her another moment to realize what it was.

"And thank you for remembering to get some veggies. And for the dessert."

"My pleasure." The big smile on his handsome face proved that she'd guessed correctly. "Let's dig in before it gets cold."

Men were like overgrown boys, seeking praise and acknowledgment from the women in their lives. First the mother, and then the wife or significant other. Women sought their men's approval too, just about different things.

After being alone for so long, Vivian had forgotten that.

Besides, she wasn't Magnus's anything. He shouldn't care whether she approved of him or not. And the same was true for her.

Except, she cared. And she approved.

If Magnus had any annoying habits or quirks, he hadn't shown them yet. He wasn't messy, he was helpful, polite, considerate...

"Aren't you hungry?" Magnus asked.

She'd been caught daydreaming. "Only a little."

As the guys exchanged knowing glances, she imagined their silent communication.

Who needs to be hungry to eat a juicy steak?

Girls are weird. They like salads.

Forking a few leaves of raw salad, she looked at Magnus across the round table. "While you were gone, I thought about how we are going to manage food-wise."

He finished chewing and wiped his mouth with a napkin. "Don't worry about it. We can have everything delivered, and there are also vending machines in the lobby that I can bring sandwiches and pastries from."

"That's nice, but I would like to prepare simple meals here. If nothing else, it will give me something to do."

He paused with another piece of steak on his fork. "What do you need?"

"Can I make you a list?"

"Sure. I can have it delivered. They deliver groceries, you know."

"Yeah, but I don't trust those services. What if they bring us rotten tomatoes and wilted lettuce?"

"We can try it once. And if it doesn't work, we will come up with a different solution."

"I like restaurant food," Parker said. "It's tasty." He cast her an apologetic look.

"Don't get too used to that. When we go back home, you'll have to make do with my cooking. We don't have the budget for dining out every day."

After that announcement, there was a long moment of silence around the table.

Magnus attacked his steak with renewed vigor, cutting away with such force, she was afraid he would cut the plate, while Parker pushed a piece of tomato around.

She wondered what they were thinking. They were probably as torn as she was. On the one hand, she couldn't wait to get Ella back, but on the other hand, she didn't want to say goodbye to Magnus. Having him around felt too damn right, and she wasn't even thinking about their mutual attraction or the great sex they'd shared.

Except, there was that too.

Parker broke the silence. "You promised to tell me how Ella called you without having your phone number."

Vivian had hoped he'd forgotten.

It wasn't going to be an easy conversation. She'd better lay it out without much preamble and then address Parker's questions and soothe his hurt feelings. "I think you've suspected what I'm going to tell you for a long time now. Your sister and I share a special connection. We can communicate telepathically."

Parker put his fork down. "What do you mean? You can talk in each other's heads?"

"Basically, yes."

"So how come you didn't ask Ella what's going on with her before?"

"Ella can block me. She only opened a channel last night when she learned that we'd escaped. Just as Magnus and his friends suspected, the people who took her were threatening to hurt us if she warned us or asked for our help. She was afraid to do anything that might look like she did."

He narrowed his eyes at her. "Since when can you two do that?"

"Ella was born with the ability. I think I got it from her when she was in my tummy. I didn't have any telepathic abilities before that." Vivian smiled. "When she first started sending me messages, I thought I was going crazy."

"Why didn't you tell me about it?"

Here goes the hard part.

"I was waiting for you to get a bit older. Your father insisted that we keep this a secret. He was afraid that once it got out, we would be subjected to experiments and maybe even forced to work as spies for the government or some other organization. As a little kid, you could not have been trusted to keep secrets."

"Do you trust me now? Or did you tell me just because I basically figured it out?"

She arched a brow. "Did you?"

"I suspected something was going on between the two of you, but I thought you had some secret hand gesture language, or that female intuition was real. I didn't think telepathy was possible."

Vivian reached for his hand. "I'm sorry, Parker. I wish I could've told you before, but it was too risky."

He pulled his hand away. "So all those times you told me that you can read me like an open book were a lie?"

"Not at all. You have a very open face, which is one of the many things I love about you."

He crossed his arms over his chest. "Nice try, Mom. I'm still mad at you."

"I know, sweetie. But I really had no choice."

"How come I don't have telepathy?"

That was what she was afraid of the most. "I don't know. I went to the psychic convention to find answers, but I didn't find any. I found Julian there, though, which proved to be a very fortunate encounter. If not for him and the help of his mom's organization, we would be in Gorchenco's clutches right now, and Ella would have no way out."

"You might develop a different paranormal talent," Magnus said. "It might manifest once you hit puberty."

Vivian frowned. He talked as if he knew that for a fact. "And you're saying this based on what?"

A fleeting look of discomfort crossed Magnus's expression, but then he smiled and leaned back in his chair. "Julian is into that stuff. He is fascinated by paranormal abilities. He told me that girls often manifest talent from a very young age, but that boys usually do so only after puberty."

"Cool. So I still have a chance. And I don't even have to

Dark Widow's Curse

wait long. I'm twelve and a half. Am I going to be telepathic like Ella and my mom?"

Magnus shrugged. "Not necessarily. You might exhibit a different talent."

"Like what?"

"There is a bunch of them. To start, you might develop a stronger telepathic ability. Your mom and sister can only communicate between themselves. You might be able to read the thoughts or just the emotions of others. Or you might be able to send messages but not receive them. Then there are other abilities, like remote viewing and precognition."

Parker listened with eyes peeled wide. "What about telekinesis?"

"Frankly, I've never heard of a proven case of someone moving objects with their thoughts. But who knows? Life is full of surprises."

14

TURNER

It had been a long day and it wasn't over yet. Turner was operating on fumes. Turning immortal had brought his energy levels to the highest they'd ever been, and his production had skyrocketed. It had been an incredible ride, making him feel like a god. But even the immortal juice had limits.

He hadn't slept in days, and although the adrenaline was keeping the brain fog at bay, he knew he needed to crash soon and let his body and mind regenerate.

"Come in," Kian called when Turner knocked on his open door.

He walked in and sat on one of the chairs facing the desk. "I know you want to join Syssi at Eva's party, so I'll keep it short."

"Aren't you coming?"

"I need to crash. If I were one of my subordinates, I would've ordered myself off duty hours ago."

Kian nodded. "That's the trouble with being the boss. There is no one to tell us when to quit."

"Except for our mates."

"They are the real bosses."

Turner tapped his temple. "It takes a smart man to know that they are always right."

"Even when they are wrong."

"Exactly."

Kian leaned back in his chair. "Did you find out more about Gorchenco?"

"I did, or rather my sources did. And none of it is good news. As I said before, he never stays more than a few days in one place and uses decoy jets and every other evasive technique known to man. A very careful fellow. The only place he stays at for extended periods of time is his estate in Russia."

"Can we get him there?"

"No."

"Because it's Russia?"

"No, because it's Gorchenco. His estate there sits on two million acres of land, and it's guarded like a top-secret military base. We can't get in there."

Kian whistled. "That's a lot of land. Still, we have Yamanu. He can't cover an area that big, but I'm sure he can deal with the actual compound. He can thrall all of Gorchenco's people."

"You forget that we are dealing with Russians. I don't know if it's their suspicious mentality or a genetic predisposition. But the fact is that they are more resistant to thralling than any other ethnic group. Yamanu might be able to thrall some, but not all of them. Then there is the problem of distance. Even if we can thrall the guards at the guard stations, we will need to drive for miles before we reach the actual compound, and there will be aerial surveillance. They will shoot first and ask questions after. And I'm not talking about bullets. They will blow us to pieces that even our immortal bodies can't put back together. And because it's Russia, he can blow up people all day long, and no one is going to intervene. It's the new Wild West, but with radar-guided rockets and missiles."

"That's a problem. And we have to assume that he has all the latest surveillance and weaponry."

"Yes."

"What about attacking one of his other estates? Those outside of Russia?"

"Timing. The moment we know he is at a certain place, we mobilize and travel to that destination, but when we get there, he's already gone. The only way to do it is to have teams in place on standby. But because we can't spread ourselves even thinner than we already do, I say we focus on the one in New York. Eventually, he will circle back there."

"What if he leaves Ella in Russia and travels without her?"

"Then we're screwed."

Kian arched a brow. "You would give up?"

"I don't like it any more than you do. But I'm a practical man. I'm not going to bang my head against a wall and sacrifice men and resources on an impossible mission."

Raking his fingers through his hair, Kian sighed. "Before, it was just a rescue operation. Now it's more. Ella might be a Dormant, which makes her, potentially, one of ours. The stakes have changed."

"I'm well aware of that. And I'm not giving up. I'm just putting it out there that at some point it might come to that."

"I can't accept it."

"There is another thing to consider. We will probably

need to kill Gorchenco and that might be even more problematic than getting Ella away from him."

"I don't see why."

"If we get her out and don't kill him, he is going to hunt her and her family down with every resource available to him, and that's a lot. It won't be just about pride for him. He can't afford to appear weak. He will have to make an example out of her so no one will dare to cross him again."

"Then we kill him. It's not like the world is going to miss the ruthless son of a bitch."

"It's not that simple. If we kill Gorchenco, we declare war on the Russian mafia. The other bosses won't like an outsider taking him out. Again, it's a matter of pride and perception of power. We take out one of them, the entire structure appears weak. They can't let it slide."

"Can we make it look as if he was killed by one of his competitors?"

"That's the approach I'm probably going to use. But I need time to make a solid plan. This is no longer about trafficking. I need to treat it as a hostage retrieval operation, and not a trafficking rescue, and those take careful planning even without the added complication of dealing with a pro like Gorchenco."

Kian nodded. "You're the expert, Turner."

"This might be the most challenging operation I've ever undertaken. I need to get some sleep before I start mulling it over."

"You do that."

Turner pushed to his feet. "I also have two scumbags in the keep's dungeon that I need to interrogate. But that's more for my personal satisfaction than anything else."

"I can have Andrew question them. He's very good at that."

"If I decide that I don't want to waste my time on them, I'll let you know, and you can send Spivak to have his fun with them."

"Or, you can take him with you," Kian suggested. "For old times' sake."

When Andrew had served under Turner, they hadn't always seen eye to eye. They respected each other, but their relationship was cordial at best. Perhaps now that both of them were immortal and members of the clan, it was time to change that.

"I'll give him a call."

15

MAGNUS

With dinner done, the table cleared, and the dishes washed, Magnus couldn't come up with more excuses to stay.

"I'd better get going. If you need anything, my door is open."

Perhaps she'd get lonely and come visit him. A guy could hope.

"Thank you. And thank you again for dinner. It was very good." She glanced at her son. "Parker, aren't you going to thank Magnus?"

The kid rubbed his tummy. "Thank you from the bottom of my stomach." He turned the screen on and started shooting.

Vivian grimaced. "Gosh, I hate those sounds. I only tolerate it because supposedly it develops dexterity and releases stress."

"It also makes him a good marksman. Did you see how well he did in the shooting range?"

She nodded. "I was impressed. He was so much better with the professional bow than with the one he'd made."

"Yeah, but he had fun making it."

"True." She looked down at her flip-flops. "Well, I guess it's goodnight."

It was still much too early to go to sleep. "How about a movie? Would you like to escape the shooting sounds and come watch a movie in my room?"

"Can I come too?" Parker asked while still twisting this way and that and shooting monsters.

It had been fun cuddling with both of them on the couch in the cabin, but Magnus had different ideas for tonight. "I think it's your mom's turn to choose a movie."

"She's going to pick a chick flick."

"As I said. It's her turn to choose."

"Fine. I'll stay here."

Vivian hesitated. "If you need us, we are right next door, and we will leave it open."

"I'll leave Scarlet with you," Magnus said.

As if she was going to budge from the couch, her paw resting on Parker's thigh as if to say he was hers.

"When can I play with my friends online?"

The keep's internet connection was safe. Magnus didn't know how it worked, but he imagined William had routed it through several servers so no one could trace the signal to the original location. But the question whether Parker could go back to playing with his friends wasn't a technical one he could address to the tech guy.

It was a question for Turner, and at the moment the guy had more important things on his mind.

"I'll check for you tomorrow."

Parker sighed. "Okay."

"Ready to go?" Magnus looked at Vivian.

"I'll make us coffee first."

"Good idea. I didn't see a coffeemaker at my place,

although I'm sure there is one." Okidu would not have forgotten an important thing like that. "Need help with the coffee?"

"No, you go ahead and browse for a movie."

"Anything in particular you would like to watch?"

"A romantic comedy would be nice."

"Chick flick," Parker muttered under his breath.

As Magnus headed to his room, he wondered whether Vivian had guessed his intentions. Not that he was so hard to figure out.

Just hard.

She looked so lovely in the red T-shirt and tight leggings, her delicate curves not hidden by bulky scrubs or a sweatshirt.

Vivian's taste in clothing was simple. But his was not. Magnus appreciated garments that were masterfully cut and made from luxurious fabrics. His friends back home used to tease him about it. Couture was not considered a manly occupation, and especially not for a Guardian.

But not everyone fitted into preconceived neat little boxes. Being a good fighter didn't preclude a man from having excellent taste in clothing.

Magnus was a fighter and a fashion aficionado.

If Vivian were his, he would dress her up in beautiful custom-made dresses and high heels.

Right.

She wasn't a doll for him to dress up. But if she was so inclined, he would love to.

Vivian entered with a steaming mug in each hand. "I don't think you'll find a movie for us to watch by staring at a blank screen."

"True." He clicked the television on. "We have everything here."

She sat next to him on the couch and put the mugs on the coffee table. "Just put something on. I know the movie was an excuse."

He chuckled. "Busted."

"You wanted to talk to me without Parker listening in."

"Talking was not what I had in mind."

"You know why there can be nothing between us."

"I don't accept it. There is no such thing as curses. And even if there were, they can't touch me. I'm invincible."

She arched a brow. "Oh, yeah? And how did you arrive at that conclusion?"

He was a damn immortal, but he couldn't tell her that. Or rather he could, but then he would have to thrall her to forget it. Besides, after all she'd been through recently, proving his immortality by showing her his fangs might be the last straw and she could snap.

"I've fought in many battles, some of them extremely brutal, and yet I came out unscathed. You can check if you don't believe me. There isn't even one mark on my body. I have no scars." He unbuttoned his shirt and shrugged it off. "Here, check for yourself."

Vivian swallowed. "It's not fair. You're playing dirty. Put the shirt back on."

That hadn't been his intention, but given her reaction, Magnus was glad he'd done it. "I have nothing to be embarrassed about." He flexed his chest muscles.

"No, you don't." She ogled him for a long moment before shaking her head. "But there is a teenage boy next door who might come in and get the wrong impression."

"I can close the door."

"Magnus!"

"All right." He shrugged the shirt back on and

buttoned it up, but not all the way, leaving enough chest exposed to keep Vivian salivating.

He was going to win this battle one way or another.

Scooting a little closer to her, he whispered, "You are not playing fair either. That red T-shirt and those leggings cling to your body and show off every curve. You can't blame me for wanting you."

With a sigh, Vivian leaned against the couch cushions and closed her eyes. "I don't blame you, Magnus. I blame myself. I shouldn't have led you on. It was a momentary weakness. I can't bring myself to regret it, but it should not have happened. Unfortunately, my curse is very real. After what happened to Ella, even she agrees with me. She said she was never going to doubt it again."

Damn. Unless he told her he was immortal and convinced her that he was indestructible, Vivian wouldn't agree to come to his bed.

But was she the one?

Until he was sure of that, he couldn't tell her the whole story or attempt her activation. Besides, he probably needed to ask someone's permission before doing either.

But whose?

Was it Kian's? Bridget's? Who made those decisions?

They really needed to have a village-square meeting and have this explained in plain language, so every clan member would know what to look out for and how to determine if the person they were interested in was the one or not.

Vivian was so strikingly beautiful that he would've lusted after her even if she were only a human and not his one and only.

Bridget would know more about that. Or maybe

Amanda? He'd heard something about affinity, but what the hell was that?

Liking someone didn't make that person the one. Magnus had liked many humans throughout his lifetime, males and females, but that didn't mean anything. Some people were likable and others were not.

He liked Vivian, a lot, and he lusted after her more than he'd lusted after any female before, but that wasn't necessarily love. How could he tell the difference between lust and love?

Some would say that he loved her if he was willing to sacrifice for her. But he was a Guardian, which meant that he would've done it regardless of his feelings for her.

Others would say that he loved her if he liked spending time with her and couldn't think of life without her.

Magnus dreaded the day he would have to say goodbye to Vivian and Parker, but that was probably because he'd felt so lonely and displaced until they came into his life.

Could love be all of the above?

He needed more time to sort out his feelings.

In the meantime, though, there must be another way to convince Vivian that it was safe for him to get intimate with her, and that sex with her wasn't going to mean a death sentence for him.

16

VIVIAN

"What if we don't have any feelings for each other? Does the curse affect anyone you have sex with?" Magnus asked.

Without opening her eyes, Vivian smiled sadly. "I wouldn't know. All three men I had sex with are dead."

"I know you loved your husband, but did you love the other two?"

God, the man was relentless, and Vivian wasn't as strong as she pretended to be. Eventually, he was going to chip away at her resistance, and she was going to succumb.

The thing was, she wanted that. She wanted him to convince her that it was okay and that nothing was going to happen to him.

"I liked them both. I don't know if I loved them. There wasn't enough time, I guess. Frank and I dated only for five months, and with Al it lasted six."

"Aha!" Magnus exclaimed. "Since we are not going to stay together nearly as long, I'm safe. Five months was the shortest period for your supposed curse to attack."

She opened her eyes. "And you reach this scientific conclusion based on a sample of only two?"

"Three. You'd been with your husband for many years before he was killed."

"Three is not big enough of a sample either."

"Why not? You decided that you are cursed based on that small sample."

She couldn't argue with that logic.

They were going to part ways soon, and until then they could enjoy each other. Hopefully, Turner would get Ella away from Gorchenco in less than a week. Two at most. As Magnus had pointed out, it seemed that her curse took longer than that to work.

It wasn't the only obstacle, though. "Parker is next door and we promised to keep the door open."

Magnus pushed to his feet. "I'll have him tucked in and asleep in no time."

"Right. And how are you going to accomplish that?"

"I have my ways."

She narrowed her eyes at him. "What do you have in mind?"

"I'll promise him a trip to the shooting range early in the morning before the other Guardians arrive. He can't be there when they are using the range. But I'll make it conditional upon him turning in early."

"Guardians?"

"That's what the fighters in our organization are called."

"I like it. Guardians sound much better than fighters."

"While I'm gone, help yourself to the bar. Okidu stocked it with a good variety."

She wasn't much of a drinker, but a glass of wine might be nice. Except, all she could find was whiskey, several brands of it and all of them naturally Scottish, and a beer called Snake Venom with an alcohol content to knock out a horse.

Since she hated the taste of whiskey, and the beer was intriguing, Vivian decided to give it a try. Just a little sip.

Oh, boy. Her eyes watered. That wasn't a beer for the faint of heart.

"Going for the real thing, are you, lass?" Magnus strutted in with a self-satisfied expression on his face and closed the door behind him.

"Did you manage to put Parker to sleep?"

"He is already snoring. I also activated the monitoring system. If he wakes up, our guy in the control room is going to call me."

"The suite is monitored?" That was news to her.

"Didn't you notice the camera mounted near the ceiling?"

"No, I didn't. Why would you have a camera in there?"

He leaned and kissed her cheek. "It's for when our guests are not here voluntarily. But don't worry. It is off unless I call security and ask them to activate it. The one in here is off. The thing is, with the door closed, we won't be able to hear what's going on outside. I didn't want Parker to wake up in the middle of the night and get scared because he couldn't get in. That's why I asked the guys in security to monitor the suite until I tell them it's okay to turn it off again."

It was like having a baby monitor. She just needed to remind Magnus to deactivate it when she got back to the room. Hopefully, there was no camera in the bedroom, or worse, the bathroom.

"Is there a camera in the bedroom?"

"No, just the living room."

"Then it's good that I made Parker sleep on the couch." She chuckled. "I can't believe he is already asleep."

"You can go and check on him. He is out."

"Are you a magician or something?"

"Or something." He reached for the bottle of Snake Venom and took a long gulp. "I love this beer." He put the bottle back on the bar's counter.

"I didn't know a beer like this existed. Where did Okidu get it?"

"There is only one importer in the area, and we need to order it by the case. It's pricey too."

"Then I'm sorry I opened it. I only took one sip."

He walked up to her and brushed her hair aside. "No worries, love. I'll finish it." He kissed her neck.

His goatee tickled her skin, but it was a good kind of tickle, and the feather-light kiss was enough to ignite sparks. "Two of those are too much. You'll get drunk. It's very potent."

"Uhm." He kept kissing her neck. "So am I."

God, she still remembered. Recalling the incredible sensation of him inside her, Vivian's core tightened with need…"Did you use a condom last time? I can't remember."

Forgetting an important thing like that was odd. She must've been really distraught or really horny not to notice.

"I didn't. But you have nothing to worry about. I'm clean. You can ask Julian to vouch for me. I had all my checkups done recently." He kissed the underside of her jaw and continued kissing up to her ear.

It was hard to think with him doing that. "I'm clean too because I haven't been with anyone except you in years. But I'm not on birth control. I hope you have condoms."

"I don't. But that's okay. I probably can't get you pregnant."

"Why?"

"I'm just not very fertile."

"How do you know that? Did you have your sperm checked out?"

Had Magnus been married before, and had he and his wife tried to conceive? It was okay if he had, but she wished he'd told her. Having been married before was an important thing to mention when entering a relationship, even if it was going to be a very short-lived one.

"Just my experience." He moved to the other side of her neck.

"Were you married before and wanted kids?"

"No, I was never married. But in my younger years, I've been with plenty of lasses without using protection, and I didn't get anyone pregnant."

"They could've been on birth control."

"Not where I come from. Trust me. You're safe with me."

With her entire body going soft, it was hard to hold on to the glass in her hand, and even harder to keep thinking straight. "That's not good enough. I can't take a chance on getting pregnant. That's what got me married at eighteen."

Wrapping his arms around her, Magnus looked into her eyes. "There are other ways to enjoy each other. I don't have to come inside of you."

"Oh God." She really wanted him to. Just to hear him say the words got her all hot and bothered.

Taking the glass from her hands, he put it on the counter, then lifted her up and carried her to his bed.

When he reached for the hem of her T-shirt, Vivian suddenly felt shy. "Aren't you going to turn the lights off?"

"I should, shouldn't I?" He looked at her for a moment longer before going for the light switch.

"Close your eyes, love."

"Why? I can't see anything. It's pitch black in here."

And it wasn't about unseemly scars. He'd shown her that he didn't have any.

"Do it anyway."

"I don't mind closing my eyes, but I need to know why you want me to, when I can't see a thing anyway."

"Because it would please me greatly if you do."

It was about dominance, then, a game. She could play along.

"Okay."

17

MAGNUS

*E*ven though it was too dark for Vivian to see, and she must've assumed that he couldn't verify her compliance, she did as he'd asked.

Delightful.

The question was whether it was okay for him to bite and thrall her again after only a one-day break in between. For repeated thralls, a much longer break was recommended, but given that he'd thralled her just once before, it should be safe.

The next time, however, he would have to either hold off on the biting, or tell her the truth. But since it was too early to do the latter, he would have to refrain from the former.

As he lay next to her, Vivian turned on her side and cupped his cheek. She rubbed her thumb over his lips. "Kiss me, Magnus."

As if he needed an invitation. Fusing their mouths together, he licked into her while reaching under the hem of her T-shirt. Her belly quivered under his touch, the skin so smooth and soft he had an urge to put his lips on it.

Sliding a bit down, he feathered kisses on her stomach, eliciting a few giggles when he touched a ticklish spot. Pushing the shirt's hem further up, he encountered satin bra cups that encased much more foam than breast. The bra was padded to the max.

She didn't need to do that, but he wasn't going to embarrass her by pointing it out. He loved her delicate build, and those nipples of hers were just as sensitive if not more so than those adorning larger mounds.

"Let's take this off." He pulled the shirt over her head and then reached behind her to unclasp the bra.

As he'd expected, Vivian tensed a little as he bared her breasts.

"Don't be shy, lass. I love your breasts." He cupped both in his hands. "They're perfect." He lifted up a little and sucked one nipple into his mouth.

She moved against him, undulating her hips in sync with his suckling.

"So sensitive," he murmured around her hard nub.

As she held his head to her breast, her sharp little nails bit into the skin of his neck. "Don't stop," she murmured.

He had no such intention.

Switching to her other peak, he swirled his tongue around it, flicking, licking, and at the same time closing his fingers around the one he'd just left wet and turgid.

She moaned as he pinched a little harder, her nails on his neck digging in deeper.

He loved the slight sting she was inflicting, wishing she had fangs, even tiny ones, so she could bite him all over.

A shiver ran through him as he imagined her teeth marks on his skin. They wouldn't last for more than a couple of seconds, but they would feel incredible for as long as they did.

Had the other transitioned female Dormants grown small fangs like those of immortal females? He hadn't checked. But no one had mentioned that, so he assumed that they didn't. It was not a necessary part of their physiology.

"Why are you still dressed?" Vivian let go of his neck to push her hands under his shirt.

He swirled his tongue around her nipple once more before letting it pop out of his mouth. "Easily fixed."

Since she couldn't see him, Magnus could undress at his supernatural speed, provided he kept his movements stealthy and the rustle of fabric to a minimum.

When he was done, he knelt at her feet and tugged her leggings down. She lifted her bottom for him, and he propped it up with one hand while pulling her pants and panties with the other.

On his palm, he could feel her center already hot and moist for him, her soft petals beckoning him to take a taste.

In his rush to get to her, he flung the leggings away too forcefully, and the whooshing sound they made as they sailed through the air startled her.

"Shh, love. It's nothing." He dove between her spread legs and pressed a soft kiss to her petals. "I love how lush your lips are." He licked along one side and then the other.

Threading her fingers through his hair, she chuckled. "Which ones? Lower or upper?"

"Both. So luscious and tempting. I couldn't wait to do this again." He licked more deeply, parting the petals with his tongue and going for the center.

Vivian groaned and arched up. "Oh, Magnus. I love it when you do that."

Her praise and the outpouring of wetness she was rewarding him with were so incredibly satisfying that he felt like thumping his chest and making a Tarzan call.

There was nothing that made a male feel more manly than pleasing his female.

It was what he was made for.

If she'd let him.

Clutching her bottom in both hands, he speared his tongue into her quivering slit, once, twice, three times, then pulled out and flicked it over the center of her desire.

Vivian cried out, her bottom clenching in his hands, but she didn't orgasm even though he knew she was close.

"Do you want to come, love?" he murmured against her soft flesh.

Her head thrashed from side to side. "Yes. No. Not without you."

So that was why she was holding back.

He kissed the top of her slit. "I love making you come. I love hearing the sounds you make, and the way you arch up a moment before you do. Let me have my fun, woman."

"You're a strange man, Magnus. And I mean it in a good way."

He peeked at her, making sure her eyes were still closed. "I'm glad you see it that way. Now, relax and let go."

"Okay."

That word was quickly becoming his favorite. He hadn't been in a relationship before, but he'd hooked up with enough women to know Vivian's easy acquiescence was uncommon. She wasn't a pushover, and she was not doing it just because he demanded it, but because she enjoyed it too.

"So sweet."

He resumed his tonguing, bringing her up to where she'd been before the brief interlude. When her moans got louder and her thrashing more violent, he pushed a finger inside her, and then another. Feeling her tender muscles tighten desperately around his invading fingers, he flicked his tongue over her clit, once, twice, three times, and then drew on it with gentle rhythmic suction.

"Oh, yes!"

As Vivian cried out, he shuddered in pleasure and kept his fingers and his tongue going until he wrung the last bit of tremors out of her.

When she lay spent and panting, he pressed a soft kiss to her inner thigh. With the words 'I love you' hovering over his lips, he stifled the impulse to sink his fangs into the soft flesh.

It had been almost as difficult to resist as uttering those words.

18

VIVIAN

Wow, and wow again. The night before last had been great, and Magnus had pleasured her probably just as expertly as he'd just done, but Vivian had been an emotional mess then, and the experience hadn't been as explosive. Or maybe it had, but the guilt that had followed had dimmed the effect.

Yeah, that was probably what had happened.

Sliding up, he lay on his side and pulled her into his arms, hugging her gently as her body slowly calmed from the explosion he'd detonated.

There was so much tenderness in the way he was holding her that she felt her eyes mist with tears. Why couldn't she have this wonderful, giving, selfless man for keeps?

"What's the matter, love? Why are you suddenly sad?"

Crap. How could he tell? She hadn't sniffled, and she hadn't whimpered, and there was no way he could have seen her expression.

Dipping his head, he kissed her eyelid, and then the

other. "Sometimes orgasms can be emotionally draining. After a high there is always a low."

It was a convenient excuse and she was going to use it. Because admitting she wanted to keep him was out of the question. The best thing would be to get busy pleasuring him until he was too mindless with it to notice a sad tear or two.

She kissed his chest, right in the valley between his pecs, which made it easy for her hands to find his nipples. They hardened under her palms, and she used the sensation to follow with her lips and her tongue.

He groaned when she licked one, then the other. Her fingers skimming his torso on a path to his manhood encountered very little hair and a lot of hard muscle. Magnus was built like an Adonis.

With her eyes still closed, her fingers did the seeing for her, and they were doing a pretty good job. It wasn't hard to imagine how beautiful he was.

As she palmed his shaft, it twitched in greeting, and as she rubbed her thumb across the head, he sucked in a breath.

His large hand, which had been resting on the small of her back, smoothed down to grab her buttocks, cupping both cheeks at once. Magnus loved holding her ass, and she loved him doing so. His hold was possessive and tender at the same time, making her feel wanted and cared for.

In her palm, his shaft continued to harden. It was so velvety smooth and hot.

Vivian licked her lips, suddenly impatient to get a taste of him. She just had to. Her mouth was practically watering.

Moving down, she first kissed the top, and then licked

it, scooping a drop of pre-cum on her tongue. He tasted sweet and tangy and potent. Swirling her tongue around it, she then licked all the way down one side and went up the other.

A growl rumbled from his chest, and a moment later she was lifted in the air and spun around to straddle his face. He blew a hot breath on her wet center, then pressed a kiss to her wet folds. "So delectable." He smacked his lips.

Vivian wasn't a novice to mutual oral pleasuring, but not like this. Not with him lying on his back and her on top of him with her legs spread wide and everything open and on full display. This was much more lewd than doing it lying on their sides.

Except, it was pitch black in the room, and she doubted he could see anything even if his night vision was excellent. No one could see in complete darkness.

The pose had one great advantage, though. The angle was perfect for taking him deep in her mouth, which was exciting. After the way he'd pleasured her, Magnus deserved a blowjob to trump all blowjobs. She was no expert, but she was going to give him her best performance.

Or at least that was the plan until he started licking into her. Concentrating on the job at hand was difficult. She would have to try and ignore what was going on at the other end of her.

Tightening her palm around the base, she took him deeper into the heat of her mouth.

A growl rumbled out from Magnus's chest, the sound sending delicious vibrations to her already overexcited core. Panting around him, she drew him even deeper down her throat, nearly choking, but forcing herself to relax the muscles and push a little further. When her eyes started tearing, she pulled back, pumping up and down with her hand as she licked all around the head, and then went down again.

When Vivian found a rhythm, taking him deep a couple of times and then licking and pumping with her hand, Magnus started thrusting up into her. He was holding back, though. His legs were quaking from the effort of not going as fast or as deep as he wanted and leaving at least some of the control to her.

She hadn't been aware of her own frantic undulations until Magnus's grip on her ass tightened, his fingers digging into her flesh.

They were going to climax together.

As Magnus's shaft thickened in her mouth and his testicles tightened in her hand, he thrust two fingers inside her, detonating her orgasm at the same time his exploded out of him.

She swallowed and licked like a woman possessed, prolonging his pleasure the same way he was doing to her. He shuddered violently with each lick.

When the quaking was over, he lifted and spun her around as if she weighed no more than a pillow.

Lying on top of him, she felt tiny in his strong arms.

"You're amazing. " He cupped her neck and kissed her deeply.

Vivian tasted herself on his invading tongue, as he must've been tasting himself. It was so damn erotic that the coil inside of her started tightening again.

The man was going to turn her into a nymphomaniac.

Pulling the blanket on top of her, he tucked the ends around them both. "Put your head on my chest."

It felt wonderful. His heart was thundering, the heartbeat still elevated from before. "I can't stay. I need to go back to my room."

"I know." His hands smoothed over her back all the way down to her bottom and cupped her there. "Stay for just a little bit longer."

As a mattress, Magnus wasn't very comfortable to sleep on, but she would've loved to anyway. Regrettably, she couldn't. "I'll fall asleep."

"This feels so good. I don't want it to end. If you fall asleep, I'll wake you in a bit."

"Promise?"

"Yes."

"What if you fall asleep too?"

He chuckled. "With your sexy little body on top of me? Not a chance."

As if to prove it, his hard shaft twitched against her leg.

"I can't believe you're up again."

His hands drew lazy circles on her back. "I told you that I'm invincible."

"I'm starting to believe it."

19

ELLA

When morning arrived, the muted British sun shining weakly through the sheers and casting soft patterns on the rug, Ella was still awake.

By now she was pretty sure Dimitri wasn't going to join her. The anticipation was what had kept her awake throughout the night, but she was too pumped with adrenaline to fall asleep.

Lying in the big bed, she stared at the ornate ceiling and counted the birds painted on the fresco. There were forty-nine of them, but she might have miscounted, so she started again. Fifty-one.

It was pointless, she was too distraught to make an accurate count. Besides, instead of helping her fall asleep, it was stressing her out.

Right, as if the number of birds on the ceiling was responsible for that.

Where was he?

This time Ella had no doubt she was sleeping in his bedroom. Just like the one in New York, this room had no personal touches, but unlike the other one, Dimitri's clothes were hanging in the master closet. One of them. She had one all to herself, including a chaise to rest on between trying on clothes, and a triple mirror on a raised platform.

Her new wardrobe had been neatly arranged by the housekeeper—another Russian woman that the boss had brought from the motherland. This one was not the motherly type like Clarissa, though. Pinched-faced and stick thin, Ilona was the epitome of efficiency and unfriendliness.

Perhaps it was a language barrier, though, and not the woman's dislike for Ella.

Ilona's English was no worse than Clarissa's, but she seemed like a prideful woman who was embarrassed about her lack of fluency.

The good news was that Misha was there to stay. He'd confirmed that the boss had assigned him to Ella as her personal bodyguard. The guy was friendly enough. He'd even joined her for dinner and tried to entertain her with his lame stories and corny jokes.

Ella appreciated the effort, but it had been difficult to even appear amused when she'd been quaking in her seat, terrified of what would happen later when Gorchenco came home.

Perhaps she should've tried harder to laugh at Misha's jokes. After all, the burly bodyguard with crooked teeth and a nose that had been broken too many times was her only friend in this place.

According to the display on her nightstand radio, it was seven-fifteen in the morning. If the routine in this place was the same as on the New York estate, she'd better get up and get dressed before Misha or Ilona came in with her breakfast.

With a sigh, Ella flung away the fluffy down comforter and swung her legs over the side of the bed. It was so tall that her feet didn't touch the floor, and she had to slide down.

The bathroom was just as extravagant as the one in New York, maybe even more so because it had a large window over the clawfoot tub, overlooking the manicured gardens outside.

Afraid Dimitri would show up, she showered quickly without washing her hair, then wrapped herself in a big towel and ducked into the walk-in closet.

There was no lock on the door, so she rushed to get dressed too. Since she didn't know what the plan for the day was, Ella opted for lounge clothing—cream-colored, wide-cut cashmere pants that were soft and comfortable, paired with a matching sleeveless shirt and a long cardigan.

Thank you, Pavel.

The guy knew how to dress a girl.

If she weren't a prisoner, she might have taken pleasure in wearing something so decadently soft, expensive, and beautiful.

When she came out of the closet, breakfast was waiting for her on the coffee table, and the French doors to the balcony were open, letting the morning air in.

The bed was made too.

Ella wondered if it had been Ilona or one of the maids. A place this size must employ a small army of those.

Whoever it was obviously had no intention of joining Ella. The table had been set for one.

Oh well, it was an opportunity to open a channel to her mother. Not that she had any news to share, but that was news too. Her mom would be relieved to hear that nothing had happened yet.

She glanced at the radio display and calculated the time. It was ten minutes to eight. Eight in the morning London time translated to midnight in California, which meant it was ten minutes to twelve at night.

Mom, are you awake?

When there was no answer, a trickle of fear ran down the back of Ella's neck.

Mom! Wake up!

Ella! Oh my gosh. I'm so sorry. I dozed off. How are you? What's happening?

Nothing. Gorchenco didn't come home last night. Thankfully, I woke up alone in bed this morning. By the way, while we are talking, I'm pouring myself coffee into a porcelain cup. This is a full-service imprisonment. I'm treated like royalty.

Is he horrible?

Ella hesitated before answering. If she lied, her mother would know. But she could choose which parts of the truth to tell her and which to omit.

He is, and he isn't. Dimitri is very polite, soft-spoken, and sophisticated. Physically, he is not big or intimidating. He's about five foot ten, stocky but not fat. He reminds me of the guy who played 007 in Skyfall, Daniel something, especially the intense blue eyes. Dimitri is not as good looking, and he's more heavily set, but you get the idea.

She could've sent her mother a mental picture, but it would've been colored by her fear of the guy. He would've come out looking like a monster.

How old is he?

I guess he's in his late forties. He is a scary man, though. A guy doesn't get to be a mafia boss without being smart, cold, and ruthless. I'm on my best behavior with him. He doesn't seem like the type who would tolerate imperfections.

Do you think you can postpone things with him? Is he patient?

He seems to be. But I doubt anything is up to me, Mom. I'm no match for him. He'll see right through me.

Oh, sweetie. I wish I could do something to help you.

You already did. You and Parker got away. Where are you?

Somewhere in a basement in downtown Los Angeles. Magnus had Parker and me blindfolded, so we wouldn't know where he was taking us. This is their secret headquarters. It's a huge underground complex, and the suite we are staying in is as fancy as what you'd expect to find in a pricey hotel.

Sounds like something from a spy movie.

I know. I shouldn't complain about a thing, though. These people are helping us, as well as other families in our situation, out of the goodness of their hearts, and they don't even seek recognition for what they do. I think it's admirable.

Her mom had a bad case of hero worship. Was it about the guy she'd mentioned before, Magnus?

Tell me about Magnus.

He's the guy assigned to keeping us safe.

I figured that out. How are you guys getting along?

Great. He taught Parker how to carve a bow out of a branch, and how to make arrows, and how to shoot them. I think your brother is ready to adopt him. Oh, and he has a puppy. A cute golden retriever named Scarlet. Parker is ready to adopt her too.

When she talked about the guy, there was a smile in her mom's mental voice. Was her mother falling for her bodyguard? Classic.

Should she tell her to be careful?

Nah, let her enjoy her time with the nice guy. Vivian had been too careful and too lonely for far too long.

There was a knock on the door, and a moment later it opened a crack.

"Ella? Are you dressed?"

"Come in, Misha.

I have to go, Mom. My bodyguard just showed up.

You have a bodyguard?

Of course. Dimitri paid three quarters of a million for me. He is protecting his investment.

"Good morning." Misha strode into the room. "I have message for you from boss. He want to take you to restaurant for dinner at seven tonight. He say to be ready at six. We take limo to London and you meet him there."

That was good news. First of all because she would have more time to herself, and later, over dinner, she would at least have a chance to get to know the man a little better before he took her virginity.

"Okay."

"Boss also ask if you need anything. Whatever you need I am to get for you."

"Some books maybe? Or even better, can you get me a reading tablet so I can download the books I want?"

Misha rubbed the back of his thick neck. "I will have to ask the boss."

20

VIVIAN

"Julian!" Vivian flung herself into the young doctor's arms. "I'm so happy you came."

He smiled and hugged her back. "With such a warm welcome, I'm glad I did."

Maybe she was overdoing it a little, but she didn't know how to express the boundless gratitude she felt toward him.

"And you too, Turner."

Vivian felt grateful to him as well, but he didn't seem like the kind of guy who liked embracing strangers. Still, she'd hugged Julian, and it would be weird to only offer Turner her hand. Instead, she gave him an awkward one-armed hug.

"Hello, Vivian." Given his stiff posture, she'd been right about him not liking it.

"Parker, this is Turner, the guy who's in charge of the operation."

"Hi." Her son waved from the couch, sparing Turner a quick glance before going back to the screen.

Turner nodded. "I hear he is a good shooter. Must be all that gaming."

Magnus chuckled. "You should've seen him on the range. The kid has great potential."

Just as he'd promised, Magnus had woken up Parker early in the morning and had taken him to the shooting range. They'd been gone by the time Vivian had gotten out of bed.

"Parker, make room." She shooed her son off the couch.

"That's okay." Turner lifted a hand. "Let's sit around the dining table. This is not going to take long." He glanced at Parker, then back at her. "I need to ask you a few questions."

His meaning was clear.

"Parker, can you please go play in the bedroom? I can't talk with all the noise you're making."

He rolled his eyes. "I told you I should've set everything up in there."

Last night, while tiptoeing back into her room and holding her breath not to wake him up, Vivian had had the same thought. It would've been incredibly awkward having to explain to her teenage son why she was coming back in the middle of the night.

Just in case he woke up, Vivian had prepared a plausible excuse about falling asleep in front of the television in Magnus's room.

And not on top of Magnus.

If not for Ella's communication, she would've spent the night like that.

"Hurry up, Parker."

"I am." He unplugged his console, lifted it into his

arms, and went into the bedroom with the wires dragging behind him on the floor.

Magnus closed the door behind him and joined them at the dining table.

"Did you hear more from Ella?" Julian asked.

"Yes. She opens the channel once or twice a day and gives me updates."

Julian's expression looked pained. "How does she sound? Can you hear her tone of voice through the mental communication?"

It still shocked her how easily everyone was accepting that she and Ella could do that. Julian claimed to be interested in the phenomenon, but Turner's reaction wasn't any different. He regarded her without a smirk or a raised brow, looking serious and severe as if she was talking about exchanging emails and not telepathy.

"She's so brave. All she cared about was us getting away. She says Gorchenco treats her well. He's supplied her with an entire wardrobe of designer clothes that are very conservative, which she takes to mean that he intends to take her to meetings and show her off as his girlfriend and not someone he bought at an auction. She says he is well-mannered, but scary. Ella doesn't dare defy him in any way."

"Smart girl," Turner said. "When you talk to her again, tell her to keep doing that. But in the meantime, she can try and accumulate information for us."

When Vivian started shaking her head, he lifted a hand. "I don't want her to do anything that might look suspicious. She shouldn't attempt to snoop around or ask questions. That's too dangerous. But if she sees or hears anything interesting, she should tell you. Most importantly, if she knows where he is taking her next, she should tell you right away. You have my number programmed into your phone. If Ella has any pertinent information, call me immediately after you talk with her."

"What if it's the middle of the night?"

"Then I leave it up to your discretion. If it's travel plans information or anything else that you think is important, call me right away. If you think it can wait, call me first thing in the morning."

"Got it. Do you have a plan?"

Turner nodded.

"Anything I can tell Ella?"

He sighed, which was not a good sign. "Unless we know where he is taking her ahead of time, the only thing we can do is wait for him to come back to his New York estate. He never stays longer than a couple of days any place other than his compound in Russia. And before you ask, we can't get to her there. It's too heavily guarded."

"That might take a long time."

His lips pressed into a thin line, Turner nodded again.

Julian groaned. "This feeling of impotence is killing me. I wish I could do something to get her out now."

'We all do," Vivian whispered through a clogged throat.

Magnus reached for her hand and squeezed it. "Courage, Vivian."

Pushing up to her feet, she walked over to the bar and filled a glass with water from the faucet. "I wish I could kill the bastard myself."

"About that," Turner said. "We will probably have to kill him even if it isn't necessary in order to get Ella back. As long as Gorchenco is alive, you and your family would have to remain in hiding. He will hunt you to the ends of the earth."

She'd been fooling herself thinking that this ordeal was going to end in a week or two. "I don't know what I'm going to do. I'm probably going to lose my job. And what about Parker? He needs to go to school. I know those sound like trivial concerns compared to what Ella is going through, and what you guys are trying to do, but I need to work for a living, and Parker needs to attend school."

Magnus got up and joined her at the bar. "Don't worry. When this is over, we will help you get back on your feet." He took her hand. "I am going to help you. You're not alone anymore."

"We can set up homeschooling for Parker," Julian said. "I know someone who is doing it now."

"Wonder?" Turner asked.

"Yes. Callie helped set her up with the program. She needed to start at the beginning."

"Didn't they have schools where she came from?" Turner asked.

"Wonder only got basic education. She started working when she was still a kid. Things were different back there."

It had taken Vivian a moment to realize that they were talking about a person named Wonder.

"Who's Wonder, and how did she come by that name?"

"It's a long story," Julian said. "I'll tell you about it when we get Ella back. What I want to do now is take a few blood samples, if you don't mind."

"What for?"

"It's for my paranormal research. I collect samples from people who have real talent and examine it."

"What do you hope to learn from that?"

"I'm trying to figure out if there are genetic similarities between humans who exhibit paranormal abilities."

She chuckled. "You say humans as if you expect animals to have them too."

Julian lifted his hands and smiled. "Who knows? Maybe they do?" He looked at Scarlet who was lying on the floor next to the bedroom door. "How about you, girl? Can you communicate telepathically with Parker?"

Scarlet wagged her tail.

"I think that means yes. I'll have to test her as well." He pushed to his feet. "I'm going to bring my equipment from the clinic and take the blood samples here."

Magnus stood up too. "I'll help you carry the stuff."

"Thanks."

21

MAGNUS

"I wanted to ask you a few questions," Magnus said as he and Julian headed for the keep's clinic.

"I figured."

"I assume that you want to take Vivian's blood work because you also suspect that she and Ella are Dormants."

"Obviously." Julian shook his head. "It explains so much. I couldn't figure out why I was obsessing about the girl's picture like some lovesick teenager over a movie star. I must've felt something."

"I've heard Amanda mention affinity, but I would think that you need to be face to face with the person and talk to them to determine if you feel an affinity toward them or not."

Julian shrugged. "If someone told me a story like that, I would've laughed it off. But I'm proof that a picture is worth a thousand words, so to speak."

"Ella is very pretty."

"I know. It crossed my mind once or twice or a thousand times that I might have gotten infatuated with her beauty. Maybe when I finally get to meet her, I'm not even going to like her."

"I don't know much about Dormants," Magnus said as they exited the elevator on the clinic's level.

This was going to be one hell of an awkward conversation. He wasn't happy about sharing his feelings for Vivian with Julian. But his ignorance on the subject might be dangerous to her.

"What do you want to know?"

"Everything. I never thought I'd find one, so I didn't bother educating myself on the subject."

Julian stopped and turned to face him. "Vivian?"

"Who else?"

"How serious is it? Did you have sex with her?"

Magnus nodded.

"I hope you used protection."

Magnus shook his head. "I never do."

"Did you bite her?"

"Yes. Only once, though."

Last night he'd managed to refrain from biting her. But it had been a mighty struggle Magnus wasn't sure he could repeat the next time they had sex, which he hoped was going to be tonight.

Julian raked his fingers through his hair. "Once might be enough. I hope she doesn't go into transition." He shook his head. "I can't believe that I said that. Of course, I hope she is a Dormant and that she'll transition. But not right now. This is a really bad time for that."

"I agree."

The only transitions Magnus had witnessed had been of thirteen-year-old boys. He didn't know what happened to an adult female.

"I assume she responded well to your thrall."

"She didn't remember the bite."

"Good." Julian started walking again. "Let's talk about it in the clinic. I'm sure this is not a conversation you want to get overheard."

There was no one around, but Julian was right that their talk shouldn't be happening in the hallway.

When they entered the clinic, the doctor opened the door to the office. "We can talk in here."

Instead of taking the seat behind the desk, Julian sat in one of the chairs facing it and motioned for Magnus to sit in the other.

"By the way. I forgot to ask Turner if the goons showed up in the cabin."

"They did. I guess they must have thought Vivian had the tracker in her purse and was coming back. They sat around for several hours, then trashed the place and left."

"That's a shame. It was a nice cabin." He had good memories from there.

Julian waved a hand. "Nothing major. Some furniture will need to be replaced and the walls repainted. At least they didn't torch the place."

"That would've been idiotic. They could've started a brush fire."

"True, but goons are usually not that smart."

"Their boss is."

"Yeah, you're right. But back to the issue of Dormants and transitioning. There are a few things that you need to know."

"Do I need to take notes?"

"It's not that complicated." Julian pushed his longish hair behind his ears. "I need to tell my mother to post a list of instructions on the clan's virtual bulletin board."

"That would be helpful. Although to tell you the truth,

I would've probably skipped it. It's not like Dormants are common. I sure as hell didn't expect to meet one." He smoothed his hand over his goatee. "Vivian is so beautiful that I would've been drawn to her even if she was just a human. Until she woke me up in the early hours of the morning and told me that Ella had contacted her telepathically, I didn't have the slightest clue."

"You didn't feel anything special for her?"

Magnus shrugged. "I'm sure I would've felt the same regardless of her being a Dormant. She is great. My perfect dream girl."

"I'm happy for you. It seems like you found your one."

"Maybe." Magnus shifted in his seat. "How can I be sure?"

"I wouldn't know. You need to ask the guys who have found theirs. Talk to Anandur."

"Yeah, I should do that." Magnus took in a deep breath. "So what are those things I need to know?"

"Use condoms. In our limited experience, it seems that biting alone is not enough to induce transition. It needs to happen together with insemination. When the time is right, and you decide that Vivian is the one, you need to tell her the truth and give her the option to either attempt transition or not. At her age, it might be dangerous, and she should be aware of the risks. Bottom line, no sex without condoms until she agrees."

"Do you have any?"

"There should be some in here, unless the other Guardians emptied the stash. Let me check." He got up and opened the door. "We should be getting back. They must be wondering what's taking us so long."

Magnus followed Julian to the supply closet, waiting outside as the doctor collected what he needed for the blood tests and loaded everything onto a tray. When Julian was done, he put the tray on the counter and opened another drawer. "Aha, here they are. How many do you want?"

"I'll take three. I know now where to get more."

Julian handed him the packets. "You should make up your mind soon. If you intend on having frequent sex with Vivian, you can't keep thralling her every time. Tell her the truth, and if she decides that she doesn't want to risk transition, you can thrall her when this is over. It's not like she can tell anyone. For the foreseeable future, she is stuck here."

Magnus stuffed the condoms in his pocket. "Should I ask Kian's permission first?"

"It's just a formality. He'll say yes. But it's good to let him know."

"Anything else I need to know about Dormants?"

Julian picked up the tray. "The first symptoms of transition are flu-like. Fever, chills, elevated blood pressure. In more severe cases there is a loss of consciousness. So if your lady gets a fever, call me right away. Sometimes the transition starts several days after the biting."

"Got it. Anything else?"

"As I said before, age is a factor. The older the body, the more difficult the transition. But on the other hand, both Turner and Andrew were older than Vivian when they transitioned. Except, Turner was in a coma for a very long time."

"So what are you saying, that Vivian shouldn't attempt it because she is too old? She is only thirty-six. That's young."

"Vivian has two kids who need her. She might not want to take the risk of leaving them orphaned."

22

ELLA

The ride to London took longer than the one from the airport to the estate. The city must be huge. Or maybe Dimitri's place was located outside of it. Ella didn't know much about London or any of the other European big cities. Now that she was Gorchenco's pet, she might get to learn about them first hand.

Heck, every cloud was supposed to have a silver lining, right?

When the limo stopped in front of a hotel, her heart sank. Did he plan on taking her up to a room after dinner?

Given the Rolls-Royces and Lamborghinis and other fancy cars parked up in front of the Wellesley, it was a ritzy place. Her Chanel suit and Louboutin shoes would fit right in.

Even Misha had put on a suit, which made him look even more of a goon. His broad shoulders strained the jacket and his biceps bulged the sleeves.

When a uniformed valet opened the door for her, Misha tapped the guy's back, motioned for him to move aside, and offered her his hand.

She took it, letting him help her out of the limo.

"The boss reserved a private room for dinner," Misha said as he led her inside.

Her mouth suddenly felt drier than sand.

It was just as she'd expected. But why had Gorchenco gone to all the trouble of reserving a hotel room for the night when he had a huge estate that was even more luxurious than this?

Except, Misha didn't lead her to the elevators. He took her to a ground level restaurant, where a host was waiting to escort her into a private dining room.

As she followed the guy, Ella let out a breath and glanced back at Misha, who had joined a group of other burly men sitting in the restaurant's main room. Gorchenco's bodyguard squad no doubt. He nodded at her and smiled, giving her a discreet thumbs up.

For a thug, he was a pretty decent guy.

As the host opened the door to the private room, Dimitri pushed to his feet, strode toward her, took her hands in his, and kissed her on both cheeks. "Thank you for joining me, Ella. You look lovely this evening."

As if she had a choice in the matter. Such a polite guy, but such a big phony.

"Thank you."

Leading her to the chair that the host had pulled out for her, Dimitri waited until she was seated and then dismissed the guy with a slight tilt of his head.

"Wine?" He lifted the bottle.

"Yes, please."

He smiled as he poured her a full glass. "Taste it. It's a very good wine."

She had no doubt. "I'm not familiar with wines."

"Good is good. I'm very glad you don't have much

experience with inferior things. I'm going to introduce you to the best things this world has to offer."

Was that a double entendre?

To hide her blush, she lifted the glass and took a small sip. "It's very good." It tasted fine, but she had no idea if it tasted better than the five-dollar bottle her mother bought at the supermarket.

He waved a hand. "Don't be shy. Drink up."

Maybe he wanted to get her drunk. Which wasn't a bad idea. On second thoughts, though, it was. Drinking lowered inhibitions, and she might say something she wasn't supposed to.

Ella took another sip.

"You don't talk much, do you?"

She shrugged.

"Is it only with me, or are you usually this quiet?"

"I'm not a blabbermouth."

Dimitri lifted his own goblet and took a long sip. "Exquisite. Just like you." He pinned her with those unnerving blue eyes of his. "I want you to feel free to say whatever you want. I can't guess what you're thinking."

"Does it matter what I think?" She regretted the words as soon as they left her mouth.

Way to go, Ella.

"It does. I want to get to know you." He looked at her for a long moment, making her squirm under his intense stare. "I don't take women out on dates, Ella. I don't have time for that. I'm making an effort for you because you're so young and inexperienced. I figured a romantic dinner would make you a little more comfortable. That is not going to happen if you sit there all stiff and stressed out."

What did he want from her? Some good acting?

Ella plastered a smile on her face. "Someone whose advice I value told me that it's better to keep silent than blurt out something inappropriate. And since I don't know what you consider appropriate, I choose to listen rather than talk."

"That's very good advice. But when we are alone, please fill free to blurt out whatever you feel like, just make sure to do it politely. I don't appreciate rudeness or sarcasm or crass language."

That limited her options. Besides, she wasn't stupid enough to fall for that. Pavel's other advice was to defer to Dimitri when she didn't know how to respond.

Guys liked to talk about themselves. Maybe asking him questions would work?

"What made you buy me? You're a handsome, rich man. You can have any woman you want." Flattery was good too. "Why spend so much money on me?"

"You don't think your beauty is reason enough?"

She shook her head. "I'm an eighteen-year-old high-school graduate. I'm not anywhere near your class. Your arm candy should be some sophisticated supermodel who went to finishing school."

Dimitri laughed. "And what would I do with a tall stick of a woman who is only interested in clothes and jewelry?" He leaned forward and took her hand. "You, on the other hand, are raw potential, and I can turn you into the perfect companion. The ingredients are all there. You are beautiful and smart, and yet you're humble and unassuming. You are not a gold-digger, and you are pure. I think I've gotten myself quite a bargain."

It all sounded very convincing. A guy with too much money and power who decided that instead of searching for his dream woman he was going to create one. But Ella still remembered his awed expression and what he had first said to her.

She reminded him of someone.

"I appreciate the compliments, but you are not telling me the entire truth. Am I right, Dimitri? Can I call you Dimitri? Or do you prefer master?"

Crap. Again her mouth had run away from her. He'd said no sarcasm.

Gorchenco laughed again. "I'm glad that you're not completely cowed by me. Please call me Dimitri." He lifted her hand to his lips and kissed the back of it. "When I want you to call me master, I'll tell you."

Oh God. Someone kill me now.

Was he into some perverted games? Or was he just teasing her?

He laughed again. "Don't look so scared. As long as you behave, you'll know only pleasure at my hands."

Damn. Could he also read minds? The guy was way too perceptive.

She needed him to start talking. "You said that I looked like someone."

23

VIVIAN

There was nothing to do, and it was driving Vivian crazy.

After the visit from Turner and Julian, Magnus had brought sandwiches from the vending machine in the building's lobby, so she hadn't even prepared lunch.

Not that she could've made something more elaborate than the sandwiches because there was no kitchen.

"I have an idea," Magnus said. "Since it seems like your stay here is going to be much longer than anyone expected, what about ordering some more things online?"

"I need school books and worksheets for Parker."

Her son grimaced. "Do I have to?"

"Do you want to fall behind in school?"

"No, but you said that we will do homeschooling. Someone is supposed to come and set it up for me, right?"

"That's what Julian said. But you will still need books and everything else."

"I thought it would all be online. You know, interactive, just me and the computer."

She had no idea. Maybe he was right. "I'll call Julian and ask him."

Parker grinned, probably figuring that he'd just wiggled out of schoolwork for another day and could spend the time playing games.

"I was thinking more along the lines of getting more clothes and other personal items." Magnus tossed his sandwich wrapper into the wastebasket.

"What for? It's not like we are going anywhere. As long as there are laundry facilities down here, Parker and I can manage with what we have."

"There are washers and dryers upstairs. I can launder your stuff for you."

She crossed her arms over her chest. "I'm restless and I need something to do. Any ideas about that? Maybe some knitting supplies? I haven't knitted in ages."

"Do you like to swim?"

She chuckled. "I haven't gone swimming in ages either. Why? Do you have a swimming pool here?"

"Olympic size."

These people had some serious funding. A huge gym, a shooting range, and a swimming pool. Impressive training facilities.

"I want to go swimming," Parker said.

"I don't have a bathing suit."

Magnus smirked. "Do you see why we need to go virtual shopping?"

Right. As if she was going to share that with Magnus. The super-padded Victoria Secret bikinis that added two cup sizes were the only kind she was comfortable wearing in public.

"Can't you go with a shirt on?" Parker whined. "I really want to go."

Dark Widow's Curse

"You don't have swimming trunks either."

"I can use the sports shorts Magnus got me."

Vivian sighed. If her son wanted to do a physical activity that involved more than his fingers, she should make an effort to find a solution.

"I guess I can wear a long T-shirt." With her padded bra under it. Luckily, the panties she'd bought were full coverage and not sheer.

"You can take one of mine," Magnus offered.

"Thank you, but I got one that's long. It will do."

"Great. I'll take Scarlet for a quick outdoor visit and get my swimming trunks from upstairs."

That was a slip of the tongue and then some. "Do you live in this building?"

"No, but I often stay here for training. One of the floors is reserved for Guardians."

That made sense. "Is swimming part of your training routine?"

"Not officially." He got up and patted his thigh for Scarlet to follow. "The official training takes place in the gym, the classrooms, and the shooting ranges. Personally, I prefer swimming to running on the treadmill. It's my endurance workout. Can you be ready in half an hour?"

Vivian waved a hand. "I'll be ready in five minutes."

"Me too," Parker said, but continued playing.

Vivian ended up fussing with her outfit a little longer. The long T-shirt was fine as a cover-up for the bra and panty combo, but it was too short to parade like that to the pool. Except, it also looked funny with pants on because it was too long for that. She tried tucking it in, but it bunched up, then she tried it with leggings instead of jeans. That was better. It would take a little wiggling around to take them off without pulling the panties down, but that was a minor worry.

When Magnus returned, looking very casual and very sexy in a pair of swimming trunks, a T-shirt, and flip-flops, Vivian slung a towel over her shoulder and handed one to Parker. Magnus hadn't brought one.

"You should grab a towel."

He lifted a brow. "What for?"

"Don't you want to get dry after getting out of the water?"

"That's what the dryers are for. We have full body ones installed."

"I've never seen such a thing. But it sounds like an awesome invention." She followed him outside.

"It certainly saves on washing towels. The less upkeep needed, the better."

"I was wondering about that," she said as they entered the elevator. "If this is your secret lair, who cleans it? Do you have a special secret-service cleaning crew?"

"In a way."

He was good at evasive answers, but she was done being polite about it. "In what way?"

"Okidu."

The elevator stopped at another underground level. As they got out, the familiar smell of chlorine served as a beacon for the pool.

"Your boss's butler? How can one guy clean up this entire place? It's huge."

"He brings help."

"Ugh, Magnus. You're a sweet guy, but getting information out of you is impossible."

He pushed the double doors open. "You think I'm sweet?"

Parker snorted.

Vivian felt her cheeks heat up. "It's a figure of speech."

She didn't mind telling Magnus that he was sweet, because he was, but not in front of Parker.

Nor could she say *wow* when Magnus took off his shirt. She'd seen him shirtless before, but then he'd had pants on. Now he was wearing short swim trunks, and all the magnificent muscles she'd felt when they'd made love were on full display.

Spectacular.

Suddenly, Vivian felt inadequate. She was short and had a stick figure with no definition. Her only asset was her face. Well, her hair was awesome too. But Magnus was the total package.

"I'm going to jump right in, if you don't mind."

All Vivian could do was nod. Her mouth was a bit dry.

"Can I jump in too?" Parker asked.

"No. You can use the stairs to get in. Only Guardians are allowed to jump." He winked at Vivian over Parker's head. "Keep an eye on Scarlet for me, will you?"

"Okay."

The dog went exploring, sniffing along the walls as if she hoped to find a hidden bone there.

As Magnus leaped into the air and dove headfirst into the water, Vivian's breath caught in her throat.

"Wow," Parker said. "Did you see how high he jumped? And he didn't even run to gain speed."

Show off.

It was so dangerous to dive into a pool like that. People broke their necks while pulling those kinds of stupid stunts.

When Magnus's powerful torso emerged from the water, Vivian let out the breath she'd been holding until he'd surfaced. But as he started swimming, she sucked it back in.

The guy was a god.

Using his powerful arms in the butterfly stroke to propel himself, he was moving at an incredible speed.

Unbidden, the image of him on top of her entered her mind, those defined back muscles working as he stroked into her. The reaction was instantaneous. Vivian crossed her arms over her chest to hide her hardening nipples. On second thoughts, though, her padded bra was already doing a good job of concealing her inappropriate response.

Still, it felt intensely awkward to think about sex with her teenage son right there beside her.

"Go!" She nudged him. "I'll keep an eye on Scarlet."

24

ELLA

*D*imitri let go of Ella's hand, lifted his glass, and emptied it. "It's a long story."

"Are you in a hurry?" She was getting cheeky with him, but he didn't seem to mind.

In fact, he seemed to enjoy it. Nevertheless, she needed to be careful not to cross the line. Except, figuring where that demarcation line lay would take time and experimentation.

Lifting the bottle, he refilled his own and topped off hers. "Drink."

"Yes, sir." She took another small sip. The taste was growing on her, and so was Dimitri. When he loosened up, the man wasn't as terrifying.

He smiled, evidently liking the honorific.

Ella stored the information for future use. Evidently, even Gorchenco could be manipulated to an extent. When she needed something from him, calling him sir might help her cause.

The good part of this evening was that Dimitri no

longer seemed made of granite. There was some humanity in him.

She was starting to relax.

As a waiter entered with two appetizer plates, Dimitri leaned back in his chair. "I hope you don't mind that I've ordered for you."

"I'm not choosy with food."

"I stayed away from foods that are known allergens. I don't have your medical file yet, and even if I did, I wouldn't have trusted it. I'll order a full physical for you."

Should she be touched or scared?

On the one hand he cared for her health, but on the other hand, he was leaving no stone unturned in his quest to own her.

Except, Gorchenco might run all of his employees through a health test, and in a way, in his eyes she was probably one too. Only in her case, he'd bought her services in advance, the contract had no expiration date, and all the proceeds had gone to the headhunter. Or seventy percent of them if she were to believe Stefano.

Ella looked at her colorful plate. "What's in it?"

The waiter bowed. "Homemade duck ravioli with beetroot and watercress purée."

"Sounds delicious." She picked up the right fork and knife.

"It is. I always order it when I'm here. One of their best dishes."

She waited for him to take the first bite. When the waiter left and closed the door behind him, Dimitri cut a ravioli in half and put the piece in his mouth. Ella did the same.

The taste was exquisite. "Oh, wow. It's even better than I expected."

"I learned to appreciate Italian food when I studied in Italy."

Ella paused with the second half of the ravioli in front of her mouth. "What did you study?"

"Medicine."

She put her fork down. "You're a doctor?"

"Not a practicing one, but yes."

"Now I'm impressed."

He laughed. "That impresses you more than the estates and the jets?"

"Well, yeah. I value education. Why Italy, though?"

"My father thought it was a good idea to get me away from the family business for a while. He wanted to give me a taste of normal life."

"Is he still around?"

"He passed away a long time ago. I run it now. Anyway, that was where I met Stefano."

Ella nearly choked on the sip of wine she'd taken. "Are we talking about the same Stefano? The one who had me lured into a trap?"

"Yes, the same one. His family owned a restaurant near the campus, and since I ate there every day, we became friends of sorts."

"You have bad taste in friends," she muttered under her breath.

Dimitri smiled. "I wasn't very choosy back then. But you're right. Stefano is not an honorable man."

"And you are?"

"In my own way, yes."

Somehow she managed to stifle the need to say 'a mafioso's honor.' That would have been crossing the line for sure.

"There was a girl." He lifted his wine glass and emptied it, then refilled it.

Ella's curiosity was whetted and then some. She had a feeling that this was going to be one hell of a story. She took a long sip from the wine glass.

"Her name was Stella. She worked in the store next door to Stefano's restaurant, selling women shoes and purses, so it wasn't as if I could go in and pretend I wanted to buy something, but I stood outside and stared through the display at her. Sometimes, she would come out to smoke, but she didn't give me the time of day. I was the Russian kid who didn't drive a Vespa or a motorcycle and was flabby and overweight from eating too much pasta and studying all day. I was obsessed with her, utterly infatuated as only a young man falling head over heels in love for the first time could be." He forked another ravioli and popped it into his mouth.

"And? What happened?"

In her excitement, Ella finished the last of the wine in her glass and held it out for Dimitri to refill.

"I knew that the only way to impress her was to throw money around." He poured wine into Ella's glass. "So I bought an expensive car that I didn't need, and I made sure she saw it parked outside the restaurant. I waited for the store to close and offered her a ride home."

"Did she go with you?"

He waved a dismissive hand. "Of course, she did. She wasn't smart like you, and she was easily impressed by money. I was aware of that, but I didn't care. I just wanted her because she was the most beautiful girl I'd ever seen, and she was kind of sweet too. For a while." He sighed. "We dated for nearly six months when things started to deteriorate. At first, she would tell me that she was too tired to go out with me after work. Then, she would say that she wanted to spend more time with her girlfriends and accused me of being overly possessive when I complained about not seeing her enough."

He probably had been possessive and then some. Gorchenco was an alpha through and through. A man like him always needed to be in charge and run the lives of everyone around him.

Ella took a sip before asking, "Were you?"

"At the time, I thought she was right. But in retrospect, I wasn't more demanding or possessive than any other guy who loves his woman and wants to spend as much time with her as possible. She just didn't feel as strongly about me as I did about her."

A knot of dread was starting to form in Ella's stomach. Gorchenco wasn't the kind of guy who would let a woman walk out on him.

"What did you do?" she whispered.

The waiter from before came in and cleared the plates, even though Ella had eaten less than half of hers. She was much more interested in the story than in the duck ravioli.

Dimitri waited for the guy to leave before continuing. "I had finals, so I didn't have time to do anything. And then my father got sick and I had to go home. I figured I'd dazzle her with a trip to Paris when I returned, and win her back. But when I returned, she was with someone else. All that talk about wanting to spend time with her friends and me being possessive had been a lie. She had a new guy."

This time Ella didn't dare to ask what he had done next. Instead, she lifted her wine glass and held it to her mouth, taking small sips so he wouldn't expect her to say anything.

Dimitri put his glass down. "I was done with my studies and had no more reason to stay in Italy. My father was ill and needed me back home. I kept tabs on her, though, waiting for her to get sick of the new guy as well. But that never happened."

"Did she marry him?"

He shook his head. "They both got killed in a motorcycle accident."

Had it been an accident, though? Or had Gorchenco arranged it?

But before he could continue the story, or rather his modified version of it, a bunch of waiters entered with the main course.

Watching Dimitri's expression, Ella didn't spare the food even a glance. There was no guilt there, only a shadow of sadness.

Maybe he hadn't had a hand in Stella's death after all.

"Another one." Dimitri pointed at the empty wine bottle.

"Yes, sir." The waiter bowed.

When the servers were gone, he continued. "I came back for the funeral. I was devastated. Until then, I'd still entertained the thought that I could get her back. But even I couldn't fight the Grim Reaper for her. She was gone for good." He leveled his intense gaze on Ella. "Until Stefano discovered you."

While the guy with the wine came back, poured it into their glasses, and left, Ella was still staring at Dimitri with eyes peeled wide.

He lifted the glass and took a sip. "When Stefano saw your picture in the magazine, he knew I would pay any price for you. You were the second chance I never thought I would get. I think you can guess what happened next."

"You were the special buyer he was talking about. So why did he go along with the whole charade of putting me up for sale in an auction?"

"To put pressure on me. If I didn't agree to the price he quoted, he was going to sell you to the highest bidder. He knew I would never allow that to happen."

"But Stefano is a nobody compared to you. You could've just taken me from him by force."

Dimitri smiled. "Contrary to what you might think, that's not how things are done in my world. And paying three quarters of a million for you was nothing for me. He could've asked for five times as much and gotten it."

Ella crossed her arms over her chest. "I hope you told him that. That would torment that scumbag to the day he dies."

Dimitri's features darkened dangerously. "Did he lay a finger on you?"

"No. But he had Romeo lure me into a trap, and then sold me like a piece of meat. And I'm not the only one. He's done it to God knows how many girls. I hope he rots in hell."

"You're not a piece of meat, Ella." Dimitri reached over the table for her hand. "You are my most valued treasure." He kissed the back of it.

25

MAGNUS

Magnus was showing off, so sue him. That was what guys did when they wanted to impress a woman. It was an impulse, an instinct, a way to prove to her that he was the best male for her.

Regrettably, there were no other swimmers in the pool for him to compete with. Without comparison, Vivian wouldn't know that his speed and form were exceptional. Among the Guardians, he was the champion in the butterfly stroke. Which meant that he was the world's unofficial record holder. Humans, even the best of them, couldn't compete with his strength and endurance. And as for immortals, other than Guardians, very few were into sports.

Doomers, as far as he knew, didn't practice competitive swimming. It wasn't likely that he would find a contender for the title among them.

On the other end of the pool, Parker dipped his toes in the water first, and then slid all the way down.

"Hey, Magnus. Can you teach me how to swim like that? I only know freestyle and the breaststroke."

Magnus flipped inside the water and swam back. Diving under Parker, he gripped his thighs and propelled him up.

The kid landed in the water like a rock, then swam back up. "What did you do that for?"

"I thought it would be fun."

"I wasn't ready."

Parker had seen Magnus coming for him, but maybe he hadn't expected the sudden lift.

"Next time I'll warn you. The butterfly stroke requires a lot of upper body strength, so it might be difficult for you to do more than one lap. But I can show you the proper form if you want."

Parker nodded.

Magnus glanced at Vivian.

She was sitting on the edge of the pool with her T-shirt still on and her legs dangling in the water.

"Don't you want to come in?"

"In a moment. I'm getting used to the water. It's cold."

It was on the tip of his tongue to tell her that he would warm her up, but he stifled it in time. With Parker around, they both needed to censor what they said to each other. But it gave him an idea. Perhaps later, he would take her for a night swim and do all kinds of wicked things to her under the water.

Damn, he shouldn't have let his mind go there. Now he had a hard-on and no way to hide it.

Turning his back to both mother and son, Magnus glanced behind his shoulder. "Watch me do it and try to do the same," he told Parker before leaping into a stroke.

If he wanted to teach the kid, he should've gone slow, but to take care of his problem, he needed physical exertion. Pushing himself as hard as if he were in a competition, Magnus reached the other side of the pool in seconds, flipped around, and went the other way. Again, and again, and again, until he was breathing hard and his impudent member was under control.

When he stopped, he was greeted by two sets of wide eyes. Parker started clapping, and a moment later Vivian joined her son.

"I've never seen anyone swim that fast," Parker said. "And I've watched swimming competitions on TV. You could've won all of them."

Magnus waved a dismissive hand. "It only looks like that because you had no one to compare me to."

Vivian shook her head. "I wish I had a stopwatch. You were flying." She narrowed her eyes at him. "What are you?"

He shrugged. "I'm athletic."

"Superman," Parker said. "You're a superhero in disguise."

Magnus laughed. "Busted. I'm the famous Captain Fancy-pants."

That got a chuckle out of Vivian. "The superhero with an Armani designed outfit. Or is it Yves Saint Laurent?"

Magnus struck a pose with his hands on his hips and his shoulders squared. "Neither. I'm a famous fashion designer by day and a superhero by night. I design my own outfits."

That wasn't a complete fantasy. He wasn't famous, but he'd designed men's clothing for his exclusive boutique, and he was an immortal Guardian, which made him a superhero of sorts.

Parker's lips twisted in a grimace. "Fashion design is for sissies."

"I thought that I taught you better," Vivian said.

"Those are gender stereotypes, and like every other stereotype, they are unfair to people. Every person should do what they are passionate about."

Magnus crossed his arms over his chest. "You should listen to your mother, Parker. What if I really like designing clothing? Does it make me less of a man?"

"Of course not. But I just thought that you invented it as a joke, and that you could've come up with something better. Like a stock market genius, or a famous software designer. Those things are cool."

"I find them boring."

"But I don't. I think clothes are boring."

"Boys," Vivian interjected. "Instead of arguing whose hobby is better, how about some swimming?" She pulled the T-shirt over her head and put it on top of her towel.

"Yeah, swimming is good," Magnus muttered under his breath.

Sexy woman in a bikini was very distracting.

Sliding into a breaststroke, Vivian swam in the other direction, which was good because his problem was back.

Magnus was going to get one hell of a workout today.

26

ELLA

By the time dinner was over, Ella was drunk.

As Dimitri had kept refilling her glass and urging her to drink, she'd been well aware that he was trying to get her inebriated, but she had gone along with it. And not only because refusing Gorchenco was a bad idea if she wanted to get on his good side.

Maybe if she got drunk enough, she could tolerate what she knew was coming later.

The story he'd told her about his lost love had softened her a little toward him, as had his pleasant attitude throughout dinner. But it didn't make him any more desirable to her. He was still a guy almost triple her age, with thinning hair and wrinkles, who was coercing her into having sex with him.

Worse, it seemed that he wanted to keep her for good.

As she swayed on her feet, Dimitri wrapped his arm around her waist. "Let me help you." He held her up with a strong arm.

As they walked toward the exit, several of his bodyguards positioned themselves in front of them, while the rest took position at their backs. The two of them were sandwiched between two walls of muscles.

"Can I take off my shoes?"

"No. Lean on me."

Ella didn't want to.

Even though she didn't hate him as passionately as she did before, Dimitri was still the enemy. But she was tired and nauseous and her head was spinning. "I don't feel so good." She let her head drop against his arm.

It didn't feel awful, but she would've preferred Misha to help her out. He was her friend, and he didn't expect anything from her.

The limo was parked right at the entry, and the driver had the back door open and ready for them to get in.

"Is the limo bulletproof?" Ella asked as she got in.

"Of course." Dimitri slid inside after her.

When they were sitting so close that their thighs were touching, he put his arm around her. "Rest your head on my shoulder."

"I can't. It's spinning every time I close my eyes."

Dimitri pulled out a water bottle from a side compartment. "Drink this. It will help."

"We should have had coffee."

"You said you didn't want any."

"Why did you listen to me? It's not like I'm the boss here."

He chuckled. "In some ways you are. If you were older and more experienced, you would've known that. But I was lucky to snag you while you were still innocent."

What the hell was he talking about? She had the voting power of an ant without her antenna.

Oh wait, she did have an antenna, a virtual one she

could use to talk to her mom. But that was a secret. Dimitri could never know.

"Was this your first time drinking wine?" he asked.

"No, I had some before. But never this much."

"What about beer? Or cocktails?"

Ella waved a hand. "We are not in Russia, and I am not a lawbreaker. I'm eighteen. It's illegal for me to drink."

He chuckled. "Eighteen is the legal drinking age in England and in most countries around the globe."

"Yeah but not in the States. I've never been anyplace else."

"You've never traveled abroad?"

"Nope."

"Well, my dear Ella. Those days are behind you. With me, you are going to travel a lot."

"Yay."

"You don't sound enthusiastic."

"That's because I'm not."

He shook his head. "You're a strange young woman. I didn't expect it to be so difficult to impress you. I'm glad at least my education managed to do that."

That wasn't the only thing, but she wasn't going to list all the things she found impressive about him because they were not good things, and he shouldn't be proud of them.

Gorchenco had such a powerful personality that it made him seem larger than life. He could've been a president, or a general, but instead he was a crime boss, using this innate power of his to do bad things. Not good.

"What time is it?" Ella asked when the limousine crossed the first gate into Dimitri's estate.

"It's after eleven."

The limo passed the second gate, and then kept going

for another ten minutes or so before stopping in front of the grand entrance.

Dimitri got out first, then offered her a hand to help her out.

"May I take my shoes off now?"

"Yes, you may."

She put a hand on his shoulder and lifted her foot, taking one shoe off and then the other.

"Misha," Dimitri called.

"Carry Ella to the bedroom."

"Yes, boss." The burly bodyguard swung her into his arms.

"Careful. I'm nauseous."

"Please, don't puke over my suit."

"I'll try." She glanced at Dimitri who went ahead of them.

Was he going to the bedroom to get undressed? Did he expect her to have sex with him tonight?

Or would he wait for her to sober up?

It was hard to think when her head was spinning and she was fighting the need to barf. "Why do people get drunk, Misha? It feels terrible."

"You need to know when to stop." He carried her up the stairs.

"And when is that? The wine tasted good. I knew I was getting drunk, but I didn't expect to feel so crappy. Is Ilona awake? Can she make me coffee?"

"Coffee don't help. You have to sleep it off."

Holding her up with one arm, he freed his other to open the door to the bedroom.

Dimitri wasn't there.

Misha put her on the bed. "I can send Ilona to help you with your clothes."

"No. I can do it myself. Where is Dimitri?"

Misha arched his brows, which made them look like a wave since they were connected. "You want the boss to take your clothes off?"

"No! I mean this is his bedroom, right? Where is he sleeping?"

"Wherever he wants."

"Ugh. I hate answers like that. Where did he sleep last night?"

Misha shook his head. "You ask the boss. I'll go get you a bottle of soda. It make you feel a little better."

"Thank you. And if you can add a glass filled with ice cubes I'd be grateful." It was a strange little thing she hadn't expected. Europeans didn't put ice in their soft drinks.

"No problem." He turned to leave.

"Misha?"

"What?"

"You are my best friend out here. I just wanted you to know that."

He chuckled. "You are drunk."

27

SYSSI

"The coffee shop is closed for a private event."

Carol put down a tray loaded with pastries and cappuccino cups, then waved her two disappointed customers away.

"Since when do you close so early? It's only five-thirty in the afternoon," Geoffrey whined.

Wonder got up. "Don't mind Carol. What can I get you, guys?" She walked behind the counter and took their orders.

"That girl is too nice," Carol grumbled. "I put a sign out saying we would be closing at five-thirty today."

Although Syssi admired Carol's assertiveness, even envying it a little, she thought it sometimes bordered on rudeness. She herself was more like Wonder and would've done the same even though it was inconvenient.

She chuckled. "It wasn't there half an hour ago when Amanda and I returned from work. How was anyone supposed to know?"

"I forgot to put it up. It's not such a big deal. They can

get stuff from the vending machines. They're just being lazy."

After Ethan's party, the girls had made plans to meet the next day for some more baby oohing and aahing. Carol had offered to close the café early and host the get-together.

Amanda lifted a cup and took a sip. "The ones from the vending machines are not as good as the ones you and Wonder make."

Carol rolled her eyes. "As if I care. It's not such a great hardship."

"It was a lovely party," Syssi said. "Little Ethan got so many cute outfits."

"I just love that name." Amanda put her cup down. "The little guy has strong features. It suits him perfectly."

The three of them murmured their agreement. Only Nathalie seemed unhappy about it. She'd wanted him to be named after Fernando, but Syssi agreed with Eva's choice.

Ethan was a good name, and it was the kind that wasn't too bombastic for a cute baby, like Benedict or Alfred.

The baby boy's arrival filled Syssi's heart with joy. Phoenix, the only other baby in the village, was growing up, and although her cheeks were still baby soft, and she was adorable, the girl didn't appreciate getting too many smooches from her overzealous aunt.

Now there was a new bundle of sweetness to cuddle.

Sipping on her cappuccino, Syssi thought about Amanda's ambivalent attitude toward babies. Where Syssi took every opportunity to hold Phoenix and now Ethan, Amanda was happy to make a few faces and make funny voices. Syssi couldn't remember her ever picking Phoenix up. In the beginning, she'd thought Amanda had been afraid to hold a newborn, but the reluctance had continued even after the child turned immortal.

"That's such a cool stroller," Carol exclaimed as Eva and Callie entered the café's enclosure.

"Hello, everyone." Eva took a seat. "I find it astounding how much things have changed since Nathalie was a baby. They have so many cool gadgets now. The crib we got for Ethan has a motor and can rock him to sleep." She turned to Nathalie. "And where is my sweet granddaughter?"

"She's with Andrew. I wanted to have some adult conversation for a change."

"Is Bridget coming?" Callie asked.

Syssi put her cup down. "No. She went to see Vivian, the woman Magnus is guarding while Turner and the Guardians are trying to get her daughter away from the scumbag who bought her."

"Why? Is she sick?" Carol asked.

Syssi leaned back in her chair and smirked. It was fun to deliver good news. "Nope. Apparently, she and her daughter share a strong telepathic connection, which makes both of them potential Dormants. Julian took blood samples from her, but Bridget went to take some more measurements."

"Freaking Fates," Amanda murmured.

Syssi understood her frustration. With all the hard work they were investing in finding Dormants, it seemed as if the research was useless, and that the Fates were responsible for all the recently discovered ones.

As Ethan started fussing, Eva took him out of the stroller.

"Is he hungry?" Nathalie asked.

"He just likes being held."

"Can I hold him?" Syssi asked.

"Sure." Eva handed her the baby. "The party was great. Thank you all for making it happen."

"It was our pleasure," Amanda said. "Next party we are going to plan will be Wonder's wedding. What's up with that? Didn't you say Annani is expecting you guys to set a date?"

Wonder put down her half-eaten pastry. "She did. But then I started the homeschooling program, and I told her that I want to get done with high school first. Annani is all for it, and she doesn't mind waiting for the wedding."

Amanda crossed her arms over her chest. "Bummer. I was getting all excited. What about Anandur? Is he fine with waiting?"

Wonder shrugged. "He said that it's up to me, but then he came home yesterday with wedding-party ideas."

"That I want to hear." Amanda uncrossed her arms and leaned forward.

"He said it would be awesome if instead of a wedding dress I wore a Wonder Woman costume, and he would come as Superman."

Amanda waved a hand. "He was just joking."

"No. He was serious. I know when he's joking." Wonder let out a giggle. "I even considered it for about a minute and a half."

It was a fun idea, but not for a wedding. "Maybe we can have superhero-themed bachelorette and bachelor parties." Syssi looked at the baby's sweet sleeping face. "Ethan can go as Jack-Jack."

Wonder shook her head. "I need more time. I'm still doing middle-school classes. It's not going as fast as Amanda said it would." She sighed. "Mainly because it's boring. I don't like sitting in front of the computer for hours."

"I can come to tutor you," Callie offered. "I'll help you go through the courses faster."

"I don't want to burden you."

"Pfft." Callie waved a hand. "It's going to be good practice for me."

"It will take you several years to complete all the classes. Why wait so long?" Amanda asked.

Syssi snorted quietly. "Look who's talking. What about you and Dalhu?"

"Dalhu doesn't want a big party. Even after all this time, he doesn't feel comfortable around too many clan members. Especially when he's the center of attention and can't slink away to hide somewhere."

"You can make it small," Eva suggested.

"I don't do anything small." Amanda crossed her arms over her chest. "I'll wait until he's ready."

Wonder smirked. "I don't know Dalhu well, but it seems to me that I'll be done with school long before he's going to be ready for a big wedding."

Syssi had to agree. Dalhu wasn't making much of an effort to get to know more people, and things were not going to improve on their own. The question was how to get him exposed to more clan members when he was spending most of his time in his studio…"I have an idea."

"About the wedding?" Amanda asked.

"In relation to it. Dalhu is not getting out and mingling with people, which means that he's never going to get more comfortable with them. You should push him to have an art exhibition. We can use one of the larger rooms in the office building and make a big production out of it. You know, with wine and appetizers. You can be the presenter, and Dalhu can stand in a corner and act as weird as he wants because he is the artist. When he sees people gushing over his work, he might get over his reluctance to mingle."

"I don't know about that. He's still insecure about his landscapes, and that's what he's been painting lately."

"Why? They are beautiful," Wonder said. "Anandur persuaded Dalhu to part with two that I liked. I hung them in our living room, and I enjoy looking at them every day."

"I'll tell him that." Amanda tapped a finger on her chin. "I like the idea. Maybe I'll have him donate half of the proceeds to our new anti-slavery mission. I'm sure that would gain him some approval. Besides, it might motivate him to actually do it. Dalhu is a big supporter of the initiative, and this will be a good way for him to contribute."

28

VIVIAN

"Come on, Parker. I'm sure you are dry already."

The few minutes Vivian had spent in the dryer contraption had dried out her skin, and she couldn't wait to get back to the apartment and smear moisturizer all over herself.

"Give me one more minute." He shook his head, trying to dry his hair.

Beside her, Magnus's phone buzzed with an incoming message.

Vivian tensed, her body responding automatically even though she knew the rescue team was not deployed yet, so there were no new updates.

"We are about to have guests," Magnus said. "Julian is bringing Bridget to meet you."

"The famous B?" Parker pulled his T-shirt on.

"The one and only."

Vivian threw her towel over her shoulder and started walking. "When are they coming?"

"They're supposed to be here at six, which gives us

about twenty minutes. The message came in an hour ago, but I was in the water."

Swimming faster than a dolphin. The man was inhumanly athletic. "We need to hurry, then. I want to grab a quick shower and change clothes."

"I'm hungry," Parker said as they walked into the elevator.

"I can get us sandwiches from the vending machines. I'll do that on the way back from walking Scarlet."

Parker grimaced. "Again? I want real food."

"How about Chinese?" Magnus asked.

"I love Chinese."

"Then I'll order a delivery. But in the meantime, I can get you a sandwich to tide you over. It may take a while until the food gets here."

"Fine."

"How about you, Vivian? Do you want a sandwich?"

"Can you pick up a few pastries? I hate not having anything to offer Julian and his mother with the coffee."

Magnus punched the numbers on the keypad to open the door to her apartment. "I'll get some."

"Thank you."

By the time he was back, Vivian had showered, including washing and drying her hair, got dressed, and even put a little mascara on. Julian's mother was probably one hell of an impressive lady. Not only was she a medical doctor, but she was also the head of the rescue organization.

Impressive, but also intimidating, especially since Vivian had nothing nice to wear. Not that she could do anything about it on such short notice. The famous B would have to forgive her schlumpy appearance.

Despite having much less time to prepare than she

had, Magnus came in looking as suave as ever in a pair of slacks, a button-down shirt, and dress shoes.

If they ever had a relationship outside of this twilight zone, Vivian would have to revamp her wardrobe. After years of not dating, her closet was full of practical, everyday stuff. The few nice outfits remaining from before were so out of fashion that Magnus would be embarrassed to be seen with her in public.

Except, all that rumination was useless, since they were not going to have a relationship once this was over. The deal was that they were going to enjoy each other just as long as their enforced cohabitation lasted.

A little after six o'clock, Magnus's phone buzzed, and he went to open the door. "Hello, Bridget." He pulled it wide open to let Julian and his mother in.

"Let me introduce you to Vivian and her son, Parker."

Looking at the young and very pretty redhead, Vivian realized that Bridget must be Julian's stepmother. There was no way the woman had given birth to him. First of all, she looked about the same age as Julian, and secondly, she was as short as Vivian, while Julian was taller than Magnus. Bridget was a redhead, and Julian's hair was light brown. The only resemblance was in the eyes. Both were blue and smart.

Vivian wondered what the story was.

Bridget must have been Julian's father's second wife, a much younger one. Was his biological mother still around? Or had she passed away?

Still, it was evident that Julian loved and admired his stepmom. Otherwise, he wouldn't have followed in her footsteps and become a doctor. Perhaps his father was a doctor too?

Bridget offered Vivian her hand. "I've heard a lot about you. It's a pleasure to finally meet you."

"Hi." Vivian smiled and shook it. "I've heard a lot about you too."

After shaking Parker's hand as well, Bridget gave Vivian a thorough look over. "Julian told me the story of how you met."

When Vivian glanced at him, she was surprised to find that he didn't appear embarrassed in the least.

"I told my mom that you looked like Kim Basinger."

Was that all he'd told her? Vivian hoped he hadn't shared with his mother the rest of the story.

"He's right. You do look a lot like her."

Vivian waved a dismissive hand. "I don't get why people think that. I look nothing like her." She motioned to the dining table. "Please, take a seat. Magnus got some pastries, and I have a pot of coffee ready."

"Thank you. That would be lovely." Bridget sat down. "I could use a cup."

When coffee was served, Bridget lifted her mug and glanced at the picture hanging on the wall over the couch. "I see that one of Dalhu's creations is still here. Are there any more in the bedroom?"

Vivian turned to look at the charcoal drawing of a stunning woman. "I thought it was an original. But I wasn't sure. I didn't want to touch it and make an accidental smear."

"That's one of the first drawings done by a very talented artist. His muse is his mate."

"You mean wife?" Vivian corrected.

"They haven't gotten around to having a wedding yet, but they're as good as married." Bridget took a sip of her coffee. "You seem to be following in their footsteps."

"How so?"

"The cabin you were staying in was where he took her after they met. And later, they lived here in this underground apartment for a while. These walls are imbued with their love. That's a lot of good juju." She winked.

Did Bridget suspect that there was something going on between Vivian and Magnus? Had that been a hint?

Shifting in her chair, Vivian grabbed a pastry. "Why did they live here? Were they in danger?"

Bridget smiled. "There was somewhat of a family drama going on. But that's a story for another time. I came here to take a few measurements Julian forgot to take." She put her mug down. "I'm also involved in the paranormal abilities research."

"You mean to do more blood tests?" Vivian cringed. She wasn't afraid of needles, but getting poked twice in one day was too much.

Bridget shook her head. "I have enough blood samples. I need other measurements. None are intrusive, though. All I'm going to use are a tape measure and a blood-pressure cuff."

Vivian frowned. "Are there similarities in size between people with paranormal abilities?" She chuckled. "I would love to hear that shorties are more paranormally talented than the tall ones."

The doctor smiled, but her eyes darted to the side. She was about to lie. "We measure everything we can think of."

29

MAGNUS

"May I be excused?" Parker leaned back in his chair and rubbed his full stomach.

Chinese cuisine was tasty, but it was heavy and oily. Even Magnus, with his fast immortal metabolism, felt sleepy. Then again, he'd had a couple of pastries with Julian and Bridget, and earlier he'd had a vigorous workout in the pool. It had been a long time since he'd exerted himself like that.

Did it mean that he was out of shape?

"Sure," Vivian said. "But go play in the bedroom so Magnus and I can talk without explosions in the background."

"I can put headphones on."

"Also without your intermittent jumps and yells."

"Fine. I'll watch something on Netflix. I'm too tired to play." He pushed to his feet and shuffled to the bedroom.

The kid must've overstuffed himself. Magnus had never heard Parker say he was too tired to play before.

"Close the door," Vivian called after him.

"Okay." The door slammed behind him.

Dark Widow's Curse

Vivian shook her head but didn't comment. "Would you like some coffee?"

"I'll make it."

She put a hand on his arm. "Please, I need to do something around here."

He took her hand and kissed it. "I like doing stuff for you."

"I know. And that's very sweet of you. But I'm not used to being useless."

He waggled his brows. "I can think of several ways you can be useful."

"You're such a scoundrel. It's only seven-thirty in the evening."

"True." And what a bummer that was. "We need to come up with an excuse to be alone. How about another movie?"

She shook her head. "Not while Parker is awake. We can't close the door on him."

"There is a movie theater two levels below. We can go there."

"And neck in the back row like a couple of teenagers?"

"Why not?"

"What if some of your Guardian buddies want to watch too? That would be awkward."

A light bulb went on in Magnus's head. "I have a great idea. I can see who's on rotation here and have them invite Parker to watch a movie with them. We will have a couple of hours to ourselves."

"He doesn't know them. And besides, how are you going to explain it to them?" She leaned closer and whispered in his ear. "I want you to entertain the kid for a while, so I can shag his mom?"

Magnus grimaced. "The truth is that Parker is bored. I

think it will do him good to spend time with other people. But first, let me check who's here this evening, and what their plans are for tonight. Usually, when the guys are in town, they go hunting at nights."

"Hunting?"

"For girls."

"Oh. Like in clubs?"

"Yeah."

She narrowed her eyes at him. "Do you do that too?"

"Where else am I going to meet eligible lasses?"

Vivian shook her head. "The life of a bachelor."

"Is not as fun as it seems. I would trade it in a heartbeat for the chance of a life-long relationship with the woman I love."

A brief look of guilt crossed Vivian's beautiful face, but it was gone just as quickly as it had appeared. "Call your friends. I'm going to make coffee."

"Yes, ma'am."

A few phone calls later, Magnus had Liam and Edward lined up for an *Avengers* marathon. That would keep Parker occupied for hours.

He knocked on the bedroom door and then opened it. "Hey, Parker, are you up for an *Avengers* marathon? A couple of my Guardian buddies are going to watch it in the movie theater we have down here. They'd be happy to have you join them."

Parker looked up at him from the bed. "You have a real theater? Like with a big screen and everything?"

"The full package, including a popcorn machine."

"I'm in!" He clicked the television closed and got off the bed. "Who are your friends, are they nice?"

"The best. They are Scots like me. Great fellows. Come

on, put your shoes on and I'll take you there. They are waiting for you to start."

"What about you? Aren't you going to watch with me?"

"Sorry, kid, but someone needs to keep your mom company. I'll stay and watch chick flicks with her." He made a face as if that was a great sacrifice.

When they stepped out of the bedroom, Vivian put down her coffee mug. "Are you going now?"

"My friends are waiting for Parker in the movie theater."

She got up. "I'm coming with you. I want to meet those friends of yours."

Parker perked up. "Are you going to watch the *Avengers* with us? It's going to be so much fun."

"No, sweetie. I'm not a great *Avengers* fan. I just want to meet the guys you're going to be spending several hours with."

"Oh." The kid looked crestfallen.

"But if you want to watch the *Twilight* marathon, I'm game."

"No way. That's so girly."

Vivian smiled. "Now you understand why I'm not as enthusiastic about watching superhero movies with you."

Down in the theater, the guys had already gotten the popcorn going, the smell of it hitting Magnus as soon as the elevator doors opened. It took Vivian and Parker a few moments longer.

"I smell popcorn," the kid said as Magnus pulled the theater's double doors open.

"Vivian, Parker, meet my buddies, Liam and Edward." He clapped each guy on the back as he said their names.

"Enchanted," Liam said as he took Vivian's hand and

kissed it. "Now I'm really peeved at Kian for not choosing me for the babysitting job."

That earned him a flick on the back of the head. Both for the leering and the babysitting comment. "Protecting a lady and her son is not babysitting," Magnus said.

Liam bowed. "My apologies."

"That's okay." Vivian smiled. "I know it's not as exciting as taking part in the action."

"I beg to differ." Edward offered her his hand. "I'd rather spend time with beauty than fight the beast."

Magnus barely managed to stifle the growl rising up in his throat. "Behave, you two. You're embarrassing the lady."

Edward smirked. "Just saying the honest truth, my friend." He wrapped his arm around Parker's slim shoulders. "Are you ready for awesomeness, my young apprentice?"

Magnus wasn't sure whether Edward was trying to mimic Darth Sidious or Yoda.

"Yes, sensei."

Apparently, Parker had decided it was the latter.

30

VIVIAN

For the first time since the journey with Magnus had begun, they were truly alone together.

It felt awkward.

"What if Parker comes back early?" Vivian asked as Magnus took her hand.

"One of the guys is going to have to accompany him. They will call. No one can open the door from the outside without the code, and I didn't give it to them."

"Clever."

As soon as the elevator doors closed behind them, he lifted her up and pinned her to the wall. "I was waiting for this all day long."

He caught her lips in an all-consuming kiss, his tongue invading, his lips hard and demanding.

Wrapping her arms around his neck, she tried to kiss him back, but he didn't let her put her tongue inside his mouth. His hand on her nape gripping harder, he held her in place for his onslaught.

Damn, the man was all dominance, and it excited her.

As lust exploded through her body, tightening her nipples and moistening her core, Vivian lifted her legs and wrapped them around his torso. Aligning his bulge with her tingling center, she rubbed herself against it to get some relief.

When the elevator doors opened, he didn't let her down. Holding her close, his lips sucking on the tender skin of her neck, he carried her down the corridor to his room.

Somehow, Magnus managed to hold her up with one hand while punching the code on the keypad with the other. As the door swung open into the dark interior, he stepped inside and shut the door with his foot, plunging them both into complete darkness.

"Aren't you going to turn the lights on?" she whispered into his ear, then nibbled on it.

"I know where the bed is." He put her down and pulled her T-shirt off.

Her bra clasp was next.

There was no fumbling in the dark. Magnus knew exactly where everything was, handling it with deft fingers. He took off her flip-flops, kissing each foot as he did, then hooked his fingers in the elastic of her leggings, pulling them down together with her panties.

Naked, Vivian rose on her knees and reached for his shirt, fumbling in the dark for the buttons.

Magnus's patience ran out on the second one, and as he pulled it over his head, she heard the unmistakable sound of little buttons hitting the floor.

"You're destroying your shirt."

"I don't care," he growled.

She heard him unbuckling his belt and then the zipper going down.

"Wait. What about condoms?"

"Got them. Julian has a stash in the clinic. I raided it."

She hoped he hadn't asked the doctor for them, but if he had, it wasn't a big deal. They were both single adults, and they weren't doing anything illegal.

"Get on your hands and knees," he commanded.

Oh, wow. She hadn't done that in forever. Normally, it would've been an embarrassing pose with a new lover, but since it was completely dark in the room, he couldn't see her, only feel.

She could deal with that.

The bed dipped as he crawled up onto it.

Vivian tensed. She was wet, but she didn't think she was ready. Would he just enter her like that?

The thought was exciting and frightening at the same time.

He didn't, though.

His warm palms resting on her ass cheeks, he gently pulled them apart, and a moment later his hot breath fanned over her moist center.

Vivian felt herself go loose. She should've known Magnus would make sure to prepare her. He was such an exceptional lover. The combination of thoughtful and giving while at the same time demanding and commanding was explosive.

In fact, he was the best she'd had, even if admitting that made her heart ache a little. Josh had been a good husband, and she'd loved him dearly, but he hadn't been as skilled and as masterful as Magnus in bed.

When his fingers joined his tongue, her hips started rocking back and forth to meet those thrusting digits. And as pulse after pulse of pleasure propelled her closer to the pinnacle, her rocking becoming more frantic, Vivian could barely recognize the sounds coming out of her throat.

The soundproof environment was so liberating. She could go wild and scream her pleasure to high heavens, and no one other than her and Magnus would hear. It was a rare luxury that she was going to miss.

Hooking his fingers inside her, Magnus pressed on a sensitive patch of nerves, detonating her climax as if he'd pushed a button, releasing the coil he'd been tightening with his skilled tonguing.

Her muscles clamping down on his fingers, she floated, drifting toward the bright lights dancing behind her closed lids and the psychedelic world they were painting.

Her limbs heavy and boneless, she would have sunk down into the mattress if not for Magnus's arm wrapped around her middle and holding her up.

He leaned over her and kissed her back, his warm palm caressing, soothing, loving.

Through the blissed-out haze, she heard the condom wrapper tear. A moment later, the head of his manhood rubbed against her entrance, and Vivian's languor turned into renewed hunger.

"I want you inside me," she murmured.

As his shaft slid easily between her wet folds, he gripped her hips, pulling her back against him and impaling her on the entire length.

"Yes," she gasped.

Despite their size differences, they somehow fit perfectly. She wasn't too small, and he wasn't too big, they were just right for each other.

Magnus pulled almost all the way out, and then slammed his hips against her backside. If not for his strong grip on her, she would've been pushed forward, but he held on tight and kept pumping into her.

With his thrusts getting faster and more powerful, the bed strained under the onslaught, rattling dangerously. Again, Vivian was grateful for the soundproofing of the place. Her only worry was that the thing was going to collapse before they both reached their orgasms.

It would be a shame if that happened, but if it did, they were going to continue on the floor. There was no stopping this runaway train.

Reaching under her, he pressed his fingers to her swollen clit, his gentle touch contrasting with the rough pummeling he was giving her.

"Oh, yes!" She bucked.

As his fingers rubbed a little harder and a little faster, her bucking followed suit until she was not sure who was fucking whom.

Colorful circles swirling behind her closed lids, Vivian felt her inner muscles clamp around Magnus's shaft, and as the explosion rattled her body once more, she let out a loud cry.

31

MAGNUS

As Vivian went lax in his grip, Magnus held her up. But as his own climax neared, he let the momentum carry them both down to the bed.

Earlier, on the way to his room, Magnus had planned on refraining from biting her, but he should have known that it would be an impossible feat of willpower to do so two nights in a row. He'd managed yesterday, but there was no stopping it now.

Clamping his lips over the tender spot where the soft flesh of her neck met her shoulder, he licked it to anesthetize it and then sank his fangs inside her and pumped her full of venom.

Vivian whimpered and tensed, but a moment later, as the venom hit her system, her body loosened under him.

That was when his seed exploded out of him, going on and on and filling up the condom, until Magnus wondered whether it could contain it all.

When he was spent, he dropped to his side, pulling Vivian with him, her back against his front. Soon, the euphoria from his bite would dissipate, and then he'd have to turn her around and thrall the memory away. In the meantime, though, he could give her a few blissful moments of soaring on the venom-induced clouds.

As he waited, he stroked her arm, her trim waist, the curve of her hip, her rounded butt-cheek, over and over until she stirred in his arms and turned around, her blissed-out expression making her beautiful face look angelic.

"My angel," he whispered and dipped his head to kiss her lips.

"Magnus." She smiled as she said his name.

Was she dreaming about him?

He took a quick peek at her mind, his shaft going hard in a nanosecond as he saw their coupling through her eyes.

Damn, that was erotic as hell, and more so given that the visuals were all a product of her imagination. With him behind her, and no mirrors on the walls, she couldn't have seen them even if there was light in the room.

Note to self. When he finally fessed up to Vivian and moved her into the village to live with him, Magnus was going to install a big-ass mirror on the wall next to their bed.

His shaft twitched, urging him to go for another round.

But first, he had to dispose of the condom and then wait for Vivian to come down from her high, thrall the memory of his bite away, and only then take her again.

This time with no biting.

Fortunately, that part of the immortal sexual urge had been satisfied tonight and there was no need for a repeat.

Withdrawing carefully, he grabbed the rubber and

tied it off. He got up, padded to the bathroom, dropped it in the wastebasket, and then returned to bed.

Spooning behind Vivian, he wrapped his arm around her and brought her back against his chest. She was still out like a light.

Perhaps when she turned immortal, he could try biting her more than once in one night.

He was getting carried away.

Even with her strong telepathic ability, there was no guarantee that Vivian was a Dormant. Besides, he wasn't sure what he felt for her.

He cared for her, and he loved spending time with her. The sex was great, and getting better because they were learning each other's bodies and letting go of inhibitions.

As he was discovering, Vivian was perfectly fine with his dominance, and he didn't need to dial it down for her sake.

Not to overwhelm her, he was getting just a little more intense each time, and each time she seemed to love every moment of it.

But was it love? Was she the one?

With her petite body nestled against his, her long hair tickling his chest, he felt as if she belonged there. And yet, possessiveness wasn't love either.

When she lifted her hand and cupped his cheek, he knew it was time to thrall her. Right now the euphoria was still twisting her perception around, but soon she would come to and remember the bite.

Winding his fingers in her hair, he cupped the back of her head and lifted it so she was facing him. It wasn't really necessary for performing the thrall, but he wanted to see her expression as he delved into her mind.

A few moments after it was done, she opened her eyes.

"I don't know why I passed out again. You have a strange effect on me."

"It's called post-orgasmic bliss."

"Well, that explains it. I don't think I've ever orgasmed as powerfully as I keep doing with you. You're something else."

Magnus's chest swelled with pride. "That's the best compliment I've ever gotten. And the feeling is mutual. You're amazing."

She rocked her hips against his hardness. "I'm starting to believe Parker's theory that you're a superhero in disguise. Unless I was out for much longer than I think I was, you have zero recovery time."

"That's because I'm with you."

It was a little white lie, but after the compliment she'd given him he wanted to give something similar back.

Vivian chuckled. "I doubt that."

He pushed her onto her back, rolled on top of her, and pulled her arms over her head. "Are you calling me a liar?"

"And what if I am?"

"There will be retribution." He dipped his head and gently nipped her lower lip, then sucked it into his mouth and licked the small hurt away. With his venom released, his fangs were no longer an issue, and he knew his eyes wouldn't glow either.

She was smiling when he lifted his head.

"Do it again."

He nipped her upper lip, then licked it and slid a little lower to feast on her nipples. He'd neglected them before, and that was unforgivable.

Rimming one stiff peak with his tongue, he thumbed

the other one until both stood to attention, and Vivian was undulating under him.

"Do you have another condom?" she husked.

"I have plenty." He licked her other nipple.

"Good. Then get it."

"In good time." He slid a little further down and kissed the top of her mound. "I can't get enough of this." He licked her wet slit.

"Stop." She threaded her fingers in his hair and pulled his head up. "Right now, I'm still too sensitive down there."

"That's a shame." He planted an open mouthed kiss on her lower lips then crawled back on top of her and kissed her mouth, sucking and licking on her lips and then thrusting his tongue inside of it as if he was treating her to cunnilingus and not just kissing her.

It had the desired effect of getting her wild with need again.

When he let go of her mouth so she could take a breath, she hissed, "Get that condom, Magnus."

"Yes, ma'am."

32

ELLA

Someone was poking needles into Ella's eyelids. Or at least it felt like it.

With an effort, she cracked her eyes open and squinted. The needles were sun rays, and the little devils were bombarding her through the large French doors.

Someone truly evil had pulled the curtains open. Probably Ilona. The woman hated her.

Ella groaned.

Ilona didn't really hate her. This was the hangover talking. She'd heard about them, read about them, but hadn't experienced one before now.

It sucked.

She had a headache, was so nauseous that barfing was imminent, and she was also damn cold and uncomfortable, but that had nothing to do with the drinking, or maybe it did. She'd passed out in her clothes. The tight skirt was twisted around her waist, and the jacket was crumpled under her shoulders.

The good news was that no one had undressed her

and she was alone in the bedroom. That alone was worth the headache and nausea.

Yay for getting drunk.

At least it had saved her from Dimitri's advances. Apparently, he wasn't into violating drunk women. One small point in his favor.

He was only ninety-five percent evil, not one hundred. The guy had been in love once, so he wasn't a complete monster, and Ella had to admit that he'd been treating her reasonably well.

Except for the buying and imprisoning part.

But then again, he'd probably saved her from a much worse fate. Any of the other perverts who bought girls at auctions would've raped her by now.

So he was only eighty percent evil.

Did coercion count as rape?

Probably.

Dimitri had been exceedingly patient up until now. But she couldn't expect him to wait much longer to claim his new toy that he had paid so much money for.

Her time was up.

Tonight, he wouldn't let her touch alcohol and would do the deed.

But that was a worry for later. Right now she needed to take off her clothes, get in the shower, and then crawl back in bed and try to sleep that damn hangover off.

The hot shower helped with the headache, and as she came out of the bathroom, breakfast was waiting for her on the table. Her stomach was too queasy for food, but she could use a good cup of coffee.

Pouring it, she wondered whether it was too late to contact her mother. It was after ten in the morning, which meant two o'clock at night over there. Her mom would definitely be sleeping, but if she didn't hear from her, she would worry.

Mom.

Ella, thank God, I was worried. What happened?

I woke up late. Dimitri had me drink lots of wine last night and now I have a hangover. Why do people drink? It's nasty.

You sound okay, so I guess nothing happened.

No, but that was because I passed out. I'm sure tonight he is not going to let me drink.

I wish there was something I could do for you. I hate being so helpless.

There is nothing to do other than hang myself in the closet. I can use one of his belts.

Don't talk like that!

Just kidding. I'm not that desperate. It's going to be okay. I would've preferred my first time to be with someone I loved, but I think I can tolerate Dimitri. After all, you always wanted me to end up with a doctor. Ella waited for the mental gasp.

I don't understand. What doctor?

Ella chuckled. *In addition to being a mafia boss, Dimitri is a doctor. He finished medical school in Italy. He told me this incredible story about a girl he'd been in love with when he was a student. She looked exactly like me, and she died in a motorcycle accident. Stefano, Romeo's so-called uncle, knew him from back then, and when he saw my picture in that damn shoe ad, he realized the potential. He knew that Dimitri would pay any price for me because I looked like the girl he'd loved and lost.*

Oh wow. This is an incredible story. Maybe you can use it to your advantage. If Gorchenco wants a redo, he might be willing to give you more time and court you like he did that other girl.

I can try, but I doubt it will work. He is not the young guy he was back then. He is hard. Ella snorted. *Oh boy, I shouldn't have said that. Talk about double meaning.*

As her mother's anguish reached her over the mental line, she regretted her choice of words. Except, what else was there to do other than joke about it and pretend as if it wasn't that bad?

Did he make any advances? Vivian asked.

No. Other than kissing the back of my hand, nothing.

Then I think you might get him to wait.

Don't stress over it, Mom. The girl I roomed with in the auction house told me to think of it as an arranged marriage, and that's what I'm going to do. In a different time, a rich, powerful man like Dimitri could come and ask for my hand in marriage, or even just send a representative, and you would've had no choice but to agree. Ella laughed. *Heck, you might have even thought that he was a good catch. A rich doctor, right? Your dream husband for me.*

Yes, but not an old mafia boss who happens to be a doctor. I wanted a young one who you'd chosen and fallen in love with.

You're too picky, Mom. You can't have everything.

I'm glad you can joke about it.

I'd rather joke than cry. I'm trying to make lemonade from the lemons fate has given me.

My brave girl. I talked with the team's leader and he said you should keep your eyes open. Don't go searching for clues, and don't ask questions that might get you in trouble, but if you see or hear something that might help us, let me know. Apparently, Gorchenco never stays long in one place, which makes a rescue operation difficult. If we know his next destination ahead of time, we can send a team beforehand.

What if he doesn't tell me?

Then we have to wait until he comes back to his New York

estate. The people helping me are sending a team that will be stationed there until he does.

That could take forever. No way could she string him along until then.

I'll do my best to find out where we are going next.

Whatever you find out is going to help, and let me know as soon as you do.

I will. Goodnight, Mom.

Wait. I just want to tell you how proud I am of you. You are so strong.

Thanks.

Ella closed the channel before the tears came rolling down. She wasn't strong. She was just dealing with the situation the best she could.

33

TURNER

Turner wasn't happy about Julian joining his meeting with Kian, but it was unavoidable.

Now that they knew Ella was a possible Dormant, Julian was convinced that she was his fated mate, and what was even worse, everyone was treating him as if he was already mated to the girl.

It was ridiculous. Julian had never even met Ella. He was infatuated with a beautiful face. That wasn't love, and certainly not true love. But there was no sense arguing with the kid until he actually met the girl and discovered that he had nothing in common with her.

"I assume you have a plan," Kian said.

Turner shifted in his chair and glanced at Julian. "I have the beginning of one."

"From the look you're giving me, I'm not going to like it," Julian said.

"Regrettably, I didn't find a solution other than waiting for Gorchenco to return to his New York estate with Ella. I tried to come up with something more expedient, but that's all I have. It might take a long time."

"Time Ella doesn't have."

"I know. But I'm not a miracle worker. The only solace I can offer you is that she is young, and with proper treatment she'll get over it."

Hopefully.

"What's the plan?" Kian asked.

"We're going to stage a fire, or have the people in the compound believe there is one. We can use Sylvia's control over electrical things to cause a short that will spark a fire, or we can have Yamanu do his thing."

"I prefer for Yamanu to thrall the hell out of them," Julian said. "I don't want Ella to get hurt accidentally."

"Yes, that's a consideration. Anyway, once they are convinced that the estate is on fire, we show up with firetrucks, dressed as firemen, get in, kill Gorchenco, and get Ella out."

Kian raked his fingers through his hair. "If you're going to kill him, why go to all the trouble of staging a fire and pretending to be firemen? Yamanu can thrall the guards to open the gates and go to sleep."

"Yes and no. We have to take into account that some of the staff may be immune to thralling or at least resistant. And secondly, I want to make it look as if Ella killed Gorchenco."

Julian's eyes widened. "Why?"

"Because we don't want the Russian mafia on our tail. If they believe a girl he'd bought used a fire scare as a chance to kill the guy keeping her enslaved, they will probably let it go. As long as it's a plausible scenario, they are not going to poke holes in it."

"What about Ella? Aren't they going to go after her?" Julian asked.

"They will, but only perfunctorily. She can hide in the

village, and in a year or so, no one will remember the incident."

"If she's a Dormant," Kian said. "If she isn't, we will have to hide her in the keep."

Julian lifted a brow. "For a year?"

"Perhaps we can find a place to relocate her to. Like South America. It will take decades before they incorporate facial recognition software over there."

"That's a discussion for later," Turner said. "We need to have a team stationed in New York. But I don't want them to sit idly on their asses until Gorchenco comes back there. I want to reshuffle things and find them rescue operations in the area."

Kian shook his head. "I don't see how that is going to work. What if Gorchenco comes back and our people are busy elsewhere?"

"I will have everything in place, including the firetrucks and uniforms and all the intelligence I can gather. When he shows up, we pull the men out of the other operations. We will schedule only simple small-scaled rescues. Nothing overly complicated. In and out in an hour kind of operations."

"Are you going with them?"

"I have to set it up." Turner pushed his hair back. "I probably need to stay too. This is an extremely complicated mission, and it's on American soil. I can't think of any of your Guardians who I can delegate this to. Unless you want to head it?"

Kian sighed. "I wish. I haven't seen any action in a long time. Not since the monastery. But I can't. I have several big deals that I'm working on right now and they need my entire focus."

"Can I go?" Julian asked.

Turner groaned. "That's not a good idea."

"I want to be there when you get Ella out. I'm a doctor. I'm not useless baggage. People might get injured, she might be in shock and in need of emergency treatment. You never know."

"Your mother is going to put me in the doghouse, and not just because you'll be in danger. You're supposed to run the clinic. It might take weeks until Gorchenco is back."

Kian cleared his throat. "I have another doctor arriving this weekend. Merlin is coming to do research, but he can cover for Julian while this is going on."

"Why didn't anyone tell me?" Julian asked.

"Your mother doesn't know about it either. Merlin wasn't supposed to come until a couple of months from now. I was just informed of his change of plans."

Julian crossed his arms over his chest. "Then it's settled. I'm going."

"By the way," Kian said. "What did you do with your prisoners?"

That was another reason Turner hadn't wanted Julian to be there. He was a doctor whose mission was to save lives, not take them. He might be appalled by what Turner had done.

"I hope they are dead," Julian hissed.

Maybe not.

"They are. Spivak and I extracted every bit of information from them and then used them for fang practice. It was the first venom kill for both of us."

Julian grimaced. "That was too merciful of a death for those cockroaches."

"I agree." Turner shrugged. "But I figured Spivak and I needed the practice, and that was a good opportunity."

"Did you learn anything new?" Kian asked.

"Yes and no. Their operation followed the standard model. What I found surprising was the level of depravity. Romeo was just a greedy sleaze bag with no morals, but Stefano was bad."

"What did he do?" Julian asked. "I mean as in worse than kidnapping girls and selling them?"

Turner felt his fangs punch out. "He'd molested his own daughter since she was a young girl and whored her out. Luckily for Ella, he wanted to sell her virginity to Gorchenco, who he feared like the devil himself. He didn't dare touch her."

34

VIVIAN

"Good morning." Magnus entered the apartment with Scarlet trotting behind him. "You look tired."

His suggestive tone and self-satisfied smirk had Vivian cast a quick glance at Parker. Luckily, her son had been distracted by the dog who'd leaped into his lap and was trying to lick his face.

"I am." But not for the reasons he was looking so smug about. "Ella contacted me at two o'clock in the morning and I had trouble falling asleep after that."

The smirk disappeared. "Did something happen?" Magnus asked in a low voice.

Parker was busy with Scarlet and watching anime, but Vivian knew he was listening. His head was tilted in their direction.

"Nothing yet," she whispered. "Would you like some coffee?" she asked louder.

"Yes, please."

She poured him a cup. "Do you want breakfast before or after the gym?"

Magnus had his exercise clothes on, and since he never wore them just for the comfort of it, he was on his way to the gym.

"I want you to join me. I promised to teach you self-defense moves, and Parker probably wants another visit to the shooting range."

"Yes, I do!" Parker moved Scarlet aside and jumped off the couch. "I'm going to put my shoes on."

When he was out of earshot, Magnus whispered, "What did she tell you?"

"After Gorchenco got her drunk on wine last night, she passed out on the bed with her clothes on. He didn't bother her and let her be, but she doesn't think that he will wait much longer. Although, after the story she told me about him, I think he might."

"A story?"

"When he was a young student in Italy, Gorchenco fell in love with a girl who looked exactly like Ella. She got killed in a motorcycle accident. I think he wants a redo, and that's why he was willing to pay so much money for Ella. He might want to court her properly."

Magnus rubbed his hand over the back of his neck. "I don't know. His sad story notwithstanding, this guy bought a girl and is coercing her into having sex with him. I doubt he is going to play nice."

Vivian sighed. "With Parker and me gone, he has no one to hold over her head, but she needs to pretend as if she doesn't know it. I wonder if he would actually force her if she said no."

She hoped that Magnus would say that the likelihood of that was slim, but he shook his head. "I don't want to give you false hope. The only thing that could stop a man like Gorchenco from taking what he wants by force is

Dark Widow's Curse

pride. I just hope he's prideful enough. Except, that's dangerous too because he might get vengeful and hurt Ella. I wish we could assume he was a decent man, but we can't. It's better to be prepared for the worst."

Magnus was unfortunately right.

Cooperating was the safest option for Ella. Anything else would get her in more trouble. If she refused Gorchenco or resisted him, and he was too prideful to force her, he might retaliate by giving her to his bodyguards.

As tears pooled in the corners of Vivian's eyes, Magnus pulled her in for a quick hug. "I'm so sorry. I wish I could tell you something to make you feel better."

She wiped the tears away with the back of her hand. "Ella is so brave. She's trying to deal with the situation the best she can. She even made fun of it, saying that I always wanted her to marry a well-educated man. Apparently, Gorchenco went to medical school in Italy. Oh, and I forgot to mention that Romeo's uncle knew him back then. That's why when he saw Ella's picture in the magazine, he decided to grab her and sell her to Gorchenco."

"So Gorchenco didn't order her kidnapping?"

Vivian shook her head. "Doesn't seem that way. It was all the uncle's idea."

"Then maybe you're right and he will wait. There is a difference between someone who sets out to buy a girl and one who is offered a doppelgänger of his lost love and can't resist the opportunity. In his eyes, he might even think that he saved her from a worse fate."

A kernel of hope sprouted in Vivian's heart. As a woman, one who'd led a pretty sheltered life, she hadn't trusted her intuition as to what a man like Gorchenco might do. But if Magnus thought there was a chance he would spare Ella, then it was a real possibility.

"What if we can find out more about that girl? Maybe Ella can use the information to string him along."

"Did he tell her the girl's name?"

"Ella didn't tell me. But I can ask her the next time she talks to me."

Except, by then it might be too late. "What about Romeo and his uncle? Turner can ask him about her."

Magnus grimaced. "I'm afraid that won't be possible."

"Why?"

"Because he's dead."

"Oh." She wasn't going to ask how that had happened. The scumbag had gotten what he'd deserved. Hopefully, Turner and his people had killed Romeo too.

Those two were not going to hurt any more girls.

"I'm ready," Parker said. "Are you coming?" He glanced at Vivian's flip-flops.

"Give me a moment to change, and I'll come with you."

35

ELLA

As Misha escorted Ella into the estate's dining room, she was acutely aware of the clicking sound her spiky heels were making on the marble floor.

The room, like the rest of the estate, was built on grand proportions and was opulent in the extreme. Above the long table, three crystal chandeliers hung from a ceiling that was at least two stories high. It had a mural of some mythical battle painted on it, with chariots and heavily muscled larger-than-life warriors wielding long swords.

Ella counted ten chairs on each side before reaching the head of the table where Dimitri was waiting for her.

"Good evening, Ella." He got up, then waited as a servant pulled a chair out for her.

"Good evening, Dimitri." She sat down.

After Misha left, two more servants entered the room, each carrying a plate. Ella dug in, glad she was spared having to make small talk with Dimitri. Even if he were a normal date, she wouldn't have known what to say. The differences between them were so vast, she doubted they had anything in common.

The food was exquisite, and Ella enjoyed every bite, but it felt beyond odd that only two people were sitting at the enormous table, while a staff of mute servants brought in one dish after another.

Just as she'd expected, Dimitri was monitoring her alcohol intake tonight. While he kept sipping on glass after glass of wine, he poured Ella only half of one at the start of dinner, and once it was gone, he didn't offer to refill it.

The smart guy that he was, Gorchenco wasn't going to repeat last night's mistake. Her choice of drinks was limited to two kinds of spring water, still or carbonated.

She could've used the wine, though. The silence stretching between them was oppressive, especially given his intense, penetrating eyes that seemed to be delving straight down to her soul.

"I like it that you don't talk much," he said when coffee was served. "I find mindless chatter annoying."

Should she thank him? Was it even a compliment?

Ella smiled and forked a piece of cake. "Thank you for the meal. It was very good."

"You're welcome." He took a sip of his black coffee. "As you can see, I surround myself only with the best. My chef studied in the famous Le Cordon Bleu, and he won numerous awards."

He reached for her hand and lifted it to his lips. "And the woman sitting next to me could've won any beauty competition in the world." He placed a soft kiss on the back of her hand. "Not only that, she is also graceful, and smart, and lovely company."

It was on the tip of her tongue to tell him that at five

foot four she would've won no beauty titles, but contradicting Gorchenco, even in the name of modesty, was not a good idea.

Instead, she smiled and said, "Thank you."

It was the right response because he looked satisfied. "As I said, smart. You know how to take a compliment gracefully." He let go of her hand. "Eat the cake. It's very good."

It was decadent, but she was full. Still, denying Gorchenco, even in a small thing like that, was scary. Ella took another tiny bite.

"You know, Ella." He pinned her with a hard stare. "I'm still looking for your mother and brother. Do you have any idea where they might've gone?"

The question came out of nowhere, scaring the shit out of her. "Maybe they went to visit my aunt? Or maybe my grandparents in the retirement home?"

He shook his head. "I checked. Your father's sister hasn't heard from your mother in years, and no one's visited your grandparents in the last three months."

That was true. Both of her grandparents suffered from Alzheimer's. They didn't remember her or Parker, and most times they didn't recognize their only daughter either. Visiting them was depressing, and Ella had been doing everything she could to wiggle out of it. She'd been a bad granddaughter.

Maybe that was why God was punishing her?

"Why the guilty face?"

Damn, the man could read her like an open book. She should stick as close to the truth as possible. "I should've made more effort to visit my grandparents, even though they don't recognize me."

He nodded. "Yes, you should have. One day soon it is

going to be too late, and you'll regret it for the rest of your life."

Was that a threat?

Would Gorchenco stoop so low?

"I know. But I can't do it now, can I?"

He shrugged. "It depends on you. If you're a good girl, I'll take you to visit them. In fact, since you've been good so far, I'll let you call your mother." He pulled a cellphone out of his suit jacket and handed it to her. "You can tell her that you're okay, and that you are being treated like a queen. I'm sure she'll be glad to hear that."

This was a test, and she'd better pull off the best acting of her life to pass it.

Widening her eyes, she looked at the phone with pretend awe. "Really? You'll let me call my mom?" She reached for it with a shaking hand. "What time is it in California? Oh, heck. It doesn't matter. She is going to be so happy to hear from me. She probably thinks I ran away with that idiot Romeo, and that I'm being a brat for not calling her."

Ella took the phone and cast another questioning look at Gorchenco. "Is this for real? You are not messing with me?"

"No, go ahead. Call her."

She dialed the number knowing her mother wouldn't answer, but pretending as if she was bursting with excitement at the prospect that she would.

"It went straight to voicemail." Ella pretended disappointment. "Hi, Mom. I wanted to tell you that I'm okay and that I'm having a great time. I'm not with Romeo. I didn't call you before because I was ashamed of the way I ran away. But I met someone new, and he's taking me around the world in his private jet, and buying me expensive clothes, and he treats me like a queen. You have nothing to worry about. I love you so much and I miss you. Tell Parker that I love and miss him too."

She ended the call. "Did I do well? I didn't know if it was okay to tell her your name."

Gorchenco eyed her for a moment longer before taking his phone back. "You can tell her who I am. It's not like she can do anything about it. Besides, she is not going to elude me for much longer. I've caught professionals who had massive resources in less time. I guess it's her lack of professional training that makes her moves unpredictable. Either that or incredible intuition."

He leaned back in his chair and lifted his porcelain coffee cup. "Eventually she'll run out of cash and use her credit cards. And when she does, my people will get her and your brother."

Despite the fear swirling in her stomach and pushing the food she'd eaten up her throat, Ella decided to take a risk. "You don't need them, Dimitri. I'm not going anywhere." She waved a hand around the room. "Who else is going to give me all of this? I meant what I told my mother. I'm living a dream, and I'd be a fool to give this up for some naive notion of one day falling in love. After Romeo, I've learned my lesson. But in a way I'm glad because it brought me to you. Having a powerful man like you want me by his side is like winning the lottery. I will never lack for anything, and no one could ever keep me safer."

Except for the bullshit about being glad and winning the lottery, everything else was true, which would hopefully cloak her entire speech in truth and would be convincing enough to pass Gorchenco's suspicious radar.

A wide grin spread over Dimitri's austere face. "You

are smarter beyond your years, Ella. I won the lottery with you as well. Except, I'm not a gambling man, and I don't depend on luck to get what I want. I go after it."

He pushed to his feet and offered her a hand up. "Come. Let's go upstairs."

Ella swallowed. Talk was easy. Now he expected her to prove she'd meant it.

36

MAGNUS

As soon as the three of them stepped out of the elevator, Magnus heard the boisterous voices of his fellow Guardians and grimaced. He should've known that they weren't going to be alone in the gym.

With the New York mission canceled, the rotations were back in force and that meant the gym level, including the shooting range, would no longer be available for his guests' exclusive use.

He put his hand on the small of Vivian's back. "We are not going to be alone in there today."

She looked up at him. "You sound upset."

"No, not really. But the guys can sometimes get rowdy. I hope they are going to behave."

"Edward and Liam are really nice," Parker said. "It was fun hanging out with them in the movie theater."

Vivian smiled. "I liked them too. I'd love to meet your other friends."

The two had flirted with her, which Magnus hadn't appreciated at all. With an inward sigh, he pushed the doors open.

Other than Liam and Edward, there were five more Guardians there. All old friends that had come with him from Scotland to join the clan's new mission. Usually, he would've looked forward to sparring with the guys, but not today. By now, the rumor about Vivian and Ella being possible Dormants had probably spread like wildfire, and unless he staked his claim, his friends were going to drool all over Vivian and probably make advances.

Just as he'd expected, the activity came to a sudden halt as soon as Vivian entered, and a moment later a stampede of sweaty males with big grins on their faces started.

Surrounded by a wall of muscle, Vivian took a step back. "Hello," she said.

Luckily for the bastards, Magnus scented no fear coming from her. In fact, she was smiling sheepishly as Liam offered his hand.

"Hello, Vivian. What a pleasure it is to see you again."

She gave him her hand. "Parker told me that he had a lot of fun with you and Edward last night."

"He is a great kid," Liam said.

Edward came forward, took Vivian's hand, and brought it up to his lips for a kiss. "Maybe next time you'll join us for a movie night?"

Magnus couldn't help the growl that started deep in his belly and made its way out of his mouth.

Edward dropped her hand. "With our buddy Magnus, of course," he added quickly.

Good. So they knew what was up.

After that, the other guys behaved themselves. There were no more kisses, and no suggestive looks, just simple handshakes and nods. Still, Magnus didn't feel like teaching Vivian self-defense with a bunch of salivating males watching.

He put his hand on her shoulder. "Let's go to the shooting range first. I'll teach you self-defense later."

"Yes!" Parker pumped his fist.

"Don't leave on account of us. We can make room," Edward said. "We will hit the weights, and you can have the mats all to yourselves."

As if he was going to let Vivian watch the guys pump iron and flex their muscles for her. Someone might get injured while showing off, either by lifting weights that were too heavy, or by getting punched in the face for trying to impress his mate.

Mate. Maybe. Probably.

He should really have the talk with her soon.

"The kid wants to do some shooting. We'll do that first and then come back here." Hopefully, when the guys were long gone.

The shooting range wasn't deserted either, but this time Magnus didn't mind Vivian meeting its sole occupant. Never mind that the only reason she was there was to take a peek at the new Dormants.

"This is Carol," he told Vivian as they watched her empty a magazine into the target, hitting the bullseye every time. "She is an excellent sharpshooter."

"Wow," Parker said. "She's just making the hole bigger and bigger. But I know now why her bow fit me. She's tiny."

Vivian patted his back. "She's not smaller than me."

"You're tiny too, Mom."

"I hate being called that," Vivian muttered under her breath.

Magnus couldn't let that go without a comment. Vivian was perfect the way she was and he wanted her to know that. Wrapping his arm around her shoulder, he whispered in her ear, "You might be small, but every inch of you is delectable."

Vivian blushed and shook her head. But she had nothing to worry about. Parker was busy worshiping Carol, his new hero.

Carol finished her round, took off her ear muffs, and sauntered toward them with a big smile on her cherubic face. "Pardon the messy hair," she said as she fluffed up her curls. "I'm Carol." She offered Vivian her hand, then pulled her into her arms. "I've heard so much about you. I was hoping you guys would show up so I could finally meet you."

Magnus shook his head. Apparently, the clan's rumor machine was working overtime.

"I hope you don't mind Parker using your bow. It was the only one small enough for him."

"Not at all, but if he's serious about archery, he should get his own fitted for him."

"Can I?" Parker looked at his mom with a pair of puppy eyes.

"I don't know how long we will be staying. It would be a waste to buy you a bow to use for a couple of weeks."

Probably wondering whether he'd told Vivian about her possible future, Carol cast a questioning glance at Magnus.

Standing behind Viv and Parker, he shook his head and mouthed, "Not yet."

Carol waved a dismissive hand. "Don't worry about it. We will buy it for him." She patted Parker's shoulder. "It's an investment in future talent. What do you like to shoot more, the bow or the gun?"

Parker grinned. "Both."

Dark Widow's Curse

"Excellent. So do I. If Magnus doesn't mind, I can train you."

"I don't. I can use the time to teach Vivian self-defense moves." Or to find a dark corner for some snogging.

"I can do that as well." Carol puffed up her ample chest. "I teach self-defense beginner classes."

"Awesome," Parker said. "Magnus can keep training me and you can train Mom."

Magnus was flattered, but that wasn't what he'd had in mind. "Carol is a better shooter than me."

"I like training with you," Parker pouted. "No offense, Ms. Carol. You're awesome."

"None taken. I understand all about male bonding." She smiled at Vivian. "After spending all your time with these two, I can imagine that you are starved for some female company."

Vivian nodded. "I am. No offense, Magnus." She glanced at him with an apologetic smile. "But I'm so bored. There is nothing to do, and the books I ordered for Parker's homeschooling didn't arrive yet." She ruffled the kid's hair. "When they do, both of us will spend much more time studying and much less time shooting."

Parker grimaced. "Can't wait."

"I have a splendid idea." Carol clapped her hands. "How about I come round later this evening and bring along several of my girlfriends? We can have a girls' fun night while Magnus takes Parker shooting to his heart's content before the books get here."

Vivian turned to look at Magnus. "Is it okay?"

"Sure. Carol's friends are all part of our organization."

"Then I would love to."

37

ELLA

When they got upstairs, Dimitri didn't get all handsy as Ella had feared. Instead, he stopped by the room's bar, took one of the bottles out of the wine cooler and two glasses from the cabinet above it, and then headed out onto the master bedroom's terrace.

"Put on something warm and join me outside," he instructed before stepping out through the opened doors.

Relieved, Ella rushed into the closet and grabbed one of the long cashmere sweaters Pavel had gotten her as lounge attire. The thing was beautiful and luxurious enough for a party, but the rules were different in Dimitri's world.

Stepping outside, Ella was surprised to find him reclining on a double lounger with a joint in his hand. She'd never seen Gorchenco smoke before. Not cigarettes, not cigars, and certainly not weed. In fact, his only vice seemed to be wine, if it could even qualify as a vice. Evidently, he was too refined for drinking vodka like any other proud Russian.

"Come." He scooted sideways, making room for her.

Briefly closing her eyes, Ella took a deep breath before joining him. *Courage. It's going to be okay.*

He motioned for her to lay her head on his shoulder and handed her the joint. "In moderation, this is harmless. It will help you relax."

As if anything could.

Taking it from him, she barely managed to keep her hand from trembling. "I only smoked once. The girl I shared a room with in the auction house gave me some to try."

"Did they treat you well in there?"

She took a puff, coughed, and shrugged. "Other than the gynecological exam, and then stripping for you in the viewing room, there was nothing overly traumatic. No one got handsy with me, if that's what you wanted to know."

"I didn't ask for the exam. It was Stefano's idea. He thought I would be willing to pay more for a virgin."

"Was he right?"

"Only in the sense that I didn't want you to get touched by anyone else. Your virginity protected you because Stefano believed you'd be more valuable untouched. I would have paid any price for you regardless."

"Thank you." And she even meant it.

"The flesh trade is a nasty business that I don't want to get involved in. But I couldn't resist buying you."

She couldn't help the words that spilled out of her mouth. "And yet you still feel the need to threaten me into cooperating."

He chuckled. "I've never claimed to be a nice guy, Ella, and you'd do well to remember that. I paid a lot of money for you and I have no intention of letting you go. Naturally, I prefer for you to come to me willingly, but if you don't, I have no problem using persuasion."

At least he was honest about it.

There was no escaping this, but maybe she could delay things a little. "I'm scared, Dimitri. Could you maybe wait a little longer? Let me get used to you?"

He turned sideways and cupped her cheek. "I know that you're scared, *lyubimaya moya*." He kissed her lips almost chastely. "It's natural. But you have nothing to fear. I will make it good for you. I promise." He smiled, the wrinkles in the corner of his eyes deepening. "That's the advantage of having your first time with an older and much more experienced man. I know what I'm doing, and I'm very patient. But I've waited long enough."

Surprisingly, even though Dimitri was still going through with his seduction plan, his words had a calming effect.

Or was it his tone of voice?

It was so calm, and at the same time so commanding. It had an almost hypnotic quality to it.

Or was it the joint?

Or the combination of it all?

It was reassuring to know that he wasn't going to attack her. Dimitri was going to take his time and ease her into it.

The problem was that she wasn't attracted to him. Maybe she could close her eyes and pretend she was in Romeo's arms?

Except, as soon as she thought of that scumbag, her momentary calm evaporated. He'd had no feelings for her, manipulated her, and lured her into a trap.

Dimitri was at least honest with her.

And if she cared to be completely honest with herself,

as ashamed as it made her feel, Ella wasn't entirely indifferent to him.

The low-dose fear Dimitri inspired, in that calm and collected manner of his, had a strange effect on her.

It was arousing.

He was the villain in her story, but he wasn't a thug. He was the evil mastermind, and she'd always found those sexy. Like Lex Luthor in *Smallville*. Heck, she'd had a crush on the actor, and the guy was close to Dimitri's age.

It was so confusing.

Was she the kind of girl who was attracted to bad boys?

"I think that's enough." He took the joint from her hand and put it in the ashtray on the side table. "I want you relaxed, but aware." He kissed her lips again. "Close your eyes, Ella, and just let yourself feel."

Yeah, she could do that. She could lie there with her eyes closed, and let him do whatever he wanted with her.

When his lips trailed down her neck, she sucked in a breath, and when his hand cupped her breast over the sweater, her traitorous nipple hardened.

It felt so wrong to enjoy this on any level. Except, she couldn't pretend that she liked his touch without actually enjoying it. She wasn't that good of an actress.

Besides, this was going to happen one way or another, so why make it worse for herself?

Because it'll make me feel dirty, that's why.

What did it say about her that her captor's hand on her breast turned her on?

Where was her pride?

Had she left it on the floor in that viewing room when she'd been forced to strip naked for Dimitri and his proxy?

"Stop thinking and just feel," he whispered in her ear.

When she didn't respond, he lightly nipped her earlobe. "The correct answer is, yes, Dimitri."

"Yes, Dimitri."

"Good girl." He kissed the small hurt away.

38

VIVIAN

Magnus's phone buzzed with an incoming message. "Your guests are here."

"Are they at the door?" Vivian asked.

The thing was so thick that it was soundproof, and knocking was no use. If anyone wanted to get inside, they needed to call.

"They are just parking the car. I'll open it." He switched to the application that controlled the door electronically.

"Did Carol tell you who is coming with her?"

"Nope. But knowing my busybody relatives, there will be quite a few of them. They are all curious about you."

She narrowed her eyes at him. "Why? Did you tell anyone about us?"

He chuckled. "The guys at the gym must've guessed it. I was acting like a jealous boyfriend."

Vivian glanced at the closed bedroom door. "Keep it down, will you? Parker might hear."

"I'm pretty sure he knows by now."

"I'm not sure at all. He didn't say a thing."

It wasn't that Vivian was ashamed of her relationship with Magnus, but since it was going to end soon, she didn't want Parker to get attached to the Guardian. Except, it was probably already too late. Her son was ready to take Magnus home with them and never let him go.

And so was she, but it was not to be.

"Come on, Parker!" Magnus knocked on the door. "We need to get out of here before the ladies show up. I'm sure you want to avoid your cheeks getting pinched." He winked at Vivian.

The door banged open. "I'm ready. Let's go." Parker practically ran out into the corridor.

"Have fun." Magnus planted a quick kiss on her cheek. "Call me when the coast is clear."

"Are you scared of a bunch of women?"

"Terrified." He winked again before following Parker out.

As she heard female voices approaching, Vivian smoothed a hand over her hair and stood by the open door to greet them.

"Hi, Viv." Carol entered first, followed by four beautiful women, each carrying a paper bag or two. "Let me introduce you to my friends." She pulled Vivian into a quick hug.

"No need." The stunning tall brunette, who looked oddly familiar, tapped Carol's shoulder. "We can introduce ourselves. I'm Amanda." She gave Vivian a one-armed embrace.

"Are you one of Magnus's cousins?"

"Yes, I am."

The blond was next. "And I'm Syssi."

"Are you a cousin too?"

"No, I'm married to one."

"My name is Wonder," the other tall brunette said without offering a hug. "And I'm not a cousin either. I'm Magnus's partner's girlfriend."

"He told me about him. Anandur sounds like a fun guy."

"He is."

"Wonder is an unusual name. Is it a nickname? Like Wonder Woman?" The girl looked like the actress that played that role in the last remake of the movie, just a lot younger.

"It's not a nickname. That's the name I've chosen for myself." Wonder didn't elaborate how or why.

"And I'm Callie." The fourth one gave Vivian a quick hug. "I'm Anandur's brother's fiancée."

"That's so nice that all of you are close," Vivian said. "Come on in." She pointed to the couch and the dining chairs she'd arranged on the other side of the coffee table.

"I forgot about that one." Amanda pointed at the picture hanging over the couch. "I thought we took everything with us when we left here."

A light bulb went on in Vivian's head. "You're the muse Bridget talked about! That's your portrait!"

Amanda smiled. "That's me."

"Bridget said something about a great love story and a big family drama. I can't wait to hear about it."

"Maybe later." Amanda lifted her paper bag and put it on the coffee table. "First, I want to show you your ticket to freedom." She pulled a dark wig out of the bag and handed it to Vivian. "I know how claustrophobic this small apartment can get." She reached into the bag again and pulled out two pairs of sunglasses. "One for you, and one for your son. I was assured by an expert that the wig and the glasses will fool facial recognition software. Your son can put on a baseball hat."

Callie took two covered trays out of her bag and put them on the table, then removed the covers to reveal a neatly organized selection of appetizers. "Bridget told me that you need help setting your son up with a homeschooling program. I can do that for you. I did it for Wonder, so I have some experience in it. But since she is all grown up, she is doing it mostly on her own."

Wonder grimaced. "And I hate every moment of it. It's so boring. I don't mind history and English, but I hate doing math problems. I wish I had someone to share the misery with."

"Maybe you can study together with Parker?" Syssi offered.

Vivian lifted a brow. The girl looked eighteen or nineteen and was probably taking advanced classes.

"Parker is good in math, but he is only twelve. He is still in middle school."

Wonder sighed. "So am I."

"How come?"

"Wonder suffered a complete memory loss," Syssi explained. "She has to relearn everything."

"I'm so sorry. That must be really difficult."

"It's okay." Wonder picked up one of the appetizers Callie had brought. "I regained a lot of it already, and I'm going through the material fast. I wouldn't mind company, though. Maybe Parker can help me out with math. It's not that I find it difficult, just tedious. Problem after problem, and the program won't let me continue until I solve them all. I can't skip anything."

Vivian stifled a chuckle. Wonder was a very pretty girl. Parker would be too busy staring and ogling to study anything. He might want to impress her with his math skills, though, so maybe it could work.

"We can give it a try. I just hope Parker doesn't get too distracted by your beautiful eyes." They were a unique shade of jade, but Vivian was more worried about her son staring at Wonder's impressive cleavage than her eyes.

"I didn't think of that." Syssi frowned. "Teenage boys are easily distracted."

Amanda snorted. "Only teenage boys? In my experience, there is no age limit on ogling."

Vivian didn't doubt that. She'd been dealing with leering looks most of her life, and she wasn't nearly as beautiful or impressive as Amanda.

Lifting the wig up, she combed it with her fingers. "Should I try it on? I wonder how I will look with dark hair."

"Magnus likes brunettes." Carol winked. "You should wait for him with it on."

Vivian felt a blush creep up her face. What was she supposed to say to that? Denying that anything was going on between her and Magnus would be a lie, but she didn't want to encourage more talk on the subject.

Ignoring Carol's remark, she turned to Amanda. "Are you sure it's okay for me to venture out of here with the wig and glasses on? Isn't it too risky?"

"With the disguise and Magnus by your side, you should be safe from mafia goons." Amanda waggled her brows. "Just not from Magnus."

Damn it. Viv needed to put a stop to that line of talk, or she'd be dodging questions and remarks all evening long.

"I like Magnus a lot. But there can be nothing between

us. Once this is over, I'm going back to San Diego to my old job and my old life, and he stays here."

"San Diego is not so far away," Syssi said.

With a sigh, Vivian put the wig back in the paper bag and sat down on a chair. "It's not only about the distance. I'm cursed. Any guy I let close to me ends up dead. I like Magnus too much to risk his life. I'd rather be alone than bury another boyfriend."

"How many were there?" Amanda asked.

"Three. My husband was first. He got killed in Afghanistan. Several years later, I dated a contractor who fell off a ladder and broke his neck. And before any of you dismiss it, it happened while he was talking with me on the phone. A couple of years after that, I met an accountant and thought that there was no safer profession. He got killed in a car accident after leaving my house. I'm a black widow."

Syssi waved a dismissive hand. "That's nonsense."

"I'm not sure," Amanda said. "As long as Vivian believes in it, it's not nonsense to her. She might be inviting negative energies. I think we should exorcize the curse."

"We could burn incense," Wonder suggested. "Some believe that it chases the evil spirits away."

Amanda waved a dismissive hand. "That's nothing. I'm talking about the real thing—a full-on witchy ritual in the woods, including dancing naked and chanting." She clapped her hands. "It's going to be so much fun. This Friday is a full moon night, which is the best time for rituals."

Syssi rolled her eyes. "You and your dancing naked in the woods. You are just looking for an excuse."

Amanda shrugged. "It's for a good cause, and it's going to be fun. What's wrong with that?"

Syssi threw her hands in the air. "The naked part! You might be an exhibitionist, but I'm not."

"No one is going to see us. I'll get a bunch of Guardians to stand guard and make sure that we are not disturbed, and if you're worried that they are going to peek, don't. No one would dare lay eyes on Kian's mate."

Syssi was the boss's wife? Vivian would've never guessed. She didn't dress or act like a millionaire's spouse. Amanda, on the other hand, did and then some.

"I like it," Carol said. "It has been ages since I've done anything exciting."

"Good. Then it's settled."

Syssi crossed her arms over her chest. "I'm not coming. I find it utterly ridiculous that an educated woman like you, a professor no less, would suggest such a thing. All along I was sure that you were just teasing."

"You're a professor?" Vivian asked. "In what field?"

"Neuroscience. I research paranormal phenomena, like the special connection you share with your daughter. I would love for you to come to my lab so I can run some tests on you."

Vivian grimaced. "The reason I never told anyone about our ability is that I don't want us to be experimented on. I prefer to keep this a secret."

Amanda patted her shoulder. "You have nothing to worry about. This is what I do, and I'm excellent at keeping secrets. Everything is kept confidential. The tests I run are only cognitive. I'm going to show you some cards and have you guess what's on them, and then I'm going to flash random images at you, and have you predict what you're going to see."

"I get visions of the future," Syssi said. "And I work with Amanda at her lab. The information is kept in strict confidentiality. Other than her obsessive fascination with the crazy idea of dancing naked in the woods, I can vouch for her being quite sensible and very responsible."

"It's not crazy, it's fun and adventurous. My sister-in-law is just an introvert who doesn't know how to have fun. We are doing this. We need more witches, though. I think the magic number is thirteen, but I have to do some research on it."

Vivian smoothed her hand over her hair. "To tell you the truth, I don't put much faith in rituals and exorcism, but I'd love to get out of here even if it's to dance in the woods. I hope you'll change your mind about the naked part, though. Is it really necessary?"

"I'm pretty sure it is, but I'll check on this too." Amanda turned to the other two women who hadn't taken part in the discussion. "How about you, Wonder? Are you game?"

"Sure. But I'd rather not do it naked either."

"Same here," Callie said.

Amanda shook her head. "You're such a sorry bunch of prudes. Where is your sense of adventure?"

39

SYSSI

Syssi glared at her sister-in-law. "You are bamboozling us into this."

"You don't have to participate if you don't want to. You can observe from the sidelines while the rest of us are having fun."

That was a relief.

As long as Amanda didn't try to pressure Syssi into taking her clothes off and joining the craziness, watching her make a fool of herself might actually be amusing.

"If you promise not to push me into it, I'll come to watch."

"I promise. Happy?"

"Not yet." She turned to Vivian. "Are you really okay with that? You don't have to do anything that you don't want to."

Vivian smiled. "Oh, I'm in. Not that I believe it will help. I just want to see if Amanda can talk thirteen women into dancing naked outdoors. Besides, I haven't done anything this silly since forever. I got pregnant before I was eighteen and got married right away."

Syssi uncrossed her arms. "As long as you're aware that this is just for fun that's fine."

"Of course. I don't believe in curse exorcizing or any other kind."

Amanda waved a hand. "And yet you believe that you're cursed. I don't see how you can believe in one and not the other."

There was a long moment of silence as Amanda waited for her words to sink in. Syssi didn't believe in it either, but then again, as someone who was well familiar with the paranormal, she shouldn't dismiss the idea of curses and their removal just because she hadn't experienced either.

Perhaps she should read about the subject before passing unfair judgment. "I'll look into this, and if I find any legitimate information, I'll forward it to all of you."

"I'd appreciate it," Vivian said. "I wouldn't know what's legit and what's not. When I tried to research information about the kind of telepathy Ella and I share, I found things from the questionable to the absurd, and none of it was helpful."

"I can provide you with plenty of information," Amanda said. "From what I understand, you and Ella actually talk through your link?"

Vivian nodded. "It's like talking on a phone. The problem is that unless Ella is in a receiving mode, I can't get through. She, on the other hand, can reach me anytime she wants. I can't block her even if I want to, which I don't."

Amanda tapped a finger on her lips. "I wonder if it's because you're the mother and therefore more open and receptive to your daughter, while Ella is a young girl who doesn't want you in her head when it's inconvenient for her."

"Ella started communicating with me when she was still in my belly. Before her, I had no such ability. That's why she's so proficient in it. To her, it's as natural as talking face to face."

"That's fascinating," Amanda said. "I've never heard of a talent developing that early. Can she communicate with anyone else?"

Vivian shook her head. "Only me."

"Hmm. I wonder what will happen if I get her together with another telepath. Although none of the ones I know can communicate as clearly. They describe it more as pictures, intentions, and feelings, and not an actual verbal exchange."

Her eyes misting with tears, Vivian nodded. "Ella would love to meet others like her. But first we need to get her back."

"Very true." Amanda glanced at Syssi. "Any predictions on that?"

Poor Vivian. Syssi wished she had some words of encouragement to give her. "Unfortunately, I didn't get any visions about Ella, but my gut tells me she is going to be okay, and that we will get her out."

"I'll pray for that," Callie said. "In the meantime, though, we need to make plans for Parker's schooling before he falls behind. I don't mind coming over before work and helping out. I work evenings."

Vivian lifted her hand. "I appreciate the offer, but I can handle this as long as I have a program to follow. The school books we ordered should arrive tomorrow, so I can start with that, but I'm rusty and need some instruction myself. Especially in math."

"I'll come tomorrow morning and set up the program," Callie said. "And I'll show you and Parker how to use it. It's not complicated, but it's easier when someone walks you through it."

"Thank you. That would be great." Vivian turned to Wonder. "Would you like to come too?"

"I can't. I work in the mornings. But I can come in the evenings and do homework with Parker."

The rest of the evening went by with Amanda telling Vivian a modified version of her and Dalhu's romance. In her version, Kian didn't want her hooking up with Dalhu because he belonged to a rival clan and there was a long history of a vendetta between the two clans. It was close enough to the truth for the rest of the details to make sense.

When she was done, Vivian shook her head. "I can't believe that he kidnapped you and you fell for him. That sounds a lot like Stockholm Syndrome to me."

Amanda smirked. "When you see my Dalhu, you'll understand. Six foot seven inches of pure masculinity, and the man lives to please me. Even though he kidnapped me, Dalhu was the perfect gentleman. I slept in the loft while he slept on the couch. He even cooked and cleaned the cabin for me. I fought the attraction, but it was just undeniable. At some point I had to admit that he was the one for me, and that I wouldn't be happy with anyone else. Kian refused to even look at me, but I didn't give up."

"Did your brother eventually accept Dalhu, or is he still giving him the cold shoulder?"

"He accepted him, but only after Dalhu proved himself."

Vivian arched a brow. "How?"

"That's a story for another time." Amanda glanced at

her watch. "As fun as this is, we should go. It's almost midnight."

"Oh, wow. No wonder my eyelids are drooping." Vivian yawned. "Time flies when you're having fun."

Syssi pushed to her feet. "Is Parker with Magnus at his suite?"

"No. They probably went to see a movie or two in the theater. Magnus is waiting for me to call him when the coast is clear."

"Then we really should get going," Wonder said. "I'm surprised Anandur hasn't texted me yet."

Callie waved a hand. "He's hanging out with Brundar and Kian. I bet you the grill was working overtime."

After a round of hugs, kisses, and settling for nine o'clock on Friday for the ritual, the five of them headed out.

"Do you really believe a ritual can help?" Syssi asked as they entered the elevator.

Amanda leaned against the wall and crossed her arms over her chest. "Vivian believes in the curse strongly. A good ritual combined with a gentle thrall could help her get rid of the debilitating belief."

"That's dishonest."

"I wouldn't say that. Rituals, when done right, have a hypnotic element. That's not much different from a thrall. Besides, this is for a good cause. We can achieve in one night what therapy wouldn't in years."

40

ELLA

A soft kiss woke Ella up. "Good morning, *lyubimaya*."

"What time is it?"

"It's early. I'm heading out for a meeting, but I didn't want to leave without checking on you. How are you feeling? Are you sore?" There was real concern in his cold, pale, blue eyes.

"A little bit."

"A bath will help with that."

"I'll take one after breakfast."

"Good plan. You can sleep a little longer, but I want you to be ready by noon. You're joining me for a business lunch in the city. Wear one of the Chanel suits."

"Okay," she murmured.

"Take pain medication if the bath doesn't help. I keep a bottle in one of the vanity drawers."

"Okay." She just wanted him to leave so she could process what had happened last night and have a good cry about it.

"After the lunch meeting we are leaving for Russia, but don't worry about packing. Your things will be brought to the plane."

"How long are we going to stay there?"

"Only a few days." He leaned and kissed her forehead. "I have a surprise for you when we get there."

"What is it?"

"If I tell you, it won't be a surprise."

"I don't like surprises." She'd had enough to last her a lifetime, and none had been good.

As usual, Dimitri read her like an open book and decided she wasn't up to any more surprises. Even good ones. "Have you ever gone horseback riding?"

"No."

"You're going to learn. I have many horses on my estate. We will choose a gentle mare, and you'll be the only one to ride her. You'll have your own horse."

"Sounds awesome." She forced a smile.

With a satisfied expression, Dimitri patted her shoulder and got up.

As the door closed behind him, Ella heaved a sigh and pulled the blanket over her head. She could cry under it and no one would hear or see a thing even if there were hidden cameras in the room.

But the tears refused to come.

Was she still in shock?

Yeah, that was probably it. She was still shocked at how easily she'd given in to Dimitri, letting him seduce her without a fight.

She'd lost her virginity to a man much older than her father, a man she didn't even like, and yet it hadn't been as horrible as she'd expected. Dimitri had kept his promise, making the experience as pleasurable as he possibly could. Naturally, losing her virginity had hurt, but it hadn't been as bad as she'd thought it would be.

Not wishing to be an active participant, she'd kept her eyes closed throughout the entire thing, and then had fallen asleep immediately after Dimitri had cleaned her up, which meant that she hadn't even seen him naked.

Was there blood on the sheet?

There must be, but she didn't feel like checking. If there was, she was going to take it to the bathroom and burn it. If Dimitri thought to keep the sheet as a memento of taking her virginity, he was going to be disappointed. He might get angry at her, but she needed some way to retaliate for what he had taken from her.

He had done his best to minimize her pain, so the physical one had been tolerable, but the emotional one was devastating.

If she let it be.

On the one hand, the feeling of devastation mitigated the feelings of guilt and shame for enjoying any of it. But on the other hand, it weakened her. A strong woman could deal with the situation without adding unnecessary drama to it.

She should think of it the way Rose had suggested. A mere century ago, most girls entered the marital bed without any feelings of love for their new husbands, or even attraction. Hell, it was still the case for millions of girls around the world, where women had no right to choose and were married off to whoever their fathers chose or whoever paid the highest price for them.

The only thing missing from this scenario was a marriage certificate.

Ella wondered if Dimitri intended on marrying her.

Not that she wanted him to, but he'd said he was never letting her go, so maybe that was his plan. If she got pregnant, he would surely marry her.

Oh God! He hadn't used any protection, and she wasn't on the pill! She could get pregnant!

No, no, no, she couldn't.

Doing a quick calculation in her head, Ella figured that she wasn't anywhere near her ovulation time in the cycle. Still, that wasn't a sure thing, as her mother had emphasized while explaining various prevention methods. Besides, weeks might pass before she was rescued, and by then Dimitri was going to get her pregnant for sure.

If that happened, she could have an abortion.

Except, the idea terrified her just as much as the unwanted pregnancy. It wasn't that she looked down on women who had them, sometimes there was no other way, but Ella knew that choosing that route would make her feel guilty until the day she died. Dimitri might be a monster under his sophisticated exterior, but his child wouldn't be.

Not if she raised it right.

Way to get carried away.

She could ask him to use protection, or to provide her with contraceptives. Eighteen was too young to become a mother, and she would point out that he might want to enjoy her girly figure for a little while longer.

Yeah, that was good. Maybe she could even throw in wanting an education before having a child. As someone who attended medical school, Dimitri obviously valued education. He also wanted to make her happy. Otherwise he wouldn't gift her a horse, which she had to admit was something she'd dreamt about when she was younger.

What girl doesn't dream of having a pony? Naturally, her mom couldn't afford even horseback-riding lessons, let alone a pony.

It was nice to be rich. She wouldn't have to pretend too hard to like it.

Slowly but surely a plan started forming in Ella's mind.

She was going to treat this as a marriage and pretend to make plans for the future with Dimitri. She would even start talking about wanting a wedding and walking down the aisle without a pregnant belly.

Maybe her change of attitude would change his as well. When he realized that she was serious about a future with him, he might relax and give her more freedom, and maybe, just maybe, an opportunity to run would present itself at some point.

Besides, she had to take into account the possibility that she was stuck with him, and that rescuing her wasn't possible without her rescuers sustaining major casualties. She definitely didn't want that on her conscience.

No one should die to save her.

One way or another, she'd save herself.

Feeling better, Ella threw the comforter off, got out of bed, and padded naked to the bathroom. It was doubtful Dimitri let anyone watch the footage from his bedroom, and he'd already seen every little bit of her.

In the bathroom, she filled up the big tub with warm water and poured in some bath salts that promised to soothe and smooth. They did, reducing the soreness to a distant echo of one.

Lying in the warm water, Ella debated what she was going to say to her mother. Telling her about last night wasn't necessary. It would only upset her. But she needed to tell her about Russia.

Mom, are you awake?

Now I am. I wanted to stay awake until you opened the channel, but I had a bunch of great ladies from the organization visit me and they stayed until late. I couldn't keep my eyes open. I didn't even hear Magnus return with Parker.

Sounds like you had a good time.

I did. Vivian chuckled. *One of them is organizing a witchy ritual to exorcize our curse. Friday night, we are meeting somewhere in the woods.*

That sounded like so much fun. *I wish I could be there.*

Me too, sweetie. By the way, did Gorchenco tell you the name of the girl you look like?

Her name was Stella. Why do you ask?

Perhaps if we find more information about her, you can use it to manipulate him.

Don't waist your time on it. Dimitri is too sharp and too guarded for me to influence in any way. He's the alpha other alphas submit to.

It must be so difficult for someone as strong-headed as you to be with someone like him. How are you holding up?

I'm okay. We are leaving for Russia late this afternoon or early evening. I'm joining Dimitri for a lunch meeting in town, and after that we are going straight to the airport.

Did he tell you how long you'll be staying there?

Only a few days.

Try to get him to tell you where he is heading next.

I will, and he might even tell me. He seems to be softening towards me. But, Mom, I don't want anyone getting killed over this. If rescuing me is too dangerous, tell the people helping you to reconsider. My situation doesn't justify anyone losing his life for me.

Oh, Ella. You're so brave.

Not really, Mom. I'm just thinking ahead. If anyone gets killed over this, my freedom will always taste sour to me. It's not worth it. I'd rather make a life with Dimitri as best I can, knowing that no one lost his life on my account.

Oh, boy. Her mother sighed. *You don't sound like you hate Gorchenco, which is bad. They are talking about having to kill him. If they don't, all of us would have to remain in hiding for the rest of our lives. As a mafia boss, he can't allow such a slight to his honor.*

I do hate him, but not enough to want him dead.

What happened, was he mean to you?

No, he was very gentle.

The tears that had refused to come before came pouring down out of nowhere.

Did he force you?

No. Well, not physically.

I want him dead. Her mother's tone, mental or otherwise, had never sounded so vicious.

No, Mom, it wasn't horrible. He really was gentle, and he did his best to make it pleasurable for me. But, you know, I hoped that my first time would be with someone I loved. But, really, Dimitri is not so bad. He said he was going to give me my own horse when we get to Russia and teach me how to ride. I think he sincerely wants to make me happy.

Regretting the momentary emotional meltdown, Ella wiped away her tears with the backs of her hands. *Life with him is not going to be so bad. He treats me like a princess, really. Maybe in time I can even learn to like him.*

Don't talk like that. We are going to get you out and he is going to end up dead for what he did to you.

The tears came back, accompanied by sobs. *I don't want him dead. What if he got me pregnant? I don't want the father of my child to die because of me. How can I live with that? What am I going to tell that child when she or he is old enough to ask who her father is and what happened to him?*

That's nonsense, Ella. Worst case scenario, you'll get an abortion. You'll have the life you always wanted. I promise.

41

VIVIAN

After talking with Ella, sleep had been out of the question, and Vivian had spent the night imagining Gorchenco's gruesome demise. Her favorite was clubbing him over the head and seeing his brains splatter out.

She'd never before hated anyone with such all-consuming passion.

At five in the morning she gave up and got out of bed. The bathroom needed cleaning, and the area rug in the living room needed vacuuming. But since there was no vacuum cleaner, Vivian was going to do it the old-fashioned way—get it out into the corridor, find somewhere to hang it, and beat the crap out of it while imagining it was Gorchenco.

She didn't have a rug beater, but she was going to fashion one out of a clothes hanger. Magnus wasn't the only one who knew how to make tools out of ordinary things. The hangers in the closet were sturdy wooden ones. They would do.

Parker was passed out on the couch, snoring through

all the noise the coffee maker made. He didn't budge when she moved the coffee table aside and rolled up the rug, but the sound of the heavy door's mechanism woke him up even though it wasn't loud at all.

"What are you doing?" he murmured sleepily.

"I'm going to take the rug outside and beat it. It's full of crumbs and there is no vacuum cleaner in here."

"Have fun." He turned around and tucked the blanket under his chin.

Dragging the rug behind her, Vivian went in the opposite direction of Magnus's room. It was early, but he didn't sleep much, so he might be awake despite the late hour he'd turned in last night.

Had he been disappointed that she'd gone to bed without him?

Probably.

But it was better that way. If she'd been with Magnus when Ella had told her about Gorchenco, Vivian would've lost her appetite for sex, and then he would've been even more disappointed. Magnus would've understood and offered his support because he was a nice guy, but still.

Damn, there was nowhere to hang the rug from, and she didn't have access to the elevators. Maybe there was something at the other end, but that meant she'd have to pass by Magnus's room.

Well, if the door was closed, he wouldn't hear her.

No such luck.

Not only was his door open, but the man himself was up and awake and so was Scarlet. Given the leash attached to her collar, he was about to take the dog out for a walk.

He stepped out of the room. "What are you doing so early in the morning?"

"I'm looking for a place to hang the damn rug from so

I can beat the crap out of it. It's full of crumbs and there is no vacuum cleaner in the apartment."

Magnus's smile turned into a frown. "What happened?" He put his hand on her shoulder. "I've never heard you use two cuss words in one sentence before."

Even though she didn't want to betray Ella's confidence, there was no use in pretending like nothing had happened.

"He did it."

Magnus, bless his heart, didn't need explanations to get her meaning. Pulling her into his arms, he rocked her in place. "Is Ella all right?"

Tearing up, Vivian nodded. "She is so brave. But I want to kill the son of a bitch with my own two hands. Do you think your boss will agree for me to join the guys on the rescue mission? I'll be forever grateful if he does."

Magnus rubbed a hand over her back. "He won't. But even if he did, you are not a fighter. Besides, Parker and Ella need you. You can't go risking your life like that."

Vivian leaned away so she could look into Magnus's eyes. "Do you know what she said? She doesn't want anyone getting killed while rescuing her. She'd rather stay with that monster than have a death on her conscience."

"You can reassure her that none of ours are going to die. Gorchenco, on the other hand, is not going to be that lucky."

"How can you say that?"

"Trust me. We know what we're doing, and the guys will have special protective suits. Think Kevlar vest, but all over and stronger."

That was reassuring. "I've never heard of protective gear like that. Aren't they too cumbersome to maneuver in?"

"A little. But the protection they provide is worth the small loss in mobility. They were made especially for us, and we haven't lost a Guardian yet."

"That's good to hear. But Ella doesn't want Gorchenco dead either."

He frowned. "She's probably suffering from Stockholm Syndrome."

"I don't think so. She says he treats her like a princess and that life with him is far from terrible. By the way, he is taking her to his Russian estate later today, and he said that they were going to stay there for a few days. He is getting her a horse."

Magnus pulled out his phone. "I need to let Turner know."

Vivian waited until he was done. "Ella is also afraid he'll get her pregnant, and she doesn't want the father of her child dead."

Magnus grimaced. "That's another complication I didn't take into consideration."

"Neither did I, but it can happen. Still, I want him dead. If he gets her pregnant, she'll have to abort it. Unpleasant, but under the circumstances there is no other way."

Looking undecided, Magnus kept rubbing her back. "She might not get pregnant, and if she does, it will be up to her to decide what she wants to do."

Vivian pushed on his chest. "Ella is just a child, and she's traumatized. Do you think she can make logical decisions?"

"We have a fantastic therapist who specializes in such cases, and who can help Ella make the right decision for her. But let's not worry about that just yet. Okay?"

"Ugh, I'm so angry. I need to punch something. Is

there anywhere in this damn place where I can hang this rug?"

He shook his head. "How about I take you to the gym so you can take your anger out on a punching bag?"

"I can do that. But what about the rug? It needs vacuuming."

"I'll get you a vacuum. Heck, I'll vacuum the sucker myself."

"Parker is still asleep. I don't want to leave him alone."

"Then wake him up. In the meantime, I'm going to take Scarlet out on her walk and grab a vacuum from one of the apartments upstairs."

"Callie is coming at ten to set up the homeschooling program for Parker."

Magnus leaned and kissed her forehead. "We will be done long before that. I don't think you need five hours with the punching bag. It's quite tiring."

42

MAGNUS

"Thank you." Vivian handed him the gun and took off her protective glasses. "The punching session in the gym, although short, was therapeutic. But this was even better. Every shot I made was aimed at Gorchenco's black heart."

He chuckled. "That explains your great aim today. Every shot found the target." Which hadn't been the case the other time he'd taken her to the range. She'd missed almost every time.

Vivian tapped her temple. "It's all a matter of motivation."

"That's true." He glanced at his watch. "We'd better head back so you can grab a shower before Callie gets here."

Parker didn't look too happy, but he was resigned to the idea that his enforced vacation was over.

"It was a good workout. I should make it part of my routine." Vivian waited for him to stow the weapons away.

As enthusiastic as she'd been with the punching bag,

she'd run out of steam five minutes into it. Still, she'd managed to work up quite a sweat.

"How are your hands?"

He'd found her a small pair of gloves, but she wasn't accustomed to punching.

"I'll live."

He wrapped his arm around her shoulders. "That's the spirit. No pain, no gain, right?"

Behind them, Parker groaned, but that was probably because the kid was about to start homeschooling and not because Magnus had an arm around his mother's shoulders.

It seemed Parker was okay with them having a relationship. He hadn't said anything yet, but he must've noticed that they were more than friends.

"What are you going to do while Callie is here?" Vivian asked.

"I'm getting together with my partner and his brother."

"Callie's fiancé, right?"

"Yes. His name is Brundar."

"Anandur and Brundar. I love those names. They are so original."

"Unlike Parker," the kid grumbled. "Couldn't you think of something more unusual for me?"

"Like what?"

"Like Benedict."

Vivian rolled her eyes. "I can just imagine the hell the other kids would have given you with a name like that. Besides, your idol, Batman, is named Bruce. Nothing unusual about that."

"Bruce would've been cool too."

The bickering continued all the way to the apartment.

"I'll see you later, Vivian." Magnus winked at her before turning to Parker. "Good luck with the homeschooling, Bruce."

That earned him a big grin.

"Did you give Callie your cellphone number?" he asked.

"I did."

"Good. I'll check up on you later and bring lunch."

"Thank you."

In his room, Magnus showered and changed into his street clothes. As soon as he picked up Scarlet's leash, she jumped off the couch and started wagging her tail.

"Are you ready for another walk?"

The wagging intensified.

He wondered whether she'd responded to the verbal communication or to the mental image he'd sent her way. Next time, he would only send the image and check her response to that. He was neglecting her training, but the truth was that his heart wasn't in it.

It was full of a petite blond lady who'd gotten so deep under his skin that he wondered how he was going to live without her. He'd miss her, and he'd miss Parker too.

Magnus kept mulling it over as he walked Scarlet and waited for her to do her business.

Ever since he'd met Vivian, she'd been constantly on his mind. Supposedly, that was what falling in love felt like. But then again, they were spending all of their time together, so it wasn't surprising that he could think of nothing else.

Did he need to get some distance to examine his feelings for her?

If they were separated, and he couldn't stand being

without her, then he would know that what he was feeling was love for sure.

Damn, just the thought of being alone again felt like a vice had been suddenly clamped around his heart, the phantom pain feeling so real that Magnus rubbed a hand over his chest.

He was in love with the woman. It was about time he stopped questioning it.

When Scarlet was done, Magnus headed back to the building's café. Sitting down with a cup of coffee from the vending machine, he waited for the brothers to arrive.

"I see that you've started without us," Anandur said as he and Brundar cleared the wall of greenery shielding the café from the rest of the lobby.

"I'll have another one with you." Magnus and Anandur clasped hands and slapped backs.

Brundar gave a curt nod and sat down.

"Where are Kian and Turner, here in the building somewhere?"

The meeting was the reason the brothers were in town.

"One of the offices in the security wing. We are free until lunch. Then we are shadowing him to a restaurant of Turner's choosing."

"Is it somewhere close? I want to bring lunch for Vivian, Parker, and Callie."

"I don't know. Kian wouldn't want to eat at the steakhouse, for obvious reasons, and there are no good vegan places around." Anandur walked over to the coffee machine and swiped his card for a cup. "How are your charges doing? Cabin fever yet?"

"They're holding up pretty well. I keep them busy in the gym, the shooting range, and the pool. Amanda brought them disguises so they could go out, but I doubt Kian will approve. I love the guy, but he is paranoid. He doesn't want Vivian and the kid to know where they are staying. He says they might be used as spies without their knowledge."

Anandur returned with two cups and put one in front of his silent brother. "Can they be thralled?"

"I didn't try thralling the kid."

Smirking, Anandur lifted the paper cup and took a sip. "You sly dog. I heard the rumors. Edward and Liam were boasting about keeping the kid occupied in the theater, while you got busy with the mother."

"I'm going to pound those two into dust. What are they, twelve?"

Anandur waved a dismissive hand. "Everyone gossips. That's just the way it is in a small community. There are no secrets in the village."

"And it doesn't bother you?"

"I have nothing to hide."

"How about you, Brundar?"

The blond shrugged. "It is what it is."

"Words of wisdom." Anandur lifted his coffee cup in a salute. "But back to Kian. If the kid can be thralled, then Kian should have no problem with you getting them out to breathe some fresh air, and then thralling them to forget the location."

"You might be right, but I need to ask permission first."

"Text him."

"What, right now?"

"Why not? Kian will probably run it by Turner, who is even more paranoid than him, but even he won't be able to find a good reason to keep them locked up. No one expected this to last so long. It's cruel to keep them imprisoned like that. Especially the kid."

"You're right. I'm going to text him right now."

Magnus wrote the message, erased it, and then rewrote it two more times before sending it to Kian. He wasn't the most articulate guy, and this was important.

The answer came much sooner than he'd expected. "He sent a thumbs up."

With a face-splitting grin, Anandur crossed his arms over his chest and leaned back in his chair. "Do I know the boss, or what? I told you he'd agree."

43

ELLA

"Hello, my old friend." The guy they were meeting for lunch clasped Dimitri's hand. "It has been too long."

The guy glanced at Ella without acknowledging her presence.

It was fine. Her job was to look pretty and smile politely. She was there as Dimitri's arm candy. Nothing more. Besides, she preferred for the guy not to pay her any attention. Instinctively, she knew it was safer for her if he ignored her.

Her reaction to him was a strange mix of wariness and attraction. Not the physical type, even though the guy was movie-star handsome, but something else. For some reason, he felt familiar, although she'd never laid eyes on him before. She would've remembered those dark, penetrating eyes, and that lithe body that moved like that of a dancer.

If she'd thought Dimitri was scary, with his pale-blue cold eyes that rarely revealed any feelings and seemed to delve deep into her soul, then his lunch guest was in a league of his own. His dark brown eyes were almost black, making the pupil nearly indistinguishable from the iris. It was an absurd notion, but she thought he looked demonic, especially since those dark eyes weren't cold. They were burning hot with superior intelligence and unbridled ambition.

"Indeed." Dimitri clapped the man's back. "I was starting to think that you'd found another supplier."

The man threw his hands in the air. "There is no one out there who can deliver the things you do." He sat down and sighed. "But finances have been tight lately. I need you to sharpen your pencil and give me better prices, or I will have no choice but to settle for one of your less competent competitors."

Dimitri pulled out a chair for her, but didn't introduce her, which Ella was thankful for. And as he sat between her and his guest, forming a protective barrier with his broad shoulders, Ella let out a relieved breath.

Funny how the enemy of yesterday felt like a safe harbor today, and that was despite what had happened last night. At least with Dimitri, she knew what he wanted from her. As long as she gave him her body, she could keep her soul.

Not so with the other guy.

Dramatic much? She felt silly even thinking that. The guy wasn't the devil out to get her soul. He was just another shady character doing business with the mafia.

"I'm already giving you the best deal I can," Dimitri said.

The guy lifted a brow. "I'm sure you can do better, Gorchenco." He then looked straight at her. "Aren't you going to introduce me to your beautiful companion?"

"Forgive me for neglecting to do so." Dimitri turned to

Ella and lifted her hand to his lips. "Ella, this is my old friend Logan. Logan, this is my fiancée, Ella."

"Fiancée?" Logan asked. "When did the two of you get engaged?"

Yeah, she wanted to know that too.

"I haven't asked her yet, but I'm about to." Dimitri kissed her hand again and then held on to it.

"Congratulations. I hope that doesn't mean you will no longer visit the island."

Dimitri chuckled. "Unless I can bring Ella with me, I'm afraid not. My bachelor days are over. Besides, I'm not leaving her behind even for a day. I want her with me at all times."

The guy leered at her openly. "You can bring Ella with you. A beauty like her would be very welcome on the island."

The smile Dimitri leveled at Logan would've turned a lesser man into an icicle. "Our friendship notwithstanding, I can't allow you to talk like that about my future wife."

As Logan kept leering despite the warning, Ella huddled against Dimitri's side. What was wrong with the guy? Didn't he know how dangerous Gorchenco was? Did he have a death wish?

Or was he even more dangerous than Dimitri?

Was it even possible? Who was he?

Eventually, Logan turned his unnerving gaze away from her and focused it on Dimitri. "That's a shame. Her beauty rivals that of Helen. Ella could inspire wars. Imagine the possibilities."

The guy was delusional. He was obviously referring to Helen of Troy, but he was talking about her as if he knew her in person.

Dimitri waved a dismissive hand. "My Ella is not a tool to be used in business or politics. She is to be my wife and the mother of my children. Nothing more. Instead of wasting time on nonsense, let's order lunch and conclude our business."

For the next hour or so, Ella listened to the two negotiate. If she were interested in business, it could've been a valuable lesson. But since she wasn't, she only paid attention whenever locations were mentioned in case something indicated Dimitri's next destination after the visit to his homeland.

When the coffee was served, Dimitri stood up, causing a shuffle of chairs behind them as his bodyguards got up and surrounded him.

"I need to visit the men's room for a moment." He leaned and kissed Ella's cheek. "Misha is here to keep you safe," he whispered in her ear.

Ella nodded. Staying alone with Logan was the last thing she wanted, but it seemed like she would have no choice but to suffer through a few moments of small talk with the creepy guy.

Logan smiled and leaned toward her, his dark eyes boring into hers. "Where did Gorchenco find a treasure like you?"

Ella swallowed. "At an art auction." Hopefully Logan wasn't going to ask her details because she knew nothing about art.

He laughed. "It was an auction, all right, but you were the auctioned art."

As Ella looked at him with eyes peeled wide in shock, Logan's kept boring into them.

He whistled. "Three quarters of a million. Impressive. You must be very important to him."

The guy was reading her mind, Ella had no doubt about it. She could actually feel his presence inside her head and tried to push him out. "Stop it!"

Logan laughed again. "Little girl, you're no match for me. But you sure are for Gorchenco. Good job on warning your mother."

"How are you doing that?"

And how come Misha wasn't reacting to any of it?

"The same way you talk to your mommy. But don't worry. I'm not going to tell Gorchenco a thing. I'm just amused that someone like you can wrap the big bad mafia boss around her little finger like that."

Ella glanced behind her at Misha and the other bodyguard Dimitri had left behind to protect her. Both were staring blankly as if they were in a trance.

"What did you do to them?"

He waved a dismissive hand. "Nothing permanent. I just wanted to keep our conversation private." Rapping his fingers on the table, Logan regarded her with his unnerving eyes. "I wonder who are the people helping your mother."

"I don't know."

"I know that you don't. I was just thinking out loud."

As he leaned forward, his eyes seemed to be glowing with an inner fire.

He truly was a demon. Was she one too?

Was that why he felt so strangely familiar?

"What are you? Are you a demon?"

Logan laughed. "You have no idea, little girl." Boring into her mind for a moment longer, he leaned back in his chair. "Forget this entire conversation, Ella."

When Dimitri returned, Logan got up and the two clasped hands and slapped backs.

"Like always, it is a pleasure doing business with you, my friend," Logan said.

"Same here. Until the next time."

As Ella and Dimitri walked out of the restaurant and into the waiting limousine, she let out a puff of air. "I'm glad that's over—what a creep. I know he is an old friend of yours, but he is not someone you should trust. The moment he doesn't need you, he won't hesitate to stab you in the back."

Dimitri lifted a brow. "What makes you say that? Did he say anything to you?"

Ella rubbed her temples. All she could remember was Dimitri getting up to go to the restroom, and an unpleasant sensation in her tummy when he'd returned.

She shrugged. "He didn't say a thing to me. It's just a gut feeling. Logan is a very dangerous man."

"You're right. I'm just surprised at your intuition. I should take you to all of my business meetings."

Ella forced a smile. "Sure. Are all of your contacts as creepy?"

He chuckled. "Some are, but Logan is in a league of his own. The guy must have signed a deal with the devil. In the fifteen years I've known him, he hasn't aged a day."

"Good genes or plastic surgery?"

"Must be excellent genes." Dimitri ran a hand over his thinning hair.

Was he concerned about losing it?

It must be difficult for a man who seemed in absolute control over his environment to succumb to aging.

For some reason, it humanized him in her eyes.

"Did you mean what you said about marrying me, or was it just to stop Logan from ogling me?"

"I want you to be the mother of my children. You're

not only beautiful but you're also smart and have great intuition. The combination of our genes will produce superior offspring."

"That's not very romantic."

Surprisingly, he seemed uncomfortable. "I know. I'm very pragmatic, but that doesn't mean that I don't have feelings for you. In time, I'm sure we will learn to love each other."

That was just as unromantic as his other statement, but then again, Ella wasn't looking for romance. What she was interested in was a way to convince him to use protection.

"I'm too young to be a mother."

"My mother had me when she was your age."

"Those were different times. I want us to focus on our relationship first. A child will require all of my attention."

"That's true."

"I'm glad you agree because I wanted to ask you to get contraceptives for me. I'm not on the pill."

He lifted her hand to his lips and kissed it. "I'll think about it. I'm not a young man, and it's time for me to father a child. But perhaps you need a little more time before motherhood."

"Thank you."

"Don't thank me yet."

44

MAGNUS

*A*s Magnus collected his packages from the guard station, the elevator opened and Julian stepped out.

"Do you need help with that?"

"Sure. I forgot to bring a bag to put everything in. Once I figured we'd be spending much longer in here than we'd estimated originally, I ordered a bunch of things."

Between the books for Parker and the clothes and shoes he'd ordered for Vivian, the guard station was overflowing with packages.

They walked back into the elevator Julian had stepped out of and went down to the general parking. Ever since the guards had been replaced with humans, using the side door labeled maintenance to circle back to the private elevator lobby was no longer safe, and another walk around had been created on parking level five away from prying eyes.

"Did you tell Vivian the truth?'

"Not yet. I'll do it tonight after Parker goes to sleep."

"Good luck."

They stepped out into the parking garage and entered the storage area. Inside one of the rooms was a door into a corridor that led to the private elevators.

"Wasn't Turner supposed to come with you?"

"There is no need. Since I'm going with them, I know all the details and can give you and Vivian the update."

"Fair enough. Is your mother okay with that?"

"Not really, but I gave her no choice. I have to be there for Ella." They exited on the dungeon level.

"You might have to wait a long time."

"Maybe not. Turner thinks that Gorchenco's next stop after Russia is going to be New York. Where do you want to put all of this?"

"Let's drop it at my place first. I left the door open."

After they'd lined the packages against the wall, Magnus called Vivian. "Julian is here. Do you want to come over here, or do you want us to come to you?"

"I'll come. Parker is napping on the couch. All that studying exhausted him."

Magnus chuckled. "I bet. Especially since he stayed up so late last night."

"Yeah, sorry about that. I'll be right there."

Julian opened the mini-fridge and pulled out a beer. "Want one?"

"No, I'll pass."

"Hi, Julian," Vivian said as she entered. "What's all that?" She pointed at the packages. "I don't remember ordering that much stuff."

Magnus smoothed his hand over his goatee. "I added a few items."

She arched a brow. "Not for me, I hope."

"Some of it." He'd ordered two pairs of jeans for himself. The rest was for her and Parker.

Vivian walked over to the fridge and pulled out a soft drink, then took it with her to the couch. "So what's the game plan, Julian?"

"Since Gorchenco is taking Ella to Russia, and they are going to stay there for at least several days, we are leaving late Saturday for New York."

She put the can down. "The same team that went before?"

"A much larger one." He sat next to her on the couch. "We shifted our rescue operations to the East Coast, so the guys are not going to sit around and twiddle their thumbs while waiting. But when Gorchenco comes back, we will have a large force available to move out quickly."

"What are you going to do? Storm his estate?"

Julian smirked. "In a way. We are going to stage a fire and then arrive with several fire engines to put it out. In the confusion, we are going to whisk Ella out and hopefully eliminate Gorchenco. When you talk with Ella, tell her not to panic when the fire alarm goes off. We will have the fire contained and she has nothing to fear."

Vivian frowned. "How are you going to ensure that the fire doesn't spread? Isn't it dangerous?"

The truth was that there would be no real fire. Yamanu would just create an illusion of one, but since Magnus hadn't told Vivian anything yet, Julian couldn't explain.

The young doctor cast him an accusing glance. "We are going to use pyrotechnics. It will be an illusion."

"How are you going to get the pyrotechnics into the compound?"

Julian sighed. "I don't have all the details, Vivian. I'm

going as the team's doctor, not as a warrior or a technical person."

"I'm sorry. I just want to understand how it's going to work."

"I know. But you can trust Turner. This is the kind of stuff he's been doing his entire career, and he's brilliant at it. Everything is going to work out fine. The only variable is the timeline. We know how we're going to do that, just not when."

Vivian lifted the can and cradled it in her hands. "Ella doesn't want anyone to get hurt on her account. She says she won't be able to live with the guilt if anyone dies on the mission."

"Tell her not to worry. The guys know what they are doing. We haven't lost a Guardian yet."

"That's what Magnus said."

"It's the truth."

Vivian snorted. "She doesn't want Gorchenco dead either, but I disagree. Kill the son of a bitch."

Julian's eyes started glowing. "What did he do? Did he hurt her?"

Magnus leaned to pick up Julian's empty beer bottle, shielding the guy from Vivian's eyes with his body. "Ella is fine, Julian. No need to start freaking out. Take a deep breath and relax."

The doctor caught his meaning and turned his face the other way, pretending to sneeze. "Can I use your bathroom, Magnus?"

"Sure."

"Thanks." Julian bolted for the door.

"What's wrong with him?" Vivian asked as the bathroom door closed behind him.

"He's emotional and embarrassed about it. That's all."

She shook her head. "He's taking this so hard, and he's never even met Ella."

Magnus sat next to Vivian and wrapped his arm around her shoulders. "I think it's love at first sight. He fell in love with her picture."

"Is that even possible?"

"Why not? As someone who has a strong telepathic ability, you should have an open mind for things like that. Maybe Ella and Julian share some other form of mystical connection?"

"Like what?"

"My clan has an old belief that some people are each other's fated mates. Maybe that's what Julian and Ella share. A destiny."

45

VIVIAN

When Julian left, Vivian went back to her place to check on Parker, but he was still snoring on the couch. "Should I wake him up?"

"Nah. Let him sleep." Magnus took her hand. "I want you to see what I got for you. Now that Kian is okay with you and Parker venturing outside, we can go out to a nice restaurant for dinner instead of ordering in. How about it? Are you game?"

"I wish I could, but Wonder is coming later to study with Parker."

He wrapped his arms around her waist and pulled her to him. "We can leave them here and go on a proper date."

That was a bad idea, and not because she didn't want to leave Wonder and Parker alone on their first study session together.

"We are not dating, Magnus."

He leaned and kissed the top of her head. "We'll see about that."

Stubborn man.

Except, a small part of her hoped against hope that

Amanda's exorcism idea would work. If there was no curse, she could date Magnus.

A bunch of butterflies took flight in her stomach. Not the nervous kind she was used to, but the excited and hopeful kind. Should she tell Magnus about it?

Amanda hadn't said anything about keeping it a secret. But it was better to check first. Vivian didn't know much about Wicca, and it was possible that the ritual needed to be a secret in order to work.

"Hold on one sec. I want to grab the wig from the bedroom. You haven't seen me in it yet."

"By all means." He waggled his brows. "I'm curious to see how you look as a brunette."

"Yeah, Carol mentioned something about your preference for dark-haired women."

"And beautiful blonds too." He gave her a small push. "Get that wig."

In her bedroom, Vivian pulled out her phone and texted Amanda. *Is it against the rules to tell Magnus about the ritual?*

I'm not sure. I'm still researching the subject. But if there is a rule against telling males, it was already broken since I told Dalhu and Syssi told Kian. Go ahead and tell him.

Thanks.

Amanda's lack of knowledge wasn't confidence-inspiring, but maybe by tomorrow she'd have all the details. After all, the woman was a professor, and she should know all about thorough research.

Magnus glanced at the paper bag. "Why didn't you put it on?"

"I'll do it at your place. By the way, Amanda came up with a crazy idea to get rid of my curse with a Wiccan ritual." Vivian chuckled. "She wants to have a bunch of her friends and family dance naked in the woods under the full moon, which it's going to be tomorrow night."

When Magnus frowned, she added quickly, "Women only, naturally."

He unclenched his jaw. "Sounds like fun. And who knows? It might even work. My mother used to participate in female-only rituals. I can ask her about it."

"Really? Is she into Wicca?"

He shrugged. "She never told me what they were doing. I always thought that they were meeting to have tea and biscuits and gossip. But then one day I sneaked out to see and saw them dancing in a circle."

"I hope they weren't naked."

"No, they were fully dressed. But they were chanting in a language I didn't understand. When I asked her about it, my mom dismissed it, saying they were just having fun and being silly."

"How old were you?"

"About ten."

"That's why. Maybe now that you're older, she'll tell you. Although it might be forbidden to share the secrets with men."

"You just told me about it."

"Amanda wasn't sure whether it should or shouldn't be a secret, and she already told her fiancé. I hope she didn't ruin it."

It occurred to Vivian that she wasn't taking this as lightly as she'd wanted to believe she did. Suddenly, doing everything by the book seemed awfully important.

Magnus rubbed his hand over the back of his neck. "I don't think the particulars of a ritual matter. What's important is the energy each participant contributes to the circle, and that depends on how strongly she believes in it. Combined, that energy has power."

"Wow, Magnus, I've never seen this side of you. Are you a mystic on top of being a Guardian?"

"There is nothing mystic about it. It's just common sense."

"Right." Men loved to claim this and that was common sense. For them, it meant the end of the discussion. "Come on. I'm curious to see what you got me, although you shouldn't have."

He put his hand on the small of her back. "It's my pleasure, Vivian. If you haven't noticed, I'm a bit of a fashion buff. I would love to dress you up."

She shook her head. "You're in the wrong profession."

"Can't I be both? Does loving one thing preclude loving another?"

She narrowed her eyes at him. "As long as we are not talking about polyamorous relationships, then of course not."

He laughed. "I'm a one-woman man. But I like it that you're getting jealous over me."

She waved a hand. "I'm not jealous. I just don't like this new trend. Suddenly half of the romance novels are about reverse harems. Personally, I don't get it. People are meant to be in couples, not threesomes or foursomes. Either a man and a woman, or two men, or two women, but that's it. Harems are about sex and ownership of people, they are not about love."

"What's a reverse harem?"

"It's when a woman takes on several male lovers."

"There are romance novels like that? What's romantic about an orgy?"

Vivian rolled her eyes. "My point exactly. But back to

what we were talking about before. Do you like being a Guardian as much as you like dressing people up?"

He smoothed a hand over his goatee. "Each fulfills a different need. Being a Guardian is a calling. I know I'm good at it, and that if I can help people, I should. But I also have an eye for aesthetics. I don't mind treating it as a hobby, though."

He lifted two of the packages and handed them to her. "Go ahead, try it on with the wig."

Magnus seemed excited, and maybe even a little nervous. It was obviously important to him that she liked what he'd gotten for her.

Vivian was more than happy to oblige him.

"Thanks." She stretched up on her tiptoes and kissed his cheek. "I can't wait to see what you chose for me." She added the packages to her paper bag and headed to the bathroom.

One contained a dress, and the other high-heeled shoes. Both were in her size. Magnus had either gone through her stuff, or he had an excellent eye. The third possibility was that he'd asked Parker to check the sizes.

When she put both on, Vivian decided it must've been the eye. The dress was the most flattering garment she'd ever owned, and the shoes were not only gorgeous but also comfortable and in her exact size.

Lastly, she used the bobby-pins Amanda had included with the wig to tuck her hair close to her scalp and put it on.

She looked sexy.

Different.

A femme fatale.

It was a shame she didn't have her makeup case with her. A red lipstick would've livened up her pale complexion, which looked even paler with the dark hair and the dark-red dress.

"Ugh, I look like a vampire."

"Let me see," Magnus said from the other side of the door.

The man had bat ears. She'd barely murmured the words.

Smoothing a crease in the skirt, Vivian took one last look in the mirror before leaving the bathroom.

Magnus took a step back. "Gorgeous." His eyes roamed over her body. "You look amazing in this dress. And the dark hair suits you."

"I'm too pale."

He chuckled. "So that's what the vampire comment was about?"

"Clingy red dress, long black hair, and translucent skin. All I'm missing are fangs."

Magnus looked away, proving that she was right. He was too kind to agree with her, but at the same time, he was too honest to deny it.

With a sigh, Vivian pulled the wig off and started taking out the pins holding her own hair up.

"Why did you do that?"

"The dark hair doesn't look good on me, and since we can't go out, I don't need to bother with it."

Between one blink of an eye and the next, Magnus was on her, kissing her like he couldn't get enough. When she ran out of air, he let go for a second and then resumed his attack.

The only thing keeping her from dragging him to bed was Wonder's imminent arrival. But maybe they could squeeze in a quickie?

"What time is it?" Vivian breathed.

"It's almost seven."

"Damn. Wonder will be here any moment."

"I'd better go up to the lobby and get some sandwiches for dinner." Magnus sounded as disappointed as she felt.

Perhaps his idea of leaving Parker with Wonder wasn't all that bad. But instead of going on a date to a restaurant, they could have one in his bed.

"Could you also get some pastries for dessert?"

"Will do."

46

MAGNUS

As Magnus collected the sandwiches from the vending machine, he decided that he was going to tell Vivian tonight. With Wonder keeping Parker occupied, they would have time to talk.

When he got to Vivian's apartment, he found only Parker and Wonder there.

"Hi, Wonder. Thanks for coming to study with Parker."

She smiled. "He is doing me a favor, and not the other way around. I hate studying alone, and I hear that he's really good at math. I could use help with some of the concepts." She winked at Magnus.

Looking dumbstruck, the kid didn't say anything. His eyes darting up and down, he was trying desperately to keep them on Wonder's face and not on her cleavage. Evidently, the girl didn't have much experience with teenage boys. Otherwise, she would've worn a dark turtleneck instead of the flimsy pink T-shirt with a low neckline.

Dark Widow's Curse

Next time, she wouldn't make the same mistake. If she noticed. Wonder seemed oblivious to Parker's struggles.

Magnus put the sandwiches and pastries down on the dining table. "Where is Vivian?"

"She said she wasn't hungry and to save a pastry for her for later. She's at your place watching a movie."

"I'll leave you guys to your studying and go join her. How long do you think you're going to spend?"

"Two hours," Parker blurted. "Maybe more."

Wonder shook her head. "I promised Anandur that I'd be back home at nine. I plan to leave at eight-thirty."

Parker looked disappointed.

"There are soft drinks in the fridge." Magnus pointed in its direction. "You can help yourself."

"Thanks. I will."

Picking up two of the sandwiches and a couple of muffins, Magnus headed out. An hour and a half should be enough time to tell Vivian all about Dormants and immortals and gods and goddesses. Hopefully, he would do a good job of it and not freak her out.

The lights were dimmed in his room, and the television was off, but Magnus could see Vivian clearly. She was reclining on the couch in a seductive come-hither pose. She had the wig on, as well as the new dress and shoes.

"I've been waiting for you," she whispered. "Close the door."

Magnus almost dropped the wrapped sandwiches and pastries on the floor. In the short time he'd known her, Vivian had never done anything to look sexy on purpose. She just was. But right now she was showing him a whole new side of herself.

Was it the wig?

Was she role-playing and channeling some movie seductress?

Vivian chuckled throatily. "Don't just stand there, close the door."

Magnus gave the heavy door a mighty push with his foot, which wasn't necessary since the hydraulic mechanism could be activated with a gentle nudge, and the door was going to close at the speed dictated by it and not the force with which it was shoved.

Dumping the packages on the bar's counter, Magnus sauntered over to the couch and lifted Vivian's legs onto his lap. "You have such beautiful legs. You should always wear skirts and dresses." He smoothed his hand over her exposed skin, pushing the hem a little higher. "It sure makes this easier." He pushed it further up, exposing her thighs.

"Is that why you got it for me?"

"I knew you would look stunning in red."

Vivian sighed and closed her eyes. "You make me feel beautiful, Magnus. Thank you for the dress, and thank you for the compliments."

"You don't need me to tell you that you're gorgeous. You must know it. And you're even more so on the inside. You're brave, and kind, and smart, and I'm so lucky to have the privilege of knowing you."

He wanted to spend a lifetime telling her how beautiful she was. But first, he needed to tell her that he'd fallen in love with her. Except, that would freak her out even more than tales of immortals with fangs and the possibility of her being one of them.

As long as she believed in the curse, she considered his love for her his death sentence.

The right way to do it was first to tell her he was

Dark Widow's Curse

immortal and therefore nearly indestructible, then wait for the ritual Amanda concocted and hope it was convincing enough for Vivian to believe in.

After that was done, he could tell her that he loved her.

She cupped his cheek. "You're gorgeous too, Magnus. Inside and out. I wish I could keep you."

That was his cue. She'd just given him the perfect opening to start his story.

"Your wish might come true sooner than you think."

She waved a hand. "I'm not putting too much faith in the ritual, and neither should you. I will not risk your life based on something so silly."

He was about to start talking when Vivian's phone rang.

"It's Parker." She clicked it open. "What's the matter?"

"We need your help, Mom. Both Wonder and I are stumped by this math problem, and we can't move on to the next section. Can you come?"

"Sure. I'll be right there."

With a sigh, Vivian swung her legs down to the floor. "And there goes my seduction plan." She pulled the wig off, and started taking out the pins holding her hair up.

Magnus caught her hand. "We can continue later, after Parker goes to sleep."

Vivian smiled sadly. "He slept all afternoon. There is no way he's going to sleep anytime soon." She lifted her head and planted a soft kiss on Magnus's lips. "You see why dating me is a bad idea? I come with teenagers. It's a package deal not suitable for bachelors."

He cupped her nape and brought her in for a proper kiss. "It would be my honor and my privilege to win this package deal. Don't ever think differently."

47

ELLA

"Good morning, *lyubimaya*." Dimitri kissed Ella's forehead. "Did you sleep well?"

She yawned and stretched her arms over her head. "Like the dead. What time is it?"

"Eleven in the morning. You were so tired when we got home last night that I decided to let you sleep late. Would you like to join me for coffee on the terrace before I leave?"

It was a command masquerading as a request. But at least he was polite.

She flung the comforter off. "I'd better get up. I need to unpack my things and hang them in the closet."

Dimitri laughed. "Sweetheart, haven't you learned yet? Everything was taken care of by the staff. Your clothes have been hung, and those that were wrinkled got steamed or pressed."

Nice. She was living a fairytale. No more dishwashing, or doing laundry, or cooking.

The truth was that it sounded boring. What did princesses do all day? Embroidery? She'd need something to keep her busy. Maybe she should bring up the topic of education.

"Let me brush my teeth and I'll join you on the terrace. Is there anything to eat? I'm starving."

"Of course. I'll have the housekeeper make a fresh breakfast for you. The other one is already cold."

So considerate. "Thank you."

Dimitri was really treating her like a princess, and since she was putting on a very convincing act of wanting a life with him, he was smiling more and treating her like a real fiancée and not his captive. He was still issuing commands and expecting immediate compliance, but that was just who he was. He treated everyone like that.

Last night, they'd landed late, then the ride to the estate's outer border had taken several hours. After they'd crossed the first gate, they'd driven for another hour only to reach the next one. At some point she'd fallen asleep and had woken up when the limousine stopped in front of the mansion.

Ella had been so tired that she'd barely had the energy to undress, put on her satin pajamas, and crawl into bed. Dimitri hadn't made any demands and let her sleep, and for that she was grateful.

The man wasn't the monster she'd first thought he was. He wasn't good either, she had no such illusions, but for a badass mafioso, he was okay.

I'm losing my freaking mind.

It was astounding how her perspective could change in such a short time. She'd read somewhere that the human mind was highly adaptive, and this was a perfect example of that. It seemed that common sense and logic were illusions. The mind found ways to cope with a situation it would've found unbearable in different circumstances, cloaking them in a different rationale.

Was that what Stockholm Syndrome meant?

Ella was familiar with the term and what it implied, but she'd never read up on it in a psychology book. What she was experiencing might be part of it. Whatever it was, though, it helped. Absolute truth was overrated. Sometimes lying to oneself was the only way to go.

Once she was done in the bathroom, she grabbed the robe someone had draped over the footboard and shrugged it on before heading out to the terrace.

The view took her breath away.

The mansion overlooked the lake, and the grounds spread out as far as she could see. In the distance, there were pastures with sheep grazing lazily, and to the left, someone was walking a horse. Except for the area right in front of the house, nothing looked planted or manicured. This was just the countryside's natural landscape.

"Beautiful, isn't it?" Dimitri poured her a cup of coffee.

"Breathtaking. How large is your estate?"

"Nearly two million acres."

That sounded huge. "I can't even imagine how big that is."

Dimitri lifted his cup and took a sip. "About three Rhode Islands."

"Is this the largest private estate in the world?"

"Not even close. But it's large enough."

She took the cup he handed her. "I bet."

Would all that belong to her if she married him? Not likely. Besides, it was meaningless. She was under Dimitri's absolute rule and had no say in anything unless he allowed it.

A prenup was not required, since the only way she

could ever leave him was for one of them to die, or for the rescue her mother was organizing to succeed. Hopefully without either of them dying, because she really didn't hate Dimitri enough to want him dead.

"I have a couple of meetings today, but I told Misha to take you to the stables once you're ready. I also ordered riding clothes for you. They should arrive later today."

"You think of everything."

Given his satisfied smile, Dimitri liked her response. Lifting her hand, he kissed the back of it. "I want you to be happy, Ella."

Maybe now was a good time to bring up education. "Is there any way I can study something? You're an educated man. I'm sure you don't want an uneducated wife."

"What would you like to study? In the viewing room you mentioned nursing, but that requires attending classes. You'll have to choose a subject you can learn online."

"Like what?"

"Business, accounting, even architecture. I can have a list prepared for you."

"I'd appreciate that."

He squeezed her hand. "Just remember. Your first priority is me. You can study when I'm away. When I'm home, you're mine."

That was a timely reminder that the fairytale came with chains, and if she didn't behave, maybe even whips.

Dramatic much? There would be no whips, but he would find a way to punish her.

Ella forced a smile. "Of course."

"Smart girl." He rose to his feet and leaned to plant a quick kiss on her lips. "I hope to be back before dinner. If

I'm delayed, I'll call the housekeeper and have her serve you dinner without me."

"Okay."

"Enjoy your day, Ella."

"You too."

When he left, she poured herself another cup of coffee and opened a channel to her mother.

Hi, Mom. I hope you're still awake.

I am. I was waiting for you to contact me. Is everything okay?

Yeah. I'm in Russia, and I overslept because we got here late last night. What time is it over there?

It's after midnight.

Here it's after eleven in the morning. I wasn't sure what time zone it was. Dimitri's estate is amazing. He has his own lake and pastures as far as the eyes can see. He says it's about two million acres.

That's huge. Her mom sounded duly impressed.

I know, right?

Listen, Ella, I need to tell you the plan. The rescue team is going to wait for you to come back to New York. Once that happens, they are going to stage a fire and come in as firefighters. Julian said that they are going to use pyrotechnics, and that you have nothing to fear because the fire is not going to be real. Just go with the firefighters when they come in.

Got it.

It sounded like a good plan. Fire and smoke would create confusion, and Dimitri's guards would let firetrucks in because it would be stupid of them not to.

I like it. That might actually work.

What are your plans for today? Are you going to tour the estate? You might want to take mental notes for future use.

True. I didn't think of that. I'm going horseback riding later on. Do you think it's okay to ride if I'm still sore?

Crap. That had slipped out without thinking. Now her mother was going to freak out and start crying.

Did he force you again? The venom was practically dripping through their mental connection. Ella had no idea her mother could get so vicious.

No. He let me sleep, and he didn't force me the first time either. I decided to pretend that I liked him, so he'd give up chasing after you and Parker. I was afraid that if he couldn't find you, he'd go after Maddie. Now he has no reason to because he thinks I want to stay with him. By the way, he kind of proposed.

What do you mean by kind of?

He didn't ask me. He just said that he wants to marry me and have children with me. I said that I'm not ready for motherhood and asked him to get me birth control of some kind.

Did he agree?

He said he'd think about it.

He's not going to do that. He wants you pregnant so you won't even think about leaving him.

Yeah, you might be right. He's very possessive.

Doesn't matter. He's going down.

I don't want him dead, Mom. Tell your people that I don't.

There was a moment of silence over the connection. *Do you want to spend the rest of your life in hiding, Ella? Because I don't. And that's exactly why Gorchenco must die.*

Unbidden, tears misted Ella's eyes. *I hate having no say in anything. And I hate having to make such a terrible choice. Your freedom or Dimitri's life. It's not fair.*

I know, sweetie. I'll talk to Magnus and ask his advice. Maybe he can come up with a different idea.

It sounded like a copout. Her mother wanted Dimitri

dead and was making false promises to ease Ella's conscience.

I'll try to think of something too. The housekeeper just came in with my breakfast. I'll talk to you tomorrow. Good night, Mom. Ella closed the connection without letting Vivian respond.

There must be a way to keep Dimitri alive.

What if she made him swear on his mother's soul that he would leave her alone if she saved his life?

Would the fighters rescuing her listen to her?

They would if she shielded Dimitri with her body. But they might just remove her by force and kill him anyway.

Crap.

What was she going to do?

Tell her mother that she'd fallen in love with Dimitri and wanted to stay with him?

Her mom would know it wasn't true. Ella could lie to her face to face, or over the phone, but not over the mental connection. More than words got through.

She had to find a solution before they returned to New York.

As a last resort, she could ask her mom to cancel the rescue operation. But then she would be trading her life for Dimitri's.

Living with him would kill part of her, she knew that. The old Ella, the one who had plans and aspirations of her own, would be dead.

48

SYSSI

"I'm not getting out of the car," Syssi said as Amanda drove into the keep's underground. "I'm going to wait for you while you get Vivian."

"Why?"

"Because we look ridiculous, and I don't want anyone to see me like this."

Amanda had bought everyone long wizard robes for the ritual. From a costume shop. Syssi had put hers over clothes, but Amanda was naked under hers, as was Carol. Kri came with the robe already on and hadn't shared her state of dress or undress.

"I beg to differ. I think we look fabulous." Amanda stopped in front of the rolling gate to the clan's private parking level in the building across the street from the keep. "But if you want to wait here all alone, you can."

The rest of the other so-called witches had headed straight for the spot in the woods Amanda had found. Altogether, she'd managed to rope fifteen women into participating in the ritual. Syssi planned on observing from the sidelines, and so did Kri, so that gave Amanda the thirteen she needed. But if any of the others changed her mind, Syssi or Kri would have to step in.

"Come on, Syssi," Carol said. "No one is going to see us."

"You can hide behind my back," Kri offered. "I'll protect you."

"Fine, I'll come. Hopefully none of the Guardians are using the gym right now."

"Make sure your robes are not dragging on the floor," Amanda said as the four of them piled into the golf cart.

Syssi held on tight as Kri zipped through the tunnel into the keep's underground. The Guardian was a good driver, but she was going too fast. Not that the cart's other occupants were complaining.

She was stuck with a bunch of risk-taking extroverts.

In the elevator, Amanda smiled at her own reflection. "I feel so magical." She turned sideways to examine the long trail of her robe.

Carol grimaced. "You're lucky to be tall. I'm going to trip on mine for sure. I wish we had time to make alterations."

"Tie the belt and pull the robe over it," Kri suggested. "That will shorten it."

"But it will make me look fat."

Amanda waved a dismissive hand. "Who's going to see you? It's only us girls and a few Guardians who couldn't care less how you look in this thing."

"I care." Carol did as Kri had suggested and pulled the robe over the belt.

As they exited on the dungeon level, Amanda sighed. "This place brings back so many lovely memories. I always get butterflies in my stomach as I think about the first time Dalhu and I had sex."

"I thought that happened in the cabin," Carol said.

"Nah. We were interrupted by the so-called rescue."

The door to Vivian's place was open, but she beckoned them from Magnus's room. "Over here. Parker is studying with Wonder."

Magnus chuckled as the four of them entered. "I see that you've gone all out. Where did you find these robes?"

"A theater costume shop," Amanda said. "A ritual is not complete without the proper props."

"Aren't those wizard robes? You're supposed to be witches. And don't you need brooms?"

"They look good." Amanda handed Vivian a folded robe. "The kind of witchcraft we are about to perform has nothing to do with brooms."

Vivian shrugged it over her shoulders. "Do I need to undress first?"

"You don't have to," Syssi said.

Amanda shook her head. "The ritual demands everyone is skyclad, which means naked. But you can keep your clothes on until we get there."

"I'm going with Vivian." Magnus crossed his arms over his chest. "Wonder can stay with Parker."

Sauntering up to him, Amanda put a hand on his shoulder. "Wonder is coming with us, and we have several Guardians to keep us safe. You have nothing to worry about."

"That's exactly what I'm worried about. Vivian is not a family member, and those bastards are not above sneaking peeks."

Amanda lifted a brow. "Really? You think anyone would dare to peek at Kian's, Anandur's, or Brundar's mates?"

"Is Anandur going to be there?"

"Brundar too."

The tension left Magnus's shoulders. "Well, that's good to hear. If they are coming, so can I. I'll call Liam and ask him to stay with Parker."

"There is no time, darling. The others are already there waiting for us."

He glared. "So they'll wait a little longer."

"I'd rather you stayed," Vivian said. "As far as Parker knows, I'm going out to have fun with my new girlfriends. He'll wonder why you are coming along."

By the sour expression on Magnus's face, he didn't like it, but he was smart enough not to argue. Vivian had sounded pretty adamant about going without him. Not that Syssi could blame her. She wouldn't want Kian seeing her making a fool out of herself either.

"Fine. I'll stay." He looked at Kri. "Keep her safe."

The tall Guardian wrapped her arm around Vivian's slim shoulders. "I will. Nothing is going to happen to your lady with me around."

"Are you armed?"

"Of course." Kri lifted the robe to reveal the two daggers she had strapped to one calf, and the handgun strapped to the other. "I never leave home without them."

49

VIVIAN

*A*manda clapped her hands. "Okay, ladies, gather around."

When they did as she asked, she took Vivian's hand. "Some of you have already met Vivian. But whether you did or did not, I want each of you to come up and hug her like you mean it. You need to absorb some of her energy, and share some of yours with her."

For the next several minutes, Vivian exchanged embraces, introductions, and words of encouragement with the women who volunteered to help lift her curse.

There was something to what Amanda had said about exchanging energy. With each subsequent hugger, Vivian could feel her emotional tank getting filled with positive energy, until it was crackling and sizzling with the warmth of it.

Could that be enough to dispel the curse?

As Amanda embraced her last, Vivian expected the same sensation as she'd gotten from the others, but it was a bit different. More powerful, purer in some way, which was odd, since Amanda gave up a strong naughty vibe. Syssi seemed like a much nicer person, but although her energy had felt strong and solid, it wasn't as electrifying as Amanda's.

"Now that we've all shared our energy with Vivian, it's time to disrobe. I know that some of you wonder why this is necessary and think that I'm just being eccentric or silly, but that's a legit requirement. In our everyday lives we clothe ourselves in customs, ideology, and comforting illusions. The naked body represents the truth, and by shedding our material and spiritual garments we proclaim our loyalty to it."

That sounded very poetic, and reasonable for someone as perfectly made as Amanda. If Vivian looked like her, she would have no problem getting naked in front of all these beautiful women either.

Syssi crossed her arms over her chest. "Not everyone is as comfortable in her own skin as you are, Amanda. All that positive energy you're talking about will get absorbed by our insecurities."

Vivian couldn't agree more. "I'm with Syssi on that."

Amanda lifted a brow. "What the hell does either of you have to feel insecure about? You're both beautiful."

Vivian cupped her breasts. "It looks like I have some curves up here because I'm wearing a push-up bra. Without it, I'm flat-chested like a boy."

Wonder snorted. "Count yourself lucky. I have big breasts, and they don't look good with my body type. If you ask me, they are nothing but trouble. Instead of looking at my face or paying attention to what I'm saying, guys keep staring at my cleavage."

"Same here," Kri said. "But I made peace with mine. I

actually use them as a distraction tactic. Besides, Michael likes me just the way I am."

"I have no butt," Callie said. "But since Brundar thinks I'm perfect, I don't worry about it."

Amanda threw her hands in the air. "You see? It's all in your heads. You are each perfect the way you are. If we all looked the same, the world would be a very boring place."

"Says the perfect woman," Syssi grumbled.

"I might be perfect for Dalhu, but another male might find me too tall, or too skinny, and most men find me intimidating and unapproachable. No one is perfect."

Vivian sighed. "Amanda is right. Before any of you spoke up, I thought that all of you were beautiful and that I would be the only one with a less than perfect body. But it seems like each woman is unhappy about something. So let's shed these limiting beliefs together with our clothes, and celebrate our femininity."

Amanda clapped her hands. "Couldn't have said it better myself."

Next to her, Syssi lifted her face to the sky in a silent prayer. "After these two speeches I feel silly about keeping my clothes on. Can you use a fourteenth witch?"

"You can take my place," Carol said.

"Why? What are you insecure about?" Syssi asked.

Carol shrugged. "Nothing except for my height. I can parade naked anywhere, anytime. My body is perfectly proportioned. But this is a breakthrough for you. In a way, you're exorcizing your demon as well. Which in your case, is shyness. I want you to participate."

"Nonsense." Amanda waved a dismissive hand. "The number is irrelevant. The more participants the better. More energy means more power. You can come in too, Kri."

"I'd better not. I'm here as a Guardian, and I'm sure bringing weapons into the circle is forbidden."

Amanda tapped a finger on her lower lip. "I see your point about the weapons, but you don't need them. We have enough men guarding the perimeter."

Kri crossed her arms over her chest. "I promised Magnus that I'd guard Vivian."

"Very well. Fourteen it is. Take your robes off, ladies, and let's form a circle."

As everyone disrobed, the full moon shone on the women's naked skin, clothing them in its gentle light and making them look ethereal.

Each one was beautiful in her own way.

As they formed a circle and joined hands, Amanda assumed the role of the high priestess. "We are gathered here to summon the Goddess's help for our sister Vivian. With her divine light, the Goddess will destroy the unhealthy energy that Vivian believes is a curse. Repeat after me, sisters. Great mother, the supreme mistress who lives in our hearts, who guides our way toward love and compassion, honor and humility, mirth and pleasure. Please bestow upon us your power tonight, chase away the darkness and replace it with your light, allow our sister to worship you freely and without fear, let her heart rejoice in love and pleasure and other delights."

At first, Amanda swayed in place as she chanted the incantation, but soon the circle started moving. Joined by thirteen voices, the chant became louder and louder with each repetition, and soon someone added a melody to it, and it became a song.

The faster the chant was sung, the faster the circle moved. Vivian got dizzy and would've stumbled if not for the hands holding on to her on both sides.

She'd never been high on anything before, but she surely was now because she was hallucinating. The chant and the dancing must've induced a hypnotic-like trance and she was seeing things. The moonlight shining on the women around her was making their eyes look as if they were glowing. Not with reflective light, but in all colors; blue, green, brown, amber.

And still the circle moved faster and faster, the sounds and colors blurring in Vivian's mind until her eyes rolled back in her head and there was only darkness.

Someone patted her cheek. "Vivian, darling, wake up."

Vivian opened her eyes and hesitantly looked into Amanda's, expecting them to glow from the inside.

Thank God, they looked perfectly normal. "Is it over? Did I ruin it?"

Amanda laughed. "Not at all. It was supposed to happen like that. The Goddess filled you with light and chased the curse away. The energy surge short-circuited your brain. Think of it as a reboot."

Vivian closed one eye and lifted the brow of the other. "Is this the professor talking or the Wiccan priestess?"

"Both. Focus inward. What do you feel?"

What did she feel?

Lightheaded, or lighthearted?

Vivian was warm and comfortable, lying on someone's robe with another robe draped over her. Her sisters in ritual were sitting around her, dressed in their robes, except for Syssi who had her regular clothes on. The robe under her was probably hers.

She felt loved, accepted, strong, and powerfully feminine.

"We are powerful," she finally said. "Women, I mean. Can men share energy like we just did?"

Amanda smiled. "Perhaps I should test it. I'm pretty sure a worthy cause is needed for people to unite like this, and especially for men. For them to put aside their big egos and combine their energies instead of competing, it must be something really important. Usually it only happens on the battlefield or in the emergency room."

50

MAGNUS

*A*fter Vivian had left, Magnus took Parker to the gym and gave him one hell of a workout. When they returned, he herded the kid into the shower, opened the sofa bed and then tucked him in.

Parker was too exhausted even to click the television on, and fell asleep right away.

Mission accomplished.

Tonight, Magnus was going to tell Vivian the truth no matter what. If she came back tired, he would make her coffee and sit her down to listen. He should've told her days ago, but it never seemed like the right time.

The truth was that he didn't know how to go about it.

He'd been wracking his brain for a way to build up to the reveal, so when he finally got to the point, Vivian wouldn't be too shocked. Except, nothing came to mind. He just wasn't great with words or with telling stories. He was a hands-on kind of guy. Give him something to create or someone to fight, and he would know exactly what to do.

How did the other immortals do it?

He couldn't imagine Brundar telling a long-winded story, and Anandur had had no need since his mate was already an immortal when he'd met her.

It seemed that he would have to just blurt it out and see how Vivian responded. Rip the Band-Aid off and then kiss the boo-boo away.

Pacing the corridor as he waited for her to come back, Magnus ran through several scripts in his head, but none sounded good to him. Should he start with ancient history? Or should he just show her his fangs?

The first approach provided the most gradual buildup, but Vivian wouldn't believe any of it until he showed her proof. So perhaps he should start with that, show her his fangs, and then go back in time to the clan's history.

Except, his fangs without the backstory first were going to freak her out.

At midnight, he got impatient and texted Anandur. *Are they done yet?*

They should be getting there any minute. Amanda wanted to stop for drinks, but Vivian didn't bring her wig, so they couldn't go anywhere public. They might want to continue the party at your place.

Thanks for the heads up. I'm going to hide the booze.

Magnus went back to pacing the corridor outside their rooms. On the one hand, he didn't want to curtail Vivian's fun, and if she wanted to continue to party with the girls, he shouldn't be a jerk and hide the drinks. But on the other hand, he wanted her alone so he could finally talk to her.

When the elevator pinged, he cringed as he waited for the doors to open. Would a boisterous gaggle of females spill out of it? Or just Vivian with whoever escorted her?

The Fates must've heard his prayer. Vivian stepped out

Dark Widow's Curse

and waved at Amanda, who stayed inside. "Good night, and thanks for everything. It was awesome."

Amanda smiled and winked at Magnus. "Good night to you too. Sweet dreams."

As the doors closed, he wrapped his arms around Vivian. "Looks like you had fun."

"I did. Amanda outdid herself."

"Are you tired?"

A seductive smile lifted the corners of her lips. "Not at all. What do you have in mind?"

"Lots of things. But first, we need to talk."

Dropping the smile, Vivian frowned. "Why? What happened? Is Parker okay? Did you get any news concerning Ella?"

"Relax. Everyone is fine. Parker is sleeping, and there is no news about Ella." He led her toward his room.

She let out a puff of air. "Don't scare me like that. If you need to say something just say it without preamble."

If he only could.

"I just want to tell you a little more about myself." That was the understatement of the millennium.

"Okay..." Vivian sat on the couch and put the bundle of clothes she'd had tucked under her arm on the coffee table. "This is a weird time for it. With Parker asleep, we could make better use of it." She waggled her brows.

"Are you naked under that robe?"

"Yes, I am. What are you going to do about it?"

Damn, she was making it really hard for him. But Magnus was determined to stick to the plan. Pulling a bottle of wine out of the fridge, he poured Vivian and himself a glass. "Let's toast the lifting of the curse."

She clinked glasses with him. "I'm not sure it's lifted, but I'll drink to it."

Magnus put his glass away and rubbed the back of his neck. "Actually, it doesn't really matter if it was lifted or not. I'm immune to it because I'm immortal. I can fall off ladders, and get into car accidents, and walk away unharmed. I might even survive a helicopter crash."

"Oh, really?"

Given her smirk, she thought he was joking. At least she wasn't freaking out.

Not yet.

"It's not a joke, Vivian. I'm immortal and so are all the women you danced naked with tonight. Remember the story from the Bible about the sons of gods taking the daughters of humans? It was partially true. In reality, both gods and goddesses took human mates and had children with them. We are the children of the gods, or rather their great-great-grand many times removed children."

Vivian put her wine glass down. "And you expect me to believe that?"

"I can prove it."

"How?"

"Have you heard about shapeshifters?"

She laughed. "Don't tell me you are one."

"No, but I can create an illusion that will make you think I turned into an animal. Do you want to choose which one?"

"Does it have to be the same size as you?"

"No. It's an illusion. I can be as small as an ant, or as big as a dinosaur."

Viv leaned back and crossed her arms over her chest. "I've recently read a sexy dragon shifter romance. Can you do a dragon?"

"Sure. Do you have a preference for any particular color?"

"Cobalt blue."

"I'm not sure what kind of blue that is." He was well familiar with the colors that went into men's tailored clothing, but cobalt blue was not one of them.

"A purplish blue. It doesn't matter. Any blue would do." She chuckled. "It rhymes. Blue, do."

Vivian sounded drunk, but she couldn't be from the little wine she'd had. "Did Amanda give you something to drink?"

"Only water, but I'm starting to think that she slipped some hallucinogenic inside it." She waved a hand. "Please continue. I can't wait to see my blue dragon."

Damn. If Vivian believed she'd been given hallucinogenics, the dragon illusion wasn't going to work, nor would cutting himself or showing her his fangs.

"Amanda didn't give you anything. Do you trust me?"

"Of course."

"Good. What I can do is similar to your telepathy. But instead of projecting verbal communication, I'm projecting an image while erasing my real one from your awareness. In short, I can manipulate your mind without the use of any chemicals. Does that make sense to you?"

She frowned. "I guess."

51

VIVIAN

"*R*eady?" Magnus asked.

What he was telling her sounded too bizarre, but given everything that had been happening in her life lately, Vivian shouldn't be surprised or dismissive of anything.

Besides, she trusted Magnus. So unless he'd ingested something or had suffered brain damage while she'd been out with Amanda and the others, he was telling her the truth.

"Sure. Dazzle me."

For a split moment, his image shimmered as if she was watching a faulty holographic projection, and then a small purple dragon appeared. Not blue with a purplish tint, but solid purple like Barney.

That was how Vivian knew it wasn't her imagination or the work of hallucinogenics. Magnus just didn't know what cobalt blue was, which was odd for someone who was into fashion, but still. If this were her imagination's creation, the dragon would have been a bright, metallic blue with a purplish hue.

"I believe you. You can turn it off."

The image shimmered again, and Magnus reappeared with a puzzled expression on his handsome face. "I didn't expect it to be so easy. What convinced you?"

"Your dragon was purple, not blue. It was nothing like what I imagined it would look like, so I know it didn't come from my imagination, but from yours."

Magnus let out a long breath. "Wow. I was wracking my brain trying to figure out how to prove to you that I'm not making it up."

She lifted a hand. "You've convincingly demonstrated your mind manipulation powers. You didn't prove your immortality, though. What's the connection?"

Believing in the power of the mind came easily to her. Immortality, not so much.

Magnus smoothed his hand over his goatee. "Maybe I should demonstrate it as well, and have someone else tell you the story. I'm no good at it. Amanda can do a much better job."

Vivian chuckled. "When I want a dramatized version of it, I'll ask Amanda. You might not be as practiced in delivering lectures, but I'm sure your story will be more of a documentary than a drama."

"This is going better than the best scenario I imagined." He sat next to her on the couch and clasped her hand between his two. "I'm so glad that you're taking it so calmly. I was afraid you were going to freak out."

"I trust you, Magnus. I know who you are on the inside, and it doesn't matter to me if you're an alien from another planet or an illegal alien from another country."

She wanted to add that she would love him no matter what he was. But Vivian was still struggling to internalize the realization. Whether the curse had been lifted for real or not, something in her mind had decided that it was, and broken open the dam she'd built around her heart.

It was okay to love Magnus.

He wouldn't die because of it.

And if he was really immortal as he claimed, then there was no reason for her to keep her heart locked up. Her curse couldn't touch him.

"As I said before, the gods took humans as mates and had children with them. Those children were immortal and had some of the godly powers, but naturally, they were diminished. But when the first generation of immortals took human lovers, the children were born human. In the beginning, they thought that this was the end of the story, and that only the unions of gods with mortals could produce immortals. But then they discovered that the children of the female immortals could be turned. I don't know exactly how that happened, it might have been by chance. An immortal male hooking up with a Dormant and biting her. Or maybe two boys fighting, one immortal and one Dormant, and the immortal bit the Dormant."

Now he'd lost her completely.

Vivian lifted a hand. "Stop, and back up a bit. What's a Dormant? And what's the deal with biting?"

"Oh, right. I jumped the gun on that. Immortal males have fangs and venom glands, as did the male gods. They serve two very different purposes. During sex the venom delivers incredible orgasms and a general euphoric feeling to the female. But during fights with males, the venom can be deadly. First, it incapacitates the opponent, who feels too euphoric to fight, and in a large dosage, it can stop the heart, even of another immortal. That's one of the few ways to kill us. The others are cutting off the head or cutting out the heart, or a massive explosion that inflicts so much damage our bodies' self-repair mechanism can't fix it in time."

"But you don't have fangs!"

He smiled broadly. "Yes, I do."

His canines were a little longer than usual, but they weren't fangs. "No you don't."

"Part that robe and then watch me. They elongate when I'm aroused."

Since her breasts weren't exactly what would make a man horny, Vivian slowly pulled up the robe, exposing her thigh and the side of her bottom, all along watching Magnus's mouth.

Just as he'd said, his canines started elongating. But that wasn't the only tell. His eyes started glowing as well.

"The women's eyes glowed. I thought the dancing and chanting was making me see things."

"All immortals' eyes glow when we get excited. But only the males have fangs and venom."

His speech sounded a little slurred, probably because of the fangs. She remembered he'd sounded that way before. When they'd been intimate.

"That's why you told me to close my eyes when we had sex. You didn't want me to see your eyes glowing."

"Right. If not for the glow, I could've gotten away with the fangs because it was too dark for you to see them."

"You didn't bite me, though. I would've felt it."

Magnus smiled sheepishly. "I did. Biting during sex is as difficult to control as ejaculating. Possible, but not fun. I erased the memory of my bite from your mind."

Oh, boy. Out of all his revelations, that one was the hardest to stomach because he'd violated her trust.

"I can understand you hiding the truth from me. I did that too about my telepathic communication with Ella. But messing with my brain and erasing memories of something you've done to me is unforgivable. What else did you erase?"

His eyes widening, he lifted his hands in the sign for peace. "Nothing. I swear. And I didn't peek at your thoughts at all. I had to erase the memory of the bites. Immortal males do it all the time. How else can we hide what we are?"

Male logic was so convoluted. Vivian rearranged her robe and crossed her arms over her chest. "If you can't refrain from biting, you shouldn't hook up with human females. Keep to your own kind."

"We can't."

Vivian rolled her eyes. "What do you mean, you can't? Human females are so irresistible to you that you can't help yourselves? That's such a load of crap."

"There are no females of our kind that we can hook up with. All the women you met are either cousins or already mated to other members of the clan."

He wasn't making any sense. "If there are no immortal females out there other than your relatives, then where did your clansmen find their mates?"

"Most of them were Dormants. And you are probably one too."

"And Dormants are what? Or rather who?"

"Remember what I told you about the second generation of children born to immortals and humans? The children born to female immortals carry the gene, but it's dormant. It can be activated by venom."

"My mother is not immortal."

"But she carries the gene. There are probably many Dormants among the human population, but it's next to impossible to identify them. Strong paranormal ability is one of the indicators. That's why I said that you might be a Dormant. And if you are, so is Parker and so is Ella."

52

MAGNUS

Wide-eyed, Vivian stared at Magnus for a long moment. "Are you saying that my children and I might be immortal?"

"Yes. If you're a dormant carrier of the godly genes, then I can induce your transformation by biting you."

Her hand flew to her neck as if a phantom memory of his bite lingered there. "What if it already happened?"

"It didn't. The transition isn't easy. Some Dormants go into a coma for many days. And the older the person the riskier the transition. It is best done at the start of puberty."

The process was different for girls, but he wasn't ready to tell Vivian about Annani and her magical influence on dormant little girls. That would complicate the story further.

Lifting the wine glass, Vivian gulped it down and then extended her arm for him to fill it up. "This is all too much. If your bite, which I'm still mad about, didn't activate my genes, then maybe I don't have them."

Damn. He'd made a mess of things.

Filling up her glass, Magnus shook his head. "I'm not doing a good job of explaining this. I should've let someone else do it."

"Why are you telling me this at all? And why now? If you suspected that I'm a carrier ever since I told you about my telepathic ability, you should've told me then."

Magnus groaned. "Because I wasn't sure that you were the one and only for me. You're so beautiful, and I didn't know if what I was feeling was just an attraction or the real thing."

"And now you do?"

He nodded. "I love you, Vivian. I know you're the one for me. If you feel the same, then I should be the one inducing your transition. If you don't, I'm supposed to step aside and let you choose another immortal male. But I don't think I can do that. Hell, I know I can't. I would fight my best buddy to the death for you."

That was probably the wrong thing to say too. But since he was doing such a bang up job of it already, Magnus figured he could at least speak his mind freely.

Vivian either accepted him as he was or not. It was her choice anyway.

False bravado notwithstanding, he turned away to avoid looking into her eyes and seeing repulsion or disappointment. Before his confession, Vivian had thought he was a nice guy.

Now, probably not so much.

As she cupped his cheek and turned his face back to her, there was a smile on her face. "That's a terrible thing to say, but it's also the sweetest thing anyone has ever said to me."

"You're a strange woman, Vivian."

"I know. I love you too."

Magnus's heart did a somersault. She loved him?

"You love me."

She nodded. "Yes, I do. Before tonight, I didn't let myself feel it because I believed that loving you would lead to your premature death. But the ritual helped. The women all shared their energy with me, and I felt uplifted, strengthened, and hopeful for the first time in a very long while."

Taking the glass from Vivian's hands, Magnus put it on the coffee table next to his and then wrapped his arms around her. "Before I continue with my story, I need to kiss you."

"Kiss away."

As he gathered her to him and kissed her long and deep, Magnus didn't want to keep on talking. Now that Vivian knew the gist of it, they could make love and continue talking in the morning, and given the strong scent of desire she was emitting, she shared his opinion.

Except, she didn't.

Vivian pushed on his chest. "Continue with your story, Magnus. I need to understand how it all works and what risks are involved. We can make love later."

"Right. The mechanics are easier to explain. In order for the venom to activate your genes, the bite has to happen together with insemination. Which means that as long as we use condoms, you won't transition."

"We didn't use one the first time."

"True, but it usually takes more than one bite, and luckily it didn't happen for you with that one."

"Why luckily? Isn't it what you want?"

"Sure, but not without your consent. And as I said before, it gets riskier the older the Dormant is at the time of transition. That being said, Turner was much older than you when he transitioned, and he made it through. But he was in a coma for a very long time. Another guy was in his early forties and he was in a coma for a few days. Even Syssi, who was in her mid-twenties, had trouble transitioning."

Vivian's eyes widened. "Now it all makes sense. I thought that Bridget was Julian's stepmom, and that his father either died or they'd divorced. But she is his real mother, right?"

"Yes."

"Oh, wow. Meeting Julian couldn't have been a coincidence. I think fate had something to do with it."

"I think so too." He leaned and kissed her lips. "It's meant for us to be together. And probably for Ella and Julian too. He is already in love with her, and they haven't even met."

Vivian put a hand over her heart. "I'm so glad that I showed him her picture. None of this would be happening if I hadn't."

"You said it. Fate."

"Exactly. When Julian said that he was too old for Ella, I told him that I had a strong feeling about him and her. And I really did. I was so sure he'd call." Vivian sighed. "But when he finally did, it was too late.

"He should've called right away. Ella would've not met that scumbag and none of this mess would be happening."

Vivian shook her head. "If we are to believe in fate, then this is how it was supposed to happen. But why would fate put an innocent girl through such an ordeal? It's so cruel."

As he thought it over, Magnus rubbed the back of his neck. "We have a belief about the Fates. Supposedly, they reward those who have suffered the most or sacrificed a lot for others. You certainly have suffered enough to merit a big-time reward from them. And so does Ella. I wish with all my heart that I was the one who paid for our happiness with either suffering or self-sacrifice, and not you. And I wish Julian paid for his and Ella's. Unfortunately, the Fates didn't give us a choice in the matter."

Her brows drawn tight, Vivian didn't answer right away. "Maybe the Fates didn't orchestrate Ella's and my misfortune. Perhaps they are only in the rewards business."

53

VIVIAN

Magnus lifted Vivian's legs and put her feet in his lap. "I guess that's a healthier way to look at it. Even as a skeptic, I always feel uncomfortable speaking ill of the Fates." He started massaging her arches. "Out of fear, of course." He chuckled. "If they are real, they might punish me."

The attention he was paying to her feet was reason enough to fall in love with the guy, but there were so many more reasons. Magnus was kind and charming and attentive, with just the right dose of assertiveness to make him sexy but not overbearing.

Vivian understood now why he hadn't told her before. Some of it was because he was clumsy with words, and some of it might have been fear of commitment, which, apparently, was a prerequisite for an immortal male to induce a Dormant's transition. On her part, she had done nothing to encourage him to commit. On the contrary. She'd done everything to discourage him.

"What about the gods? Are they still around too?"

Magnus shook his head. "Only one remains, the

mother of our clan. The rest were wiped out by a single god whose quest for power brought an end to their era."

"That's sad. So all of you are her descendants?"

"Yes. And that's why we can't seek partners among ourselves. There is a genetic explanation for why even those who are generations removed from each other can't join, but Bridget or Julian can explain it much better than I can."

His mention of generations brought about a new question. "How old are you, Magnus?"

He smiled. "In immortal terms I'm very young. I'm two hundred seventy-two."

Wow, that was ancient. But Magnus didn't act or sound like an old man. He was a little old-fashioned, but just enough to be polite. Was it an immortal thing? Or did people adapt to the way they looked and felt rather than their chronological age?

"Does that bother you?" he asked.

"It's a bit of a shocker, but compared to all the rest it's nothing." She chuckled. "There are advantages to being so old. You can help Parker with his history projects."

"I doubt it. First of all, I'm most familiar with Scotland's history. And secondly, what's written in the books is very different from what actually happened. I'd be doing him a disservice."

Bringing up Parker raised a whole new line of questioning. Under normal circumstances, she wouldn't have asked about intentions and future plans as soon as a guy told her he loved her, but these were as far from normal as it got, and those questions needed to be asked.

"What's the purpose of all this disclosure, Magnus? Are you asking me whether I want to be immortal or not?

Are you offering to induce my transition? What are your intentions for me?"

He sighed. "I thought it was self-explanatory. But I guess it's not. You are the one for me, Vivian. I want to spend the rest of my immortal life with you, so naturally, I want you to transition. And the reason I brought it up now, instead of waiting for us to get Ella back first, is that I can't keep biting you and then erasing the memory of it from your mind. Too much thralling can cause brain damage. We can't start your induction before we get Ella because you might slip into a coma, and we need you to communicate with her."

As if she would've agreed to do that while her daughter was being held captive. In fact, given the risks Magnus had mentioned, she shouldn't consider it at all. If something happened to her and she didn't make it, Parker and Ella would be all alone in the world.

He paused, rubbing her toes. "Don't say anything about this to Ella when you communicate with her. She might blurt something out. Our existence must be kept secret."

"I understand perfectly. If anyone discovered the existence of immortals, you'd get dissected like lab rats to discover the secret to your immortality. That's the reason I kept the telepathy secret."

"I'm glad you understand. Because that brings me to the downside of you knowing about us. Until you transition, you need to either stay under our watch or have your memories of us erased before we let you go."

"Then I guess you'll have to erase the memory of what you've told me because I don't intend to transition until my children are independent and don't need me anymore. And that might take a very long time."

"Not really. Ella can transition right away. At her age there is practically no risk, and she and Julian are almost certainly meant for each other. Parker is almost ready to transition as well. We usually induce boys at thirteen."

She was sure that the process for inducing boys was different than the one for women, but that explanation could wait for later.

"That's less than six months away. But even so, Parker will still need me."

"He will always need you, Vivian. You're his mother. And the same goes for Ella. The longer you wait, the higher the risk. Although we haven't lost a Dormant yet, I don't want to pretend like there is none. But on the remote chance that you don't make it, Ella and Parker will not be alone. They'll have an entire village of immortals to take care of them."

"A village? As in a community, or as in a real physical location?"

"Both. We have a beautiful village hidden somewhere in the mountains of Malibu, and most of the American arm of the clan lives there. You're going to love it."

"Do immortals need a dental hygienist?"

"No, but I'm sure you'll find something else to do. And you can work in the city if you want. But only after you transition. As long as you're human, you won't be allowed out. Not with your memories of us intact, that is."

"What about Parker? Are there any boys his age in your village?"

"Regrettably, no. Until he transitions, he'll have to do homeschooling. After that, we can drive him to school in the city. We have special self-driving vehicles that turn the windows opaque in the village's vicinity, so its location is kept secret even from us."

"I hope you're not suggesting that he can go to school in a self-driving car."

"No, of course not. Someone must be with him. The self-driving engages only near the village. I'll drive him whenever I can, and when I'm on duty we can arrange carpooling. You're going to love it up there. The village is beautiful and the people are awesome. The only downside is the gossip. There are no secrets in a small community."

She chuckled. "Living with a bunch of immortals, I don't need to worry about that. My only secret is my telepathic connection with Ella."

It was tempting. Even more tempting than the prospect of immortality. She could live free from fear of discovery, among other people who were different from the rest of humanity.

No wonder she'd felt so good hanging out with Magnus's relatives. The feeling of connection hadn't been an illusion. That was where she belonged.

But most importantly, she could have a life with Magnus. The man, or rather immortal, took on the father role so naturally. He was already talking about Parker and Ella as if they were his kids.

"I'll come with you to the village, but I'll wait with my transition at least until Ella goes through hers. If I don't make it, she'll be there for Parker."

54

MAGNUS

Magnus pulled Vivian into his arms and squashed her to him. "Thank you. I love you so much." He kissed her hard.

It took him a moment to realize she was pushing on his chest. "I'm sorry." He loosened his embrace. "Did I squish you?"

"Yeah, you did. Is super strength part of being immortal?"

"It is. I'm so sorry that I got carried away. Most of the time I remember to watch it."

"Am I going to get stronger when I turn?"

"Stronger, faster, better eyesight, superior hearing and sense of smell. There are many advantages to immortality."

"I bet. So when can we move to the village? As comfortable as it is in here, I would rather Parker breathed fresh air and spent some time outdoors."

Damn. In all the excitement, Magnus had forgotten that Kian hadn't approved moving them to the village yet. What if he said no?

Vivian frowned. "What's the matter? You seem worried suddenly."

"I didn't ask the boss if I can bring you to the village. I need to call him." He reached into his pocket.

"It's after one o'clock in the morning, Magnus. You can't call him now. It can wait until tomorrow."

Right. Besides, he hadn't tried thralling Parker yet, and that would be Kian's first question.

"I won't be able to sleep until I talk to him. I should've cleared it with him before telling you about the village."

"Do you think he might object?"

"Kian's first priority is to keep his people safe, and he's paranoid about it. But finding Dormants is also a priority. I have a feeling he'll agree, but it's not a sure thing."

He wasn't going to tell her about Kian's crazy theory that maybe she and Parker were being used by the Doomers like a Trojan horse.

Putting her head on his chest, Vivian snuggled closer. "If he agrees, hiding from Gorchenco will not be an issue. Once Ella is in that hidden village of yours, I assume he can't find her. Right?"

"Correct."

"Then maybe there is no need to kill him."

"I thought you wanted him dead."

"I do, but Ella doesn't. She'll be traumatized enough as it is. Feeling guilty for Gorchenco's death will make it worse."

"We need to discuss it with Turner and get his opinion."

"It's Friday night. Does he work on weekends?"

"I think he always works. And so does Kian. They only take short breaks to spend time with their mates."

"What a waste of their immortality. When time is of no consequence, why not take things easy?"

He rubbed her back. "Time is always of consequence. The faster we do things, the more lives we save and improve. That's what our clan strives to do. That's the mission our Clan Mother undertook after realizing that she was the last one of her kind and the custodian of her people's knowledge. She alone stood against the forces of darkness, helping humanity progress while they wished to enslave it."

"Who are they?"

"Our enemies. But that's a long story."

"We have all night."

He leaned and kissed her forehead. "Aren't you tired?"

"I am. But with all the questions still swirling in my head, I won't be able to sleep either."

Magnus shifted to make them both more comfortable on the couch. "Do you want me to start from the beginning?"

"Yes, I do. I want to know everything."

He smiled. "A long, long time ago, in a land far, far away, there lived a beautiful princess..."

The end...for now...

COMING UP NEXT
THE CHILDREN OF THE GODS BOOK 25
<u>DARK WIDOW'S BLESSING</u>
BOOK 3 IN MAGNUS & VIVIAN'S STORY

Dark Widow's Curse

To read the first 3 chapters
JOIN THE VIP CLUB AT ITLUCAS.COM
AND GAIN ACCESS TO THE **VIP** PORTAL

If you're already a subscriber and forgot the password to the VIP portal, you can find it at the bottom of each of my emails. Or click HERE to retrieve it.

You can also email me at isabell@itlucas.com

Dear reader,

Thank you for joining me on the continuing adventures of the ***Children of the Gods***.

As an independent author, I rely on your support to spread the word. So if you enjoyed the story, please share your experience, and if it isn't too much trouble, I would greatly appreciate a brief review on Amazon.

Click here to leave a review

Love & happy reading,

Isabell

Don't miss out on
The Children of the Gods Origins
1: Goddess's Choice
2: Goddess's Hope

SERIES READING ORDER

THE CHILDREN OF THE GODS ORIGINS

1

GODDESS'S CHOICE

When gods and immortals still ruled the ancient world, one young goddess risked everything for love.

2

GODDESS'S HOPE

Hungry for power and infatuated with the beautiful Areana, Navuh plots his father's demise. After all, by getting rid of the insane god he would be doing the world a favor. Except, when gods and immortals conspire against each other, humanity pays the price.

But things are not what they seem, and prophecies should not to be trusted...

THE CHILDREN OF THE GODS

1

DARK STRANGER THE DREAM

Syssi's paranormal foresight lands her a job at Dr. Amanda Dokani's neuroscience lab, but it fails to predict the thrilling yet terrifying turn her life will take. Syssi has no clue that her boss is an immortal who'll drag her into a secret, millennia-old battle over humanity's future. Nor does she realize that the professor's imposing brother is the mysterious stranger who's been starring in her dreams.

Since the dawn of human civilization, two warring factions of near-immortals - the descendants of the gods of old - have been secretly shaping its destiny. Leading the clandestine battle from his luxurious L.A. high-rise, Kian is surrounded by his clan, yet alone. Descending from a single goddess, clan members are forbidden to each other. And as the only other immortals are their hated enemies, Kian and his kin have been long resigned to a lonely existence of fleeting trysts with human partners. That is, until his sister makes a game-changing discovery - a mortal seeress who she believes is a dormant carrier of their genes. Ever the realist, Kian is skeptical and refuses Amanda's plea to attempt Syssi's activation. But when his enemies learn of the Dormant's existence, he's forced to rush her to the safety of his keep. Inexorably drawn to Syssi, Kian wrestles with his conscience as he is tempted to explore her budding interest in the darker shades of sensuality.

2

Dark Stranger Revealed

While sheltered in the clan's stronghold, Syssi is unaware that Kian and Amanda are not human, and neither are the supposedly religious fanatics that are after her. She feels a powerful connection to Kian, and as he introduces her to a world of pleasure she never dared imagine, his dominant sexuality is a revelation. Considering that she's completely out of her element, Syssi feels comfortable and safe letting go with him. That is, until she begins to suspect that all is not as it seems. Piecing the puzzle together, she draws a scary, yet wrong conclusion...

3

Dark Stranger Immortal

When Kian confesses his true nature, Syssi is not as much shocked by the revelation as she is wounded by what she perceives as his callous plans for her.

If she doesn't turn, he'll be forced to erase her memories and let her go. His family's safety demands secrecy – no one in the mortal world is allowed to know that immortals exist.

Resigned to the cruel reality that even if she stays on to never again leave the keep, she'll get old while Kian won't, Syssi is determined to enjoy what little time she has with him, one day at a time.

Can Kian let go of the mortal woman he loves? Will Syssi turn? And if she does, will she survive the dangerous transition?

4

DARK ENEMY TAKEN

Dalhu can't believe his luck when he stumbles upon the beautiful immortal professor. Presented with a once in a lifetime opportunity to grab an immortal female for himself, he kidnaps her and runs. If he ever gets caught, either by her people or his, his life is forfeit. But for a chance of a loving mate and a family of his own, Dalhu is prepared to do everything in his power to win Amanda's heart, and that includes leaving the Doom brotherhood and his old life behind.

Amanda soon discovers that there is more to the handsome Doomer than his dark past and a hulking, sexy body. But succumbing to her enemy's seduction, or worse, developing feelings for a ruthless killer is out of the question. No man is worth life on the run, not even the one and only immortal male she could claim as her own...

Her clan and her research must come first...

5

DARK ENEMY CAPTIVE

When the rescue team returns with Amanda and the chained Dalhu to the keep, Amanda is not as thrilled to be back as she thought she'd be. Between Kian's contempt for her and Dalhu's imprisonment, Amanda's budding relationship with Dalhu seems doomed. Things start to look up when Annani offers her help, and together with Syssi they resolve to find a way for Amanda to be with Dalhu. But will she still want him when she realizes that he is responsible for her nephew's murder? Could she? Will she take the easy way out and choose Andrew instead?

6

DARK ENEMY REDEEMED

Amanda suspects that something fishy is going on onboard the Anna. But when her investigation of the peculiar all-female Russian crew fails to uncover anything other than more speculation, she decides it's time to stop playing detective and face her real problem—a man she shouldn't want but can't live without.

6.5

MY DARK AMAZON

When Michael and Kri fight off a gang of humans, Michael gets stabbed. The injury to his immortal body recovers fast, but the one to his ego takes longer, putting a strain on his relationship with Kri.

7

DARK WARRIOR MINE

When Andrew is forced to retire from active duty, he believes that all he has to look forward to is a boring desk job. His glory days in special ops are over. But as it turns out, his thrill ride has just begun. Andrew discovers not only that immortals exist and have been manipulating global affairs since antiquity, but that he and his sister are rare possessors of the immortal genes.

Problem is, Andrew might be too old to attempt the activation process. His sister, who is fourteen years his junior, barely made it through the transition, so the odds of him coming out of it alive, let alone immortal, are slim.

But fate may force his hand.

Helping a friend find his long-lost daughter, Andrew finds a woman who's worth taking the risk for. Nathalie might be a

Dormant, but the only way to find out for sure requires fangs and venom.

8

Dark Warrior's Promise

Andrew and Nathalie's love flourishes, but the secrets they keep from each other taint their relationship with doubts and suspicions. In the meantime, Sebastian and his men are getting bolder, and the storm that's brewing will shift the balance of power in the millennia-old conflict between Annani's clan and its enemies.

9

Dark Warrior's Destiny

The new ghost in Nathalie's head remembers who he was in life, providing Andrew and her with indisputable proof that he is real and not a figment of her imagination.

Convinced that she is a Dormant, Andrew decides to go forward with his transition immediately after the rescue mission at the Doomers' HQ.

Fearing for his life, Nathalie pleads with him to reconsider. She'd rather spend the rest of her mortal days with Andrew than risk what they have for the fickle promise of immortality.

While the clan gets ready for battle, Carol gets help from an unlikely ally. Sebastian's second-in-command can no longer ignore the torment she suffers at the hands of his commander and offers to help her, but only if she agrees to his terms.

10

Dark Warrior's Legacy

Andrew's acclimation to his post-transition body isn't easy. His senses are sharper, he's bigger, stronger, and hungrier. Nathalie fears that the changes in the man she loves are more than physical. Measuring up to this new version of him is going to be a challenge.

Carol and Robert are disillusioned with each other. They are not destined mates, and love is not on the horizon. When Robert's three months are up, he might be left with nothing to show for his sacrifice.

Lana contacts Anandur with disturbing news; the yacht and its human cargo are in Mexico. Kian must find a way to apprehend Alex and rescue the women on board without causing an international incident.

11

DARK GUARDIAN FOUND

What would you do if you stopped aging?

Eva runs. The ex-DEA agent doesn't know what caused her strange mutation, only that if discovered, she'll be dissected like a lab rat. What Eva doesn't know, though, is that she's a descendant of the gods, and that she is not alone. The man who rocked her world in one life-changing encounter over thirty years ago is an immortal as well.

To keep his people's existence secret, Bhathian was forced to turn his back on the only woman who ever captured his heart, but he's never forgotten and never stopped looking for her.

12

DARK GUARDIAN CRAVED

Cautious after a lifetime of disappointments, Eva is mistrustful of Bhathian's professed feelings of love. She accepts him as a lover and a confidant but not as a life partner.

Jackson suspects that Tessa is his true love mate, but unless she overcomes her fears, he might never find out.

Carol gets an offer she can't refuse—a chance to prove that there is more to her than meets the eye. Robert believes she's about to commit a deadly mistake, but when he tries to dissuade her, she tells him to leave.

13

Dark Guardian's Mate

Prepare for the heart-warming culmination of Eva and Bhathian's story!

14

Dark Angel's Obsession

The cold and stoic warrior is an enigma even to those closest to him. His secrets are about to unravel...

15

Dark Angel's Seduction

Brundar is fighting a losing battle. Calypso is slowly chipping away his icy armor from the outside, while his need for her is melting it from the inside.

He can't allow it to happen. Calypso is a human with none of the Dormant indicators. There is no way he can keep her for more than a few weeks.

16

Dark Angel's Surrender

Get ready for the heart pounding conclusion to Brundar and Calypso's story.

Callie still couldn't wrap her head around it, nor could she summon even a smidgen of sorrow or regret. After all, she had some memories with him that weren't horrible. She should've felt something. But there was nothing, not even shock. Not even horror at what had transpired over the last couple of hours.

Maybe it was a typical response for survivors--feeling euphoric for the simple reason that they were alive. Especially when that survival was nothing short of miraculous.

Brundar's cold hand closed around hers, reminding her that they weren't out of the woods yet. Her injuries were superficial, and the most she had to worry about was some scarring. But, despite his and Anandur's reassurances, Brundar might never walk again.

If he ended up crippled because of her, she would never forgive herself for getting him involved in her crap.

"Are you okay, sweetling? Are you in pain?" Brundar asked.

Her injuries were nothing compared to his, and yet he was concerned about her. God, she loved this man. The thing was, if she told him that, he would run off, or crawl away as was the case.

Hey, maybe this was the perfect opportunity to spring it on him.

17

Dark Operative: A Shadow of Death

As a brilliant strategist and the only human entrusted with the secret of immortals' existence, Turner is both an asset and a liability to the clan. His request to attempt transition into immortality as an alternative to cancer treatments cannot be denied without risking the clan's exposure. On the other hand, approving it means risking his premature death. In both scenarios, the clan will lose a valuable ally.

When the decision is left to the clan's physician, Turner makes plans to manipulate her by taking advantage of her interest in him.

Will Bridget fall for the cold, calculated operative? Or will Turner fall into his own trap?

18

Dark Operative: A Glimmer of Hope

As Turner and Bridget's relationship deepens, living together seems like the right move, but to make it work both need to make concessions.

Bridget is realistic and keeps her expectations low. Turner could never be the truelove mate she yearns for, but he is as good as she's going to get. Other than his emotional limitations, he's perfect in every way.

Turner's hard shell is starting to show cracks. He wants immortality, he wants to be part of the clan, and he wants Bridget, but he doesn't want to cause her pain.

His options are either abandon his quest for immortality and give Bridget his few remaining decades, or abandon Bridget by going for the transition and most likely dying. His rational mind dictates that he chooses the former, but his gut pulls him toward the latter. Which one is he going to trust?

19

Dark Operative: The Dawn of Love

Get ready for the exciting finale of Bridget and Turner's story!

20

Dark Survivor Awakened

This was a strange new world she had awakened to.

Her memory loss must have been catastrophic because almost nothing was familiar. The language was foreign to her, with only a few words bearing some similarity to the language she thought in. Still, a full moon cycle had passed since her awakening, and little by little she was gaining basic understanding of it--only a few words and phrases, but she was learning more each day.

A week or so ago, a little girl on the street had tugged on her mother's sleeve and pointed at her. "Look, Mama, Wonder Woman!"

The mother smiled apologetically, saying something in the language these people spoke, then scurried away with the child looking behind her shoulder and grinning.

When it happened again with another child on the same day, it was settled.

Wonder Woman must have been the name of someone

important in this strange world she had awoken to, and since both times it had been said with a smile it must have been a good one.

Wonder had a nice ring to it.

She just wished she knew what it meant.

21

DARK SURVIVOR ECHOES OF LOVE

Wonder's journey continues in *Dark Survivor Echoes of Love*.

22

DARK SURVIVOR REUNITED

The exciting finale of Wonder and Anandur's story.

23

DARK WIDOW'S SECRET

Vivian and her daughter share a powerful telepathic connection, so when Ella can't be reached by conventional or psychic means, her mother fears the worst.

Help arrives from an unexpected source when Vivian gets a call from the young doctor she met at a psychic convention. Turns out Julian belongs to a private organization specializing in retrieving missing girls.

As Julian's clan mobilizes its considerable resources to rescue the daughter, Magnus is charged with keeping the gorgeous young mother safe.

Worry for Ella and the secrets Vivian and Magnus keep from each other should be enough to prevent the sparks of attraction from kindling a blaze of desire. Except, these pesky sparks have a mind of their own.

24

DARK WIDOW'S CURSE

A simple rescue operation turns into mission impossible when the Russian mafia gets involved. Bad things are supposed to come in threes, but in Vivian's case, it seems like there is no limit to bad luck. Her family and everyone who gets close to her is affected by her curse.

Will Magnus and his people prove her wrong?

25

DARK WIDOW'S BLESSING

The thrilling finale of the Dark Widow trilogy!

FOR A **FREE** AUDIOBOOK, PREVIEW CHAPTERS, AND OTHER GOODIES OFFERED ONLY TO MY **VIP**s,

JOIN THE VIP CLUB AT ITLUCAS.COM

TRY THE SERIES ON

AUDIBLE

2 FREE audiobooks with your new Audible subscription!

FOR EXCLUSIVE PEEKS
JOIN T*HE CHILDREN OF THE GODS VIP CLUB*
AND GAIN ACCESS TO THE VIP PORTAL AT ITLUCAS.COM
CLICK HERE TO JOIN

INCLUDED IN YOUR FREE MEMBERSHIP:

- **FREE** NARRATION OF GODDESS'S CHOICE—BOOK 1 IN THE CHILDREN OF THE GODS ORIGINS SERIES.
- PREVIEW CHAPTERS.
- AND OTHER EXCLUSIVE CONTENT OFFERED ONLY TO MY VIPs.

Printed in Poland
by Amazon Fulfillment
Poland Sp. z o.o., Wrocław